GENTLY DOWN THE STREAM

GENTLY DOWN THE STREAM

RAY ROBERTSON

Cormorant Books

THE CANADA COUNCIL | LE CONSEIL DES ARTS
FOR THE ARTS | DU CANADA
SINCE 1957 | DEPUIS 1957

ONTARIO ARTS COUNCIL
CONSEIL DES ARTS DE L'ONTARIO

The publisher gratefully acknowledges the support of the Canada Council for the Arts and the Ontario Arts Council for its publishing program. We acknowledge the financial support of the Government of Canada through the Book Publishing Industry Development Program (BPIDP) for our publishing activities.

Printed and bound in Canada

LIBRARY AND ARCHIVES CANADA CATALOGUING IN PUBLICATION

Robertson, Ray, 1966–
Gently down the stream / Ray Robertson.

ISBN 1-896951-67-8

I. Title.

PS8585.O3219G46 2005   C813'.54   C2004-906523-8

Cover design: Bill Douglas @ The Bang
Text design: Tannice Goddard, Soul Oasis Networking
Printer: Friesens

CORMORANT BOOKS INC.
215 SPADINA AVENUE, STUDIO 230, TORONTO, ON CANADA M5T 2C7
www.cormorantbooks.com

M.K.

Troubled cure
For a troubled mind

I

SHE SAYS SHE DOESN'T understand why I worship the dead.

I tell her I don't, of course, tell her that I only have a healthy amount of respect for all those who have stood in there and taken one for the team like a good lead-off man should. While I'm at it, I ask her if she knew that Eddie Cochran wrote *For God so loved the world he gave his only begotten son: Eddie Cochran* on the inside upper left-hand corner of his King James Bible.

"Who's Eddie Cochran?" she says.

I stop my lip walk down her stomach and raise a single eyelid; squint down between her breasts at her head resting on the pillow. Both of her eyes are wide open and staring at the ceiling.

"He sang 'Something Else,'" I say. "'C'mon Everybody.' '40-Flight Rock.' 'Summertime Blues.'"

"How come I've never heard of him?"

"He helped invent rock and roll," I say. "Without him there wouldn't be rock and roll as we know it."

"He sounds pretty conceited to me."

I pluck a single hair from my mouth and flick it aside on the third attempt. The hair could be either hers, mine, or Barry's, our dog's. The room is dark except for a couple of candles and the red and green glow of the stereo, Booker T. and the MG's deep in the groove and doing their best to get and keep us in the mood, but the hair seems more coarsely black than finely brown and therefore one more reason why a ninety pound black Labrador retriever shouldn't be allowed to sleep in the same bed as his human companions and why we're one of those couples whose house has what guests kindly refer to on their way home as "that funny smell."

"Why are you stopping?" she says.

I wait a moment before answering, not knowing I am going to stop until she said that I had. I rest my head on the mattress, between her legs. Against her thigh, "You're not into it," I say.

"Why don't you let me be the judge of that?" she says. Lifting a leg, rubbing a big toe back and forth over one of my nipples, "C'mon, baby," she says, "I was enjoying myself. C'mon, come back."

"Your eyes were open."

"So?"

"You were bored. If you weren't, your eyes wouldn't have been open."

"So my eyes were open. It doesn't mean I didn't like what you were doing."

"It means you were bored."

She lifts her head and leans back on her elbows.

"How do you know my eyes were open?" she says.

"I saw you."

"So how do you know you weren't the one who was bored?"

BUT THAT'S NOT RIGHT, that's not Mary, that's not what Mary is like.

Mary's always loyal to the home team. Mary really wants to believe everything the shiny magazines at the check-out counter at Loblaws have to tell her about all of the models who are secretly intelligent, the actors who have integrity, the endangered species making a last-minute comeback. Mary calls the Humane Society whenever she sees an animal that's lost its way.

Once, out taking Barry for his after-dinner walk in the park near our house, Mary spotted a dog enjoying a leisurely piss in the empty soccer field, no watchful master in sight. Recognizing him from the neighbourhood, first she attempted to corner and corral him so she could clip Barry's leash onto his collar and at least prevent him from running into traffic, but this only resulted in the dog, a small, scruffy, older mutt, scrambling away to another part of the park to continue his sniffing and peeing. Figuring that if he got there by himself he probably knew his way back, Plan B was to just keep him moving, right out of the park and safely across the street and all the way home.

They herded the dog across the road and down several streets, Mary all the while calmly assuring him that it was all right and not to worry but to go home now, go on home now, the dog every hundred feet or so stopping his trot and risking a quick peek over his shoulder at the two mad bastards on his tail. Fifteen minutes later the dog turned into the half-opened black iron gate of a white brick house, barked once at the aluminum door, and disappeared inside.

The elderly Portuguese woman who appeared on the front step holding a broom in both hands listened in silence to Mary's tale of shepherding her dog home from the park and how she might want to be careful about keeping her gate closed all the way because no one would want to see him get run over by a car and how the OSPCA came by the park all the time now and carted away dogs whether they had a collar and tag or not.

The old woman seemed to consider all this for a moment. Finally:

"Shame, *shame*. You crazy? You crazy lady, hey?" She jabbed a forefinger at her own head several times. "Crazy. Crazy lady, hey? Go now, you go. Shame you, *shame*." Just to be sure Mary knew how she really felt, she thrust the broom a couple of times in Mary's direction. "Shame, *shame*."

"Christ," I said, when Mary got back. I was lying on the couch, the sports section a mess in three different pieces across my lap. "Did you tell her to go screw herself?"

"Of course I didn't," Mary said, taking off her coat. "She probably didn't even know what I was saying. She was probably just worried about her dog."

"If she was so worried about her dog, she wouldn't let it run all over the neigbourhood just because she's too lazy to walk it."

Mary eased into the big red leather reading chair opposite and undid her bun; slowly combed out a flood of chestnut hair with both hands, brown streams of it flowing through her fingers.

"You can't get mad at people for not knowing any better, Hank," she said. Barry was lying at her feet licking his paws and washing his ears and face like a cat. Barry always follows Mary around, is always sitting at her feet. She leaned over and rubbed him underneath his chin. "And we're just glad her poor dog got home all right safe and sound, aren't we, Barry Boy?"

Barry shut his eyes, lifted his chin higher.

ALL RIGHT, THE PARK.

On a typical springtime or summertime or even late fall evening, the park, Sorauren Park, is a living thing: screaming packs of six-year-olds chasing around a single, elusive soccer ball; little league baseball teams decked out in brightly coloured jerseys coughed up by neigbourhood businesses; babies in carriages like little popes in their little popemobiles going for fresh-air rides; and a loose circle of grown-ups and their dogs gathered together in the middle, near the drainage grate.

Mary and I don't have kids and don't even know the names of the other dog owners who come to the park every night like us, just like they don't know ours. Dog owners know other dog owners by their dogs' names. Here comes Rocky and his mum, you'll say. Or, Did I tell you Bracken's dad was ahead of me in line today at the beer store? He bought a twelve-pack of Amsterdam Blonde.

Tonight, a November drizzle steadily turning into a cold, autumn rain, there's just us, the dog people — Fraser and his dad, the big cop wearing his York weight belt as usual over top of his sweaty grey track pants and PROPERTY OF TORONTO POLICE DEPT. sweatshirt; Lucille and her mum, the redhead from Quebec who's always complaining in broken English between drags on her cigarette how unfriendly Torontonians are; and Rover and his mum and dad, Casey and her family, and Hunter and his parents. And me and Barry, Mary at a friend's art opening. And somebody new whose dog I don't even know.

The woman is tall and thin and strawberry blonde, her bright blue eyes the perfect facial accessory. Her hair is long and loose and hangs in ringlets that she pushes away from her face with one hand while being tugged around our little circle by her border collie puppy yanking on the other. Lucille's mother is saying something about how in Montreal people work to live, not live to work, when the woman's puppy pulls her my way on the far edge of the crowd. I'm glad there are the dog people — Barry spends most of his time with me and Mary, so it's good for him to have some quality time with his own species — but I'm not good at saying nothing, a prerequisite for standing around in the middle of a park with a bunch of strangers in the rain.

Naturally, the puppy goes right for Barry's pecker and starts slurping away like a hungry calf to a cow. Less than half Barry's size, all he has to do is stick his head underneath and turn it sideways and — Action! — instant doggie porno heaven. Then Barry disengages himself and returns the favour, if with some difficulty. Of course. I've yet to run into an attractive woman walking her dog when I'm out with Barry and not have the situation almost instantly degenerate into a sloppy canine sixty-nine. Only the puppy not being big enough yet to accommodate a reciprocal lap job saves me that particular embarrassment this time around.

"Omar, will you stop that," the woman says with what I think is an English accent, the puppy going back for seconds now, she pulling at the dog's leash with both hands to little effect.

"Barry, come," I say in my best alpha dog baritone, and Barry follows me a few feet further away from the crowd. The woman's leash looks expensive, long and thin and made of polished brown leather, and she gives the puppy the slack he needs to quickly find several other willing partners back in the inner circle.

"I wish I could get him to listen to me like yours listens to you," she says.

The accent *is* English; like most people who aren't really from anywhere, accents impress me, make it sound like there's more to what someone is saying than there likely is. This is my theory as to why most documentaries are narrated by the British.

"He just turned ten," I say. "Yours will slow down. That's why nature made puppies so cute — so people don't kill them."

The woman sweeps some of her hair off her face and smiles, not just with her mouth, but with her eyes. I like looking at beautiful women and think everyone should — just like I believe that no one should go more than a month without watching the sun come up, that a life without the Beach Boys' *Pet Sounds* in it doesn't make sense, and that everyone, regardless of any dietary or ethical concerns, should make a point of occasionally washing down a fat slice of pizza, the greasier the better, with an ice cold can of Coke classic. But looking isn't the same as flirting, so I cut my eyes from hers to the ground.

For some reason I'm stunned at how incredibly green the grass is. I know it's just because of the sewage stream running directly underneath this section of the park, which is also why the grass is so much longer and thicker, but it's so brightly green, it's like it's almost glowing. There's no way, part of me is saying, that the accumulated shit of six or seven blocks of houses can be responsible for something so ridiculously alive. There's just no way.

"Any tips, then?"

I look up. I have to think for a moment. "Use a firm voice," I say, "the lower the better. Let him know who's in charge. Dogs want discipline, they want to be told what to do. Even puppies."

The woman turns toward her dog and the group. "Omar, come," she says, more loudly than before. The puppy stops sniffing Hunter's ass long enough to raise its ears, but a moment later is back at it. "Omar, come," she repeats, surprisingly deeply, this time even louder, jerking the leash at the same time. Omar recovers from the jolt of being yanked from his feet, shakes his head a couple of times, and jogs over to where we are, his little white tail wagging. The woman smiles at me again.

"Beverly," she says, offering her hand.

"Hank," I say, taking it.

TO MARY, TO MYSELF, to the government, on credit card application forms, on our answering machine, I'm Hank, Hank Roberts. Only to my mother on the telephone when she's worried I haven't gotten my flu shot like she told me to or haven't done my taxes yet, and to Phil, because he'd insisted from the start that Hank was no name for a philosopher, am I Henry.

I call Philip Phil even though, unlike me, he ended up being what he'd set out to be — a poet — because when we met he was just Phil. When exactly he became Philip Sumner, I don't remember. When we met, though, he was definitely just Phil.

I was going to be Bertrand Russell and he was going to be Charles Baudelaire. And if an English logician and a French symbolist aren't the first two things that come to mind when conjuring up images of ideal intellectual amigos, we made up the difference by having in common what we weren't: well-off, getting laid, and who we wanted to be.

I was drinking a bottle of Budweiser by myself on a snowy Saturday afternoon in February at an upstairs Vietnamese pool hall on Spadina Avenue that I liked to go to. It was only a five minute walk from the philosophy department, but I was usually the only white person there and didn't understand a word anyone said. All the appeal of human contact without any of the hassle of having to pay attention to what anyone else was up to.

Phil recognized me first, from our Introduction to Moral Reasoning class. He stood beside my table with one hand on his pool cue and the other on his hip.

"Let me guess," he said. "Too much epistemology, therefore the pool table beckons, just like John Locke."

"You mean David Hume," I said. "And I think he played backgammon."

"Well, do *you* play pool?"

"Not really."

He looked around him. "Let me guess again. You come here for the atmosphere."

The walls were covered in fake walnut panelling, the low, white-tiled ceiling with large brown water stains. No matter where you looked, skinny Asian men armed with pool cues and with Marlboro cigarettes hanging from their lips bent over one of the ten or so tables or squinted through the smoke sizing up their next shot, the crack of the balls and the violent grunt of impenetrable Vietnamese syllables the room's only sounds.

"Cheap beer and a good place to hide," I said, lifting my bottle, taking a drink.

"Now what could a philosopher possibly have to hide from?"

It was like the first time your dad says *fuck* in front of you or you're allowed to slide from the little people's table over to where the grown-ups are eating — instant, tacit admittance to the big leagues. My parents told their friends I was away at university, I told people I wanted to impress — girls, usually, who weren't — that I was studying philosophy, but no one, not even myself, dared call me a philosopher. Phil did.

Like me, he was from the suburbs, commuting downtown every day from his parents' place in Etobicoke, but he was also the first person I ever met who described himself as a poet like somebody else might say that they were twenty-two years old or liked Pepsi better than Coke. Where I grew up, Chatham — a small town three hours southwest of Toronto — poets only existed in high-school textbooks and were almost always dead, insane, or from somewhere other than where you were, usually all three at once.

He left me and came back with two more Buds and two glasses and sat down at the rickety table. Pouring his beer, "Be always drunken," he said. "Nothing else matters: that is the only question. If you would not feel the horrible burden of Time weighing on your shoulders and crushing you to earth, be drunken continually. Drunken with what? With wine, with poetry, or with virtue, as you will. But be drunken."

"Wow," I said. "Is that yours?"

He concentrated on filling his glass to the brim, stopping

only when the thin line of foam seemed certain to spill over. It didn't.

"Let's hope you're a better pool player than an identifier of verse," he said. He stood up and grabbed his cue leaning against the table. "And let's not mess around, all right? Straight pool, I'll shoot first, first one to twenty thousand wins."

"Twenty thousand," I said. "How long does that usually take?"

"I'm not sure. No more than twenty years, anyway. First one there buys the next round."

NOPE, NO IMMEDIATE OPENINGS for occasional inscribers of thoughtful *bon mots* today; nor for people who like to read late-nineteenth century Russian novels and talk about them while tramping through the leaves in High Park, bondable individuals with a background in mid-period Rolling Stones (knowledge of *Beggars Banquet* through *Exile on Main Street* essential), or men or women with a strong interest in drinking cold beer in their backyard on warmish but not yet hot late-summer evenings.

Meat and fish cutters, though; a part-time driver to deliver pre-assembled children's playground equipment, however; self-motivated telemarketers who want to earn a minimum of one thousand per week from home, on the other hand ... But I don't eat meat and, even if I did, don't have the necessary minimum two years' experience; must have my own car and don't; and don't really want to earn one thousand dollars or more per week, just enough to add my fair share to Mary's toward the monthly household bills. Which probably just goes to show I'm not all that self-motivated either.

I shut the pages of yesterday's classifieds and place it and the rest of the newspaper in the recycling bin beside the fridge, click off the radio perched on top. Its white plastic casement is more a weathered yellow now, and it's cracked down the back and has to be at least twenty-five years old, but it sounds as good this afternoon as the day I brought it home from a yard sale four years ago this summer. It's not so ancient that it doesn't pick up FM as well as AM, although the little black frequency switch rarely ever gets clicked to the right. Music is an upstairs thing, whether headphoned alone or loud enough to make Mary's plants dance along the bookshelves supporting the speakers. And forget the news. Ignorance and ugliness travel fast enough without inviting them into your home. The radio is for the Fan 590, all-sports radio, all sports all the time, twenty-four loop-to-loop hours of who won, who lost, and plenty of gossipy guesses why.

I grab a plastic grocery bag from the stash we keep underneath the sink. "C'mon, Barry," I say, "let's go for a walk." When in doubt, do a dog a favour.

Midday walks are a bonus for Barry, an after-breakfast and after-dinner pooper, but I always make sure to take a bag along with me whenever we head out. You don't need an animal in the picture to spot another dog person — just look for the white plastic bag stuffed into their pants pocket or hanging out of their jacket. The mark of the beast.

It's as nice a November afternoon as can be expected — not too overcast, crisp but not cold, the sidewalks dry — and, allowing for a sufficient amount of time for pissing and sniffing, we hit Roncesvalles within a few minutes. The best thing about living in a city is being able to live in a neighourhood. When Mary and I visit my parents we have to use the rental car just to get a newspaper in the morning. The sundry joys of small-town suburban life don't, unfortunately, include busy sidewalks at three o'clock on a workday afternoon, Korean fruit markets where the owner knows you like your Spartan apples especially hard, and a used bookstore cum music store staffed by the sort of people who will argue with you for as long as you've got about the greatest rock and roll live album of all time.

And today is Thursday, Simon will be working, we could pick up where we left off Tuesday trying to name every Dylan cover we could come up with. I stop in front of a Polish bakery while Barry checks out the scent on a cement planter, and the neat row of glazed Pazlockies in the window, a diabetes-inducing Polish version of a triple-strength jelly donut, reminds me that I don't have to be walking the streets looking for ways to escape jobless melancholia, that I do have things that need to get done at home.

Mary is a full-time painter and a part-time graphic designer at the Canadian Cancer Society. One of the side benefits of her job is the occasional report or study or educational brochure the company hires out to be edited when things get harried, ideal nickel-a-word labour for idle husbands. I've done a lot of things to help pay the rent since graduation — freelance high-school tutor, community newspaper proofreader, library researcher for hire, and, most recently, a brief stint as an English as a second language instructor where my own unique contribution to ESL pedagogy, speaking louder and louder in proportion to a student's increasing grammatical confusion, failed to impress my employers — and line-editing and style-conforming isn't the worst. Still, pity the man who grows up fantasizing about one day trying to come up with a more reader-friendly way of saying *Increased gamma-glutamyl trans-ferase can be elevated by high doses of sugar diabetes, non-alcoholic liver disease, obesity, and medications such as phenytoin, as well as having a sensitivity in detecting alcoholic consumption of five or more drinks per day.*

Of course, desirous of something a little more creatively fulfilling, there are three uncorrected, uncommented upon — in fact, unopened — manuscripts on my desk at home just awaiting my sage response. Before passing through to full-time versifier status, Phil taught a poetry workshop at U of T's School of Continuing Studies, and, upon leaving for greener poetic pastures, passed on my name as not only an up-and-comer in the world of philosophy but also a remarkably adept fellow in all matters literary. Ergo, my present status as instructor of the Independent Writer's Classroom, a creative writing correspondence course that not only provides my sole steady trickle of income at the moment, but also allows me the pleasure of witnessing first-hand the blossoming literary careers of more than one retired elementary school teacher, businessman, and artistically stifled stay-at-home mum.

The planter passes Barry's sniffing inspection and we continue our way down Roncesvalles before stopping again less
than a minute later beside a bunch of newspaper boxes. Dogs
apparently experience the world most vividly through their
sense of smell, so, bags of rotting garbage excepted, Barry gets
free rein to linger and whiff whenever we're out. Two walks
a day of no less than half an hour each is a better deal than a
lot of dogs get, but do the math and it still means that he's
housebound twenty-three hours out of twenty-four. One of
the least commented upon but nonetheless wonderful things
about dogs is that they don't know what a lawyer is. Good
thing, too. By rights, Barry probably has more of a legal claim
to our place than we do.

It's too early in the afternoon to register today's new and
improved bad news yet, so I keep my eyes off the newspaper
boxes and on a pack of kids jostling around outside the take-
out window of the Red Flame Grill instead. Waiting for their
little yellow paper boats of French fries soaked in gravy and
ketchup and their tin-foiled cheeseburgers and hot dogs, the
stupid, grinning health of the young isn't easy to look at straight
on. Every one of their coats unbuttoned to the last, every one
of them in nothing warmer than running shoes, none of them
soft around the middle, slow in the remembering, careful what
they put inside their stomachs — why do I have to wear a scarf
even if it's not really cold out yet and can't forget to put on my
warm winter boots although it's not even snowing, and how
come I have to be sure to take my echinacea and mega-dose of

vitamin C for my immune system and olive oil and lemon juice for my cholesterol and pumpkin seeds to fend off prostate cancer, and have already cut out dairy (to reduce pleghm) and hard liquor (to reduce hangovers)? Because, I calculate, not one of these little bastards is likely more than fourteen years old and I'm double their age and a half. I run through the numbers again but they aren't any prettier the second time around. I'm 250% older than every one of them.

So, today's headlines, right on down the line:

SCIENTISTS SAY OZONE LAYER O.K.
— the *Post*
CHER'S NEW BOY TOY LIKES T.O.
— the *Sun*
KYOTO WILL CRIPPLE ECONOMY, THINK TANK SAYS
— the *Globe and Mail*

Thankfully, the *Star* box is empty.

We move along and pick up the pace, Barry getting an unaccustomed hard yank when he attempts to pull to the right to say hello to a black poodle coming down the sidewalk. He gags at the jerk but recovers in time to be as startled as I am by the neigbourhood's most conspicuous street person, a very tall and very thin middle-aged man in a torn, much-too-short black overcoat and dirty Nike high-tops and a drooping goatee, screaming at the passersby.

"C'mon, Jesus," he yells, "everybody's got a video game by now! Let's get this revolution on the road!"

I dig a loonie out of my pocket and drop it in the upside down baseball hat on the ground in front of him, don't stop to disagree.

THURSDAY IS THE LAST day of Mary's work week and we usually celebrate by not dirtying the pots and pans and going out for dinner. Except celebrate isn't really the right word. Four eight-hour days per week of doing her part to try and make the planet a better place, the rest of the time happily oblivious behind her studio door (from eye to brain to the paintbrush in her hand, the paintings she makes and shows and more than sometimes sells), Mary's yin gets along just swell with Mary's yang, both of Mary's feet are firmly planted on the ground, Mary not only has priorities, she has the right ones and has them in order. Mary, as my father has told me more than once, has got her shit together.

Walking down Roncesvalles, in the direction of the lake: Thai, East Indian, Polish (several), Chinese, Italian, and three good quality grease pits, each specializing in such North American delicacies as all-day breakfast with a bottomless cup of bad coffee, anything that can be fried, fried, and with cole slaw, a dill pickle, and french fries on the side, and, an entire hour before most of the bars open up, hangover-melting Labbat Blue and Labbat Blue Light on tap if you need it. Tonight, though, we keep moving and hang a left at Queen, a half a block later plopping ourselves down at one of the coveted window tables at Easy, neo-hippie home of the best Huevos

Divorciados with ancho sauce and vegetarian breakfast burritos in Parkdale. Leaving the neighbourhood is like going on vacation — half the appeal is being glad to get back home. Get right out there as soon as the meter on the weekend starts ticking and remind yourself that you're not really missing anything by not being out there.

After the menus have arrived but not our water, I spot Phil and his girlfriend on the other side of the street attempting to cross against traffic.

"Shit," I say.

"What?" Mary says, looking up from her menu. Mary always orders the Huevos with rye toast, not wheat, and coffee, with milk not cream, but pores over the entire menu every time anyway. It's the same way she always insists upon carefully reading through the entire set of instructions for anything new we buy. This is why, unlike lesser mortals, she knows how to set our VCR to record when we're not home and how she discovered that she can claim forty percent of her entertainment expenses on her income tax but only one quarter of the cost of her studio space in our apartment.

"Self-described experimental novelist at three o'clock," I say.

Mary looks out the window, sees what I saw.

"I think I'll have a pint with dinner tonight," she says, closing the menu.

"We could escape through the kitchen."

"And I suggest you stick with water."

Technically, it's not too late to pretend to bump into them at the door while rubbing our faux-full stomachs and plucking imaginary bits of tortilla from between our teeth and cursing our bad dining timing, but Mary, naturally, wouldn't hear of it, so I don't bother pleading. We stay where we are, brace ourselves for the blast of cold air that'll announce the opening of the door.

Simultaneously peeling free their black scarves and undoing the top buttons of their matching long black wool overcoats and surveying the room for an empty table, Phil and Rebecca see us. "Hey, you two," Phil says.

"Hey," I say, shaking Phil's hand, standing up to greet Rebecca.

I've never really understood the whole cheek kissing phenomenon. A firm handshake for either sex has always seemed to me one of the few sensible things North Americans have over Europeans. And how to do it if you do decide to do it? The rules seem to change every season. A peck on each cheek, or just one? Phantom kisses puckered over each of the other's shoulders? And do you hug, too, on top of everything else? I decide to hedge my bets, sort of hold Rebecca loosely by the shoulders as I plant a wet one on her jaw, just below her right earlobe. She manages a thin, pained smile that says, Nice try, Bubba, and leans over to share a reciprocal hug hug, kiss kiss with Mary.

It takes two more menus, four glasses of ice water, several How are you?'s and just as many Good, how are you?'s before Rebecca starts my temples throbbing. No one can enrage quite like the absolutely clueless. The vanity of vacuity.

"Are you still painting, Mary?" Rebecca says, eyes on her menu.

"Mary just had a show, in August," I say.

"That's right," Rebecca says, "we were in New York." She peeks over top of the menu. "And where was that again?"

"The —"

"The Carbert Gallery," I say, finishing Mary's sentence. She lowers her eyes to the edge of the table.

Rebecca puts two fingers to her temple — no, literally, she puts two fingers to her temple. "The Carbert," she says, "the Carbert ... We've had this conversation before, haven't we? No, I don't think I know it."

"She got a great review in *Canadian Art*," I say, putting my arm around Mary's shoulder, pulling her close. I can feel her wiggle a couple inches away from me on the bench.

"Good for you," Rebecca says. "I'm sure it can't be easy trying to create lasting art when you have to cope with the pressures of a nine-to-five Joe job. I know I couldn't do it."

The waiter, a blond guy with greasy hair and sleepy eyes in torn blue jeans and a paint-splattered T-shirt who obviously puts a lot of time and effort into looking unkempt, takes each of our orders in spite of having a hard time taking his eyes off Rebecca. Bounteous of body in all the places she's supposed to be and personal-trainer lean everywhere else, with pouty lips and high, model cheekbones and a long, thin neck — say what you want about her novels, the woman definitely does take a great author photo.

"What are you two up to this evening?" Phil says, running his hand back and forth across Rebecca's resting on the table.

Up until he and Rebecca started dating, anytime Phil and I would be out somewhere and some couple would be pawing away at each other in the corner, Phil was fond of quoting Baudelaire's "Ah, sexuality — the lyricism of the masses." Now whenever I'm around the two of them I'm constantly having to stop myself from slapping his hand. It seems fairly clear that if they end up having children someday they're going to be one of those couples who think that it's just adorable to include their baby's name on their answering machine message. *Hi, you've reached the residence of Philip, Rebecca, and Penelope. We're not home right now …*

"We're both working tonight," I practically shout. They're both decked out like they've got a heavy duty social scene to tend to, but double-date nightmares dancing in my head mean I just can't be too careful about being too obvious.

"Ah, yes," Rebecca says, smiling, cutting her eyes Mary's, then Phil's way. "The mysterious meisterwork of Mr. Henry Roberts. Any news on when the world will finally get a glimpse of your magnum opus, sir? Now, this is the same book you've been working on that started out as your undergraduate philosophy thesis, correct?"

I nod. "Actually, I'm in the revision stage right now."

"It's been in the revision stage since the late eighties," Phil says, stroking Rebecca's bare forearm.

"That's not true," Mary says, joining the fun. "The eighties were when Hank was editing. The nineties were when he revised. The new millennium is for spell-checking."

Giggles all around.

"Joyce spent thirteen years on *Finnegans Wake*," I say, drinking from my glass, clamping on a piece of ice between my molars.

"Well, let's hope your book is a little less self-indulgent," Rebecca says. "My theory is, get in, get out, and move on. This guarantees a certain freshness, an immediacy of expression, don't you think?" She looks around the table for confirmation, and Phil must have given it to her because she kisses him full and long on the lips. The sound of their kiss is like a toothless man dying of thirst. "Besides, life is too short," she says.

To read the tripe you call your novels, it is, I think.

"I've forgotten, Henry," Rebecca says. "What is the name of your book again?"

I bite down hard on the piece of ice, part of which ricochets directly down my windpipe and sends me into a coughing fit. Everyone at the table is very concerned and most helpful, all three of them loudly encouraging me to drink from their glass of water, each one tinkling to the top with several more little chipped pieces of frozen choking hazards. I wave away their concern and wordlessly insist upon walking to the bathroom by myself. By the time I return, red-faced but at least not gagging anymore, the food is on the table and cooling, but no one has so much as lifted a fork.

Mary stands up when she sees me. "Hank, are you all right?" she says, a tentative touch of her hand on my shoulder.

"*Work in Progress*," I say, sitting down, picking up my burrito.

"What?" Phil says.

Mary is still standing beside me.

"I beg your pardon?" Rebecca says.

"You asked me what the name of my book was," I say. I take a bite. Out of the side of my mouth, "*Work in Progress*," I say.

"SO THIS NEWFIE COMES to Toronto and goes into a gay bar. The bartender sees the guy sitting next to the Newfie say something to him, and then all of a sudden — Pow! — the Newfie goes nuts — punches the guy square in the face, hits him in the head again as he's going down, and then won't stop kicking him once he hits the floor. So the bartender, he jumps over the bar and grabs the Newfie and pins him against the wall with his arm behind his back.

"'Look, Buddy,' he says, 'you're way out of line. I don't think you know where you are. This is a gay bar. What did that guy say to you, anyway?'

"'That sonofabitch,' the Newfie says, 'he offered me a job.'"

Everybody sitting at the bar laughs — me, Julio, even Lenny, who's still sober at quarter to ten and who usually needs a gallon or so of draft beer in his bloodstream before what qualifies for him as a sense of humour is encouraged to make its alcohol-abetted nightly appearance. Even Frank, sitting by himself at the table closest to the bar, laughs, careful, as usual, to put a little distance between himself and our idiocy, only not so much so that he can't help but be part of the half-witted chorus.

But, then, homosexual jokes or jokes about Newfoundlanders or, for that matter, jokes about anyone who isn't exactly like the person telling the joke are pretty much always a sure bet around the Duke. Even if none of us cares enough to care if anybody at the bar was gay. Even if everybody knows Julio is from Newfoundland.

The same eight pickled eggs that no one ever eats swim in yellow brine in a clear glass jar on the bar. There's a toilet that's backed up three nights out of seven and that never stops running. There's a framed black velvet print over the cash register of several dogs in green eye shades and red smoking jackets playing poker. And there isn't any Becks, Guinness, or Corona, even if you ask nicely, or any wine that doesn't come in a cardboard box.

Sam, the teller of the tale and the owner of the Duke, takes a long pull from his bottle of Labbatt Ice; beverages with a higher than usual percentage of alcohol are real popular at the Duke. Duke patrons don't pretend that they're there for any other reason than getting messed up. No one has ever said "Let's drop by the Duke for a beer" and literally meant it. Honest desperation is the Duke of Connaught's one and only charm.

"How come we never see Mary around here anymore, Hank?" Frank says from his table.

Frank's an old hippie who's done it all — hung out in Yorkville, attended Rochdale, spent the seventies in a commune in Northern California, made a nice chunk of change in the eighties smuggling dope into Canada from the Middle East — only to end up as the skinny guy at the bar who tends not to eat when he's on a big drunk and who's always got his nose stuck in a book. Whenever the stupidity of the Duke gets just a little too stupid, Frank and I will sit together and shoot the shit, mostly about what he's been reading, mostly heavy-duty, What's-it-all-about? stuff. Somehow he's gotten the impression that my getting my B.A. in philosophy qualifies me as intelligent. I have read a lot of the same books he's partial to — Neitzsche, Schopenhauer, Plato — but I usually end up having to bluff my way through our conversations anyway, the voices of all of his brand new friends so clear, so insistent in his own head, old acquaintances of mine I haven't spoken to in years, voices I sometimes have a hard time even placing. If he's drunk enough, he'll confide to me how someday — someday soon — he's going to dry out and get himself together and buy a little piece of land up north and make his own bread and grow his own vegetables and weed again.

"She's probably at home with her boyfriend," Sam says, looking straight ahead, at the bottles of liquor in a row behind the bar. Intimating that someone's wife or girlfriend is being flagrantly unfaithful is another surefire Duke thigh-slapper.

Lenny pours himself a half-pint and drinks it off standing at the tap; I count his adam's apple rise and fall three times. He wipes the foam from his beard on the sleeve of his size xxxL black long-sleeved T-shirt adorned with the teardrop-shaped, big-eyed universal symbol for a space alien.

"I doubt it," he says. "She barely had time to put her clothes on and get out of the can with those two skinheads before Hank got here."

A big group guffaw, and I lay a five on the bar. Lenny hits a key and the old cash register bangs open. He knows what I need. He drops two toonies and a loonie in the palm of my hand.

"Oh, he's taking his change and going home," he says, hand on the tap, refilling his glass. Lenny's been the only bartender at the Duke for as long as I've been coming here, nearly fifteen years, and he and Sam have an understanding. Sam doesn't provide any employee benefits or pay more than minimum wage, and Lenny gets to drink for free. Initially, I think Sam came out on top, but these last few years, I'm not so sure.

"You going home, Hank?" Julio says.

Julio is the only one at the bar without a beer in front of him. Social assistance checks don't get mailed for another couple of days, so he's nursing his usual end-of-month pint glass of tap water with a lemon slice. Julio has a jagged blue prison tattoo of his given name, Jules, on his right forearm, and a ten-second reality delay due to once too often being on a two-week binge and coming up a little short and having to substitute Scope or Listerine or plain old rubbing alcohol for his preferred Molson Dry.

"He's going to sit with all his friends," Lenny says, motioning with his chins in the direction of the rear of the room, empty but for several vacant tables and chairs and the jukebox. Except for maybe a few pieces of Queen West human driftwood washed up at a table or two and the odd university student or young musician taking it all in, the only time there's ever more than the regulars at the bar these days is Friday night, when what's left of the Toronto punk scene jams the place. Mary and I happened to be there once and left after one drink. Forty year-old bicycle couriers with clip-on cell phones whose receding hairlines mean they don't have to shave their heads anymore isn't a happy sight.

Last night, going through my albums again, attempting once more to slim them down enough so that our two bedroom, partial-basement apartment won't feel like it quite so much, I had to force myself to read twice what my mind couldn't compute the first time: that the Ramones' debut album, the one with "Blitzkrieg Bop," "Beat on the Brat," and "Now I Wanna Sniff Some Glue," came out over a quarter-of-a-century ago. And in just the last few years, Joey, Dee Dee and Johnny, three-quarters of the original band, just three more cold clumps of rock and roll worm food.

I set my bottle of Budweiser down on one of the sticky tabletops and stand before the jukebox. I don't know why I bother flipping through the stacks of disks before I drop in my loonie; it's like Mary and the menu at Easy. I always start off with something lighter — tonight, "About a Girl," from Nirvana's unplugged album — move on to some crunchy Stones, and then finish things up with a nice big hunk of Hendrix. I program a fully balanced musical meal and sit down before the first song is served.

First it was just Phil and me.

Walking down Queen Street one afternoon, loaded down with the spoils of the annual book-buying splurge we allowed ourselves every fall semester when our OSAP checks would finally arrive, it had started to pour on the way from Pages to our next stop, a second-hand bookstore a bunch of blocks away, and we'd ducked in for a quick beer to wait out the rain. Five hours and four pitchers later the Duke of Connaught was our bar.

There was a guy in a wheelchair drinking scotch and milk and screaming at *Wheel of Fortune* on the TV mounted on the wall over the pool table. There was an old man with one arm rolling his own cigarettes and laughing at something no one else could hear. There was an unbroken procession of staggering drunks, homely prostitutes, and all sorts of off-centre citizens you didn't ordinarily get a chance to rub elbows with during epistemology class. If Raskolnikov had been alive and unwell and living in Toronto in 1988, he'd have been here too, stewing away in the corner in his sour psychological juices over the cheapest pint on Queen Street, trying to decide whether killing off God was such a hot idea or not.

When I met Mary a year later, standing in the cafeteria line downstairs at Hart House, a big book of Gehardt Richter reproductions under one arm and all her long brown hair tied up into a fluffy fountain on top of her head, I made our first date for at the Duke. She was twenty minutes late and I wasn't sure she wasn't going to stand me up. I can still remember how good it felt — relief, excitement, equal measures of each, rocketing off from the bottom of my gut before finally touching down as a goose-pimply crown on the top of my head — to see her come through the doorway wearing her beat-up black biker jacket with the broken zipper and in blue jean cut-offs pulled on over top of black tights. I shut the copy of Freud's *Civilization and Its Discontents* I'd been using to avoid the hands on the clock on the wall and watched her walk toward me and into my life. The next week I introduced her to Phil.

And what better place for a nascent poet, philosopher, and painter to follow Rimbuad's wise counsel and get busy systematically disordering our senses?

Except, poets who have to attend a black-tie fundraiser at eight p.m. sharp for something called the Mid-Career Atlantic Female Writer Distress Fund with their novelist girlfriends, and painters who have several freshly gessoed canvases waiting at home and who want to get started on a new series of diptychs before Monday morning and another work week rolls along, can't be as systematic in their disordering as they used to be. In the case of the latter, sometimes can't even take the side of the argument that till death do us part so obviously demands.

"What do you care what she thinks?" Mary had said, meal done, Phil and Rebecca bye-bye in a cab, and she and I walking the other way, home.

"I *don't* care what she thinks," I said. "Why would I? The women is a pompous idiot."

"Then don't let her get under your skin."

"I'm not," I said, loud enough that a man walking his golden retriever on the other side of Sorauren Avenue looked over.

"Yeah, I can tell," Mary said.

"Look, anybody who has half a brain knows her stuff is

terrible," I said, careful to sound as nonchalant as possible. "Who cares if her eight-by-ten is a knockout or that critics who wouldn't know a well-written book if it buggered them in broad daylight fall for her act?"

"Obviously, you."

"You're missing the point," I said. I watched a single leaf hanging from the end of an otherwise bare branch fall to the sidewalk and then be blown by the wind onto the road, only to be swallowed up underneath a speeding SUV.

"Which is?"

"Which is ... I mean, how can Phil possibly be happy?"

"Well, he is. He seems to be, anyway. And that's what's important, isn't it?"

"But my point is, how *could* he be? He's our friend, Mary."

"And he always will be. But people change, Hank."

I stopped walking; Mary, reluctantly, too.

"Meaning Phil is as full of shit as she is," I said. "That he's as much a no-talent, careerist phony as her."

"Is that what you think?" she said.

"Of course not. Why would you even say something like that?"

"I didn't. You did."

Therefore, an evening alone at the Duke, and Don't wait up, and Don't worry, I won't.

The jukebox coughs out the opening Fender Stratocaster whacka-whacka-whack of "Voodoo Chile' (Slight Return)," and Jimi hurls down a perfect storm of electricity straight from heaven, making us all tremble and wonder and smile.

I take a drink, and remember that today, November 26, would be his sixtieth birthday. I could sit here all night, I think, and I'd never be able to imagine it.

IF I DON'T TOUCH the brown stuff, I'm all right. A little slow the next day, a bit less on the ball even than usual, needing a nap after dinner to make it through the evening maybe, but no more agonizing over the toilet bowl about such absorbing metaphysical questions as *Did I really say that?* and *Why am I such a fucking fool?*

Liquor circumvents the body's natural anti-asshole system. Shoot, swallow, make a face — the human brain doesn't stand a chance. Pints of beer, on the other hand, take time to consume, to be metabolized, make you bloated and sleepy rather than prone to stand atop your chair in the middle of a crowded barroom, empty shot glass in hand, screaming *Who's gonna smoke my hog tonight?*

I take Barry with me to Loblaws in lieu of his usual morning walk in the park in deference to the cobwebs still in my head, and as I'm tying his leash to a pole by the automatic doors, a woman around my age pushing a baby stroller the size of a Buick says to me, "Beautiful day, isn't it?"

I hadn't really noticed, but, yeah, it is; has to be nearly sixty degrees with a moist, almost warmish breeze. Except that it's the end of November and the only reason we're not up to our necks in sleet and snow is because the parking lot is packed with fully-loaded, fossil-fuel-gulping SUVs and minivans which their proud owners tell themselves they can't live without because how else could they lug back to their overheated homes their fifteen plastic bags of pre-packaged goodies with which to gorge themselves in front of 242 channels of must-see TV?

I secure Barry's leash and snap back at the woman, "Thank global warming," and she lights up even brighter than before, says, "It's lovely, isn't it?" I tell my mouth to say *cheese* and go inside and grab a basket and hit the aisles.

When I come back out, I've got the Soya milk and romaine lettuce and raw oats I came for, but also a litre of chocolate milk, a box of double-fudge Pop Tarts, and the biggest, most expensive, most disgusting-looking bone the guy behind the meat counter will sell me.

Back home, at the kitchen table, working on my second glass of milk and third Pop Tart, my gut groans and I touch it with four fingers and I think that my belt is too tight until I see that it's tied at the notch it always is; also, that the bone Barry is working on is probably all that's left of some poor beast who'd spent every moment of his miserable life locked away in some dark shed no bigger than his ass-end and whose entire existence was all about leading up to this — some bozo blowing his stupid, trusting head off and sawing up and selling off the bloody body parts to the highest bidder so that I could buy a nice chewy treat for my pet. I wipe off my chocolate milk moustache with the back of my shirt sleeve and announce to Barry that we're going out.

Ordinarily, anything beyond his standard couple of walks is

cause for tail-banging celebration. This time he pretends like he doesn't see me standing there and keeps chomping away at the bone with his eyes practically rolling back in their sockets in some kind of extended doggie orgasm. Finally, I bark, "Barry, now!" and he reluctantly gets up and comes, licking his lips all the way out the door.

Later that night, lying in bed with Mary already asleep beside me, I wonder where the woman with the baby stroller grew up and if she ever thought that who she is now was who she was going to be. I fall asleep to the sound of Barry sucking the last bits of bone and beef from his teeth before coming to bed.

THE ENVELOPE, YES, THE envelope. A nine inch by twelve inch manila envelope that can't hurt anyone as long as they don't let it. I tap the thing twice, with a single forefinger to the right, from its resting place for over a week on the left-hand corner of my desk, until, two more taps, it's directly underneath the glare of my gooseneck lamp. The thing stares back up at me.

> Hank Roberts
> c/o School of Continuing Studies
> 158 St. George St.
> Toronto, Ont.
> M5S 2V8
> IMPORTANT DOCUMENTS WITHIN

Now *there's* some convincing fiction, I think.

I tug open my desk drawer looking for a letter-opener that I don't own and push both hands into the chaos like a swimmer into the surf, set to work lining up all the pencils with all the other pencils, the pens with the pens, putting the differently coloured rubber bands into their own separate pile, the stapler with no staples and the broken calculator with no batteries in another. When I'm sure that the envelope isn't looking, I tear it open, pouring out its contents in one swift swoop onto the desk.

Every student who enrolls in the Independent Writer's Classroom is entitled to seventy-five professionally perused pages or three months enrollment, whichever comes first. Along with their initial submission, every student is asked to include a Writer's Profile, a mini-biography of no more than three-hundred words detailing their aims for the course, previous writing experience, and a few of their favourite writers or books. Along with learning that Lenore Shipely has "always loved the idea of writing, of being a writer, of the very act of creation itself, as far back as I can remember!" and that, among other things, "raising three grown-up boys has provided me with more ideas for stories than I know what to do with!" just a few of the authors that Lenore regularly turns to for both emotional sustenance and aesthetic inspiration are "Anne Michaels, Timothy Findley, M. Proust (*Remembrance of Things Past* especially), and Rebecca James."

I place the profile on top of the paper-clipped manuscript and slide both back inside the envelope. It's only a little past one in the afternoon, and the curtain hanging in my basement window is parted as wide as it can go, but a single, dirty headlight of sunlight is all that manages to sneak into the room from the alley outside. I click off the desk lamp and concentrate on the dull beam, on the quiet chaos of a million dancing dust particles its own wordless world; until a car slows down in the alley for a speed bump and the room goes dark, the window-rattling, bass-thumping blare coming from the car the only sensation in the universe left to remind me that I'm not just another speck of dust too.

"Screw this," I say, although the only one in the room besides me is Barry, curled up asleep on the couch with his nose tucked tightly underneath his front paws. I push open the double doors of my office and switch on the kitchen light.

When Mary and I moved in here nearly four years ago we carved it up so that a two-bedroom apartment translated into a studio for her and a small writing room for me in the basement, the book-lined living room upstairs doing double duty as our bedroom. Aside from the lack of natural light, other major gripes include having to cook in a carpeted basement kitchen with a ceiling so low that Phil, who's six two, has to duck every time he comes downstairs, and a bathroom approximately two feet away from the dinner table, the bathroom exhaust fan brilliantly devised to blow out what it was intended to blow out directly into the room where we prepare and eat our food. Plus, Mary, from Victoria, where her parents and sister still are, grew up making things grow, and, indoor sunshine scarcity notwithstanding, our backyard is barely big enough for Barry to take the occasional non-walk-induced dump. We've talked about moving a bunch of times, about maybe someday even owning our own place, but the rent is cheap, and the only neighbourhood we want to live in is this one, and even if I did have a real job like Mary, there's no way we could compete with the Yuppies plucking up the For Sale signs in Roncesvalles as fast as they get planted.

I pour a glass of Brita water from the plastic pitcher in the refrigerator and go upstairs. I don't call Barry's name, let him stay downstairs sleeping in my room in the dark; as soon as he realizes I'm gone he'll wake up and shake his head and stretch his legs and head upstairs. Living with a dog means never feeling unwanted. That Hitler knew this and always kept several dogs of his own around doesn't make it any less true.

After the last dim hour downstairs, the gush of light flooding the living room hits me like a hallucinogenic. I ignore the chatter of the bookshelves and the siren song of my album collection and plunk myself down in the reading chair near the big window looking onto the backyard and feel good feeling stoned, feeling the sunshine soak through my skin to my bones to my mind made almost instantly mellow.

Only the jingle of Barry's collar as he starts up the stairs a few minutes later makes me forget that, even in Kierkegaard's hands, as fine a prose stylist as nineteenth-century philosophy knew, if you're fortunate enough to find yourself alone in a warm room on a cold winter afternoon in a wise sunlight bath, existential dread is just some idea some guy wrote about in some book a long, long time ago; some poor old dead guy; old, dead, gone.

ALL OF WHICH IS the opposite of sex. Which, all things considered, isn't something Mary and I have ever had to worry about. We're fine, we're okay, we're good.

Sure, ten years on, no couple couples like they did at the start, carries on as in the beginning, when the scent of fresh sex has yet to become merely another smell, when every kiss, lick, and stroke isn't born of a precisely intended effect, when the small of her back, the hollow behind her knee, the pink skin underneath her earlobes isn't as much your's as her's.

All that said, on the right night of the week, with the right mix of intoxicants, the right CD on the stereo, the right amount of nourishing sleep a few nights running leading up to — everything else being equal, in other words ...

Everything, everything, everything.

"IT'S ROVER," I SAY, tugging Barry along, cutting short his sniffing at the base of the water fountain.

"Where?" Mary says, eyes suddenly everywhere.

"Over there," I say, pointing, "by the trees, near the garbage pail."

Spotting him, "Oh, Rover," she says. "C'mon, Barry, let's go see Rover."

It's the park and it's his after-dinner walk, so Barry's game for anything except turning around and going home, but he's nearly sixty in human years and other dogs don't do it for him anymore like they do for Mary and me, even if the dog in question happens to be Rover, our current Sorauren Park favourite.

Rover is a West Highland terrier who once upon a time was undoubtedly ivory white and silky snugly but now, fourteen, fifteen, maybe even sixteen years post-puppyhood — his owners don't know for sure — is covered in a matted — where it isn't thinning and patchy — coat that somehow manages to appear simultaneously greasy and dry, and who has a soiled brown beard earned from thousands of happily gobbled meals. Rover doesn't fetch a stick, catch a Frisbee, or even chase a ball; instead, once a day, usually just before sundown, Rover's elderly dad carries him under his arm to the park, sets him down gently on the ground, and, with his equally aged wife, watches Rover sniff a dandelion, hike a stiff leg to pee against a tree, or just lie silently in the cool evening grass of summer or on winter's snow-covered earth, content to watch the other dogs take their turn in time running and jumping and chasing after one another in long, happy circles.

"Hi, Rover," Mary says, squatting down, holding out a hand for him to smell. Rover looks up from his sniffing only long enough to note Mary and then both of his parents still standing nearby before sticking his nose back in the frozen grass. He finally finds a spot that makes the grade and raises his back right leg no more than three inches before producing an eye-dropper's spurt of pee; gives two slow-motion kicks with his back legs after he's done — first the left, then the right, each equally feeble — and then starts sniffing all over again. Mary and I look at each other and smile. Rover's parents keep their eyes on Rover.

The man and the woman aren't typical dog people, don't make small talk about the weather or ask you what your dog's name is or how old he is or even say all that much to each other. They're like one of those ancient couples you see at cheap restaurants who sit down and order and eat and pay and leave without speaking more than six words to each other but who you know — you *know* — have somehow managed to yak away the entire dining time in their own secret lonely language.

Mary stands up. "Bye, Rover," she says, smiling at the woman, who returns the favour. The old man doesn't break his vigil over his dog. Barry, busy up to now gnawing at the end of a fallen branch, gets up when Mary does, and we start our counter-clockwise walk around the dirt track that encircles the park. Why we always walk counter-clockwise, I don't know, only that we do. A girl on a bicycle races by us through the icy mud, screaming the name of another kid on another bicycle a hundred feet or so ahead of her. Attached to the ends of her handlebars are bright blue streamers that flutter in the wind. I'd thought that sort of thing was all over. Mary takes the hand I'm not holding Barry's leash with.

"Do you think they have any children?" she says.

"Who, Rover's parents?"

"Uh huh."

"Maybe," I say. "If they do, they're probably older than us."

We stop when a Jack Russell coming our way slows down to greet Barry. On the other end of its leash is a middle-aged woman in a designer blue track suit and expensive-looking white running shoes talking on a cell phone, her only concession to the season a ridiculously long red scarf that, in spite of being wrapped around her neck several times, still hangs to her waist. "Of course," she says into the phone, "that's what he wants you to believe."

"I like to think that they don't," Mary says. "I like to think that they've always had Rover and that all three of them are going to grow old together."

"No," the woman on the phone says. "Absolutely not, no." Barry has finished sniffing her dog's butt, and now it's the Jack Russell's turn to get its whiffs in.

"They probably got him when they were in their fifties," I say. "Probably after their kids finished university or got married and moved away. Rover was probably some kind of surrogate kid."

Barry and the Jack Russell done with their sniffing inspections, we continue with our walk, the woman with the cell phone and her dog carrying on the other way.

"I don't want Barry to die before we do," Mary says.

"I don't want him to die either," I say. "But considering he's only got about three or four more years left, I'm kind of hoping he does." I reach down and pat him on his back end. "No offence, Bubs."

Barry is, variously, Bubs (or, alternatively, "the Bubs"), Bubba, Bubaloo, Sweetest Baboo, Bubbles, Barry Boy, Bare, the Barester, and Barryrama.

"I know, but I don't want him to ever die," Mary says. "Or I want all three of us to die at the same time."

"Well, we can hope for the house to burn down while we're all sleeping, I guess."

Mary drops my hand. I laugh, slip my arm around her waist.

"C'mon," I say. "I'm just saying that, considering that the odds of that happening aren't too high, I just hope he has a bunch more good years left in him and that when he's gone we get another dog half as great as he is."

"I could never love another dog as much as I love him."

"That's what you told me you thought about Tyga when you were growing up."

"I don't care," she says. "I want us to be like Rover's mum and dad. I want to be an old bag like her and for you to be a grumpy old man like him and for Barry to be just like Rover."

We're three quarters of our way around the park when a woman standing a little off to the side of the dog people waves in our direction.

"Who's that?" Mary says.

It takes me a moment to remember the woman with the British accent and the uncontrollable puppy. I wave back.

"Just somebody from the park," I say.

"AND THAT," PHIL SAYS, driving the ball into the left corner pocket, "is that." He straightens up and stands there for a moment, admiring the empty table.

"One more?" I say.

"Nah."

"C'mon."

"I need time to regroup," he says. "You're creeping up on me."

Actually, he's up 14,892 to 12,236 lifetime and I've never trailed by less than a thousand points. Still, in the last couple of years, even as we play less and less often, I do seem to be winning more than I lose. Maybe it's just because I'm finally getting better, although the way he always manages to win the final game, no matter how many I've won up to that point, makes me wonder if he isn't laying off.

"All right," I say, shrugging, putting my cue back on the wall.

Phil unscrews his stick. The eighteen-ounce, jointed cue with its own black leather case is a recent gift from Rebecca. She loathes the Duke and can't understand what Phil gets out of playing pool, here or anywhere else, but figured that if he was going to waste his time, he might as well do it properly. Phil wipes down the stick with a miniature white towel produced from the case and lays it delicately inside, like an old-time gangster his prized Tommy gun.

Back in the fall I'd arranged for Mary and me to hook up with him and Rebecca for a drink at the Duke before a poetry reading he was supposed to give at Harbourfront. To me, it was a no-brainer: Phil's first big-time reading, and there we'd be, toasting him where it all began, youthful den of dreaming and scheming iniquity. Except that Rebecca didn't believe she couldn't get a Crantini, complained that the jukebox was too loud, and refused to use the bathroom despite whining every five minutes that her bladder was about to burst. Worse, Mary wouldn't take off her coat, kept asking if they'd always kept it this cold, and Phil kept looking at his watch. He and Rebecca had to meet the other writers he'd be reading with for dinner, he explained. It was, Rebecca added, something everyone who is invited to read at Harbourfront is expected to do.

Phil and I sit down at our usual table by the jukebox. Up until the early nineties it had still been stocked with 45s. You'd drop in your quarters, punch in your selections, and a little black platter of wax would herky-jerky fall into place, spinning and spinning and waiting for the diamond-tipped kiss of the needle to ride it to life. Now, you feed your loonie into the machine, program what you want to hear, and the CD does the rest. The sound is better, but something's missing. Number 272 used to be "The Weight" by The Band. We knew the sound of the two pops and one long crackle that preceded the acoustic guitar opening almost as well as we did the song.

A few good gulps and our glasses are empty. I pick them up and start for the bar. Table service, like sanitary washrooms and clean ashtrays, has yet to catch on at the Duke. Phil holds up his hand.

"I'm done," he says.

"You've had two pints."

"So?"

"So, since when do you have two pints when we play pool?"

"We're done playing pool."

"So have another one anyway."

"I can't. I've got stuff to do when I get home."

"What kind of stuff?"

"Stuff, stuff, I don't know — stuff. Stuff I can't do if I'm half in the bag and falling asleep."

"So why did you say yes when I asked if you wanted to play pool tonight?"

"Because I wanted to. And we did play pool. You won two out of three games, remember?"

"You know that's not what I mean."

Phil stares at the flashing, silent jukebox; me, at the bar. Lenny is flipping the remote control looking for nudity, violence, or coarse language, preferably all three at once.

"If only in theory," Phil finally says, "is it possible for us to meet up once in a while and not get pissed?"

"Okay, Mary, I'll keep that in mind."

"Mary's a smart woman."

"Yeah, and ...?"

Phil looks into his lap. I'm still standing there with the empty glasses in my hand. He pulls on his ankle-length overcoat and picks up his stick.

"You do know that that coat makes you look queer, right?"

He says nothing to me, something to Lenny behind the bar

that I can't make out that Lenny merely grunts at, and is gone.

I put the glasses on the counter and pull a twenty out of my pocket, lay it down.

"These two and one more," I say.

Lenny succeeds in placing the two dirty empties in the steaming washer to the left of the bar and pouring me a fresh draft without either removing the cigarette from his mouth or taking his eyes off the TV. He puts my beer on the bar and draws himself a half pint. I push the bill closer.

"You want me to ring it in for you, too?" I say.

He swallows his beer in three mouthfuls; burps. Every atom of air around me is instantly infused with the smell of rotting kielbasa sausage marinating in a warm can of beer with a cigarette butt floating on top.

"Phil already paid," he says, still staring at the screen.

"I didn't see him pay."

Lenny helps himself to another. "Well, I guess you weren't looking."

IT'S NOVEMBER BUT FEELS like February. The hike home from the Duke is no stroll in the best of weather, but I let the street-car clank past anyway and keep walking.

The usual scene along Queen as the bars begin to shut down — people being squeezed like toothpaste back onto the street, high-fiving cabs, buying hot dogs from bored street vendors in snowsuits, ducking into steamed-window pizza places to shake off their brrrs and grab a booze-sopping slice, shouting and laughing and flirting on the sidewalk, anything but having to go home to the alarm clock and tomorrow.

I walk and walk and do my best Zen imitation. Every time my mind hiccups from nothingness to everything I don't want buzzing around in my brain right now, I hum whatever's handiest and get back to as blank as I can be. Right now, that's "Fire and Rain," compliments of the radio playing behind the cash register of the convenience store I'd stopped into for a half litre of skim milk for Mary's coffee in the morning. Getting old means running errands for the missus after you've shut down the bar and not being enraged when you can't get a James Taylor song out of your head.

Twenty minutes later and deep into Parkdale, the Indonesian restaurants and martini lounges transformed into scaldingly bright all-night donut shops and small, dark bars where there's usually a handwritten sign in the greasy front window announcing WE RESERVE THE RIGHT TO REFUSE SERVICE TO ANYONE! I stop for a red light at the corner of Queen and Gladstone. The muted chorus to Conway Twitty's "It's Only Make Believe" pushes Sweet Baby James from my mind and I look around to see what I hear.

Close to a century old and five stories high, I've walked by the Gladstone Hotel dozens of times, even sipped cheap draft beer there once or twice with Phil years before as a slumming undergrad. Downstairs, it's a cavernous beer hall looking out onto Queen Street through a large street-level window and dotted with Parkdale regulars nursing dollar glasses of Export, checking out their horoscopes and Biodexes at the back of the

Sun, and generally trying to beat back the glooms. Upstairs, there are small rooms for rent with a shared bathroom at the end of each floor and no electrical cooking devices whatsoever please. Once upon an entirely different demographic, travelling salesman and itinerant labourers of long-dead decades slept and socialized upstairs and down. Now, anybody who needs a place to fuck, shoot up, or spoon out their welfare check by the week calls the Gladstone home.

I wander over to the window. A woman in tight acid-washed jeans and white plastic pumps and a peach polyester blouse with a face like a rotten apple core smeared with red lipstick where her mouth is supposed to be is holding a microphone to her lips and reading from a teleprompter while she sings. Badly. To the accompaniment of a karaoke machine operated by a seated, middle-aged man with a '70s porn star moustache and a blow-dryed and feathered toupée. The woman belts out the song's last line and places the mike back in the stand and steps off the little raised stage, and the half-full room of the usual Parkdale suspects erupts in applause and whistles and beer-bottle table banging.

"That's it for tonight, folks," the man says into his own microphone. "You don't have to go home, but you can't stay here." In spite of his limp, an elderly bald waiter rushes around the room, busily removing bottles and glasses from the tabletops, loading up his brown plastic tray.

"And don't forget," the man says. "Everybody's a star every Friday and Saturday night at the Gladstone Hotel."

I walk the twenty minutes more it takes me to get home trying to remember what other songs Conway Twitty sang.

I'M IN THE BACKYARD stooping and scooping some recent and not-so recent Barry do-do when the wooden gate creaks open. I turn around, look up.

"Oh, hey, George," I say.

"Hello," George says.

"How's it going?"

"It is fine."

I nod a couple of times and wait for George to say something else that I know that he won't. I stick my hand inside a white plastic bag and use it as a glove to pick up another few lumps of near-frozen dog turds. George stands at the gate, hands in the pockets of his new tan winter coat, and watches me work.

George lives a couple of streets over with his daughter and her husband and George's teenage grandchildren, but he used to live here, at 81 Parkway, with his wife and his children, although the garage Mary and I call home was still an actual garage then, George's garage. He must have enjoyed spending time out there when he did live here because it was our living room he showed up in one day unannounced not long after we moved in, and not the living room in the house itself around front. I was downstairs doing something in the kitchen when I heard the screen door open and close. I just assumed it was Mary and Barry back from their walk and waited for Barry to come barreling down the stairs for his post-hike drink. When no one came down and I didn't hear Barry's collar and tag rattling around upstairs, I decided to check things out.

"What are you doing here?" An elderly man with a thick Polish accent turned around from the window.

"I live here," I said. "What are you doing here?"

I was more surprised than scared. The old man was wearing chocolate brown polyester slacks and a light brown cardigan sweater buttoned almost all of the way up over top of a white golf shirt. What little thin, black hair there was still left on his head was neatly parted to the side. The laces of one of his black dress shoes were undone. His hands were deep in his pockets.

"I live here," he said, not aggressively, just matter-of-factly, looking back out the window. "I just do not know why I built this window. How am I going to park my car in here now?" He turned around to face me again. "And all of these books and all of these things. Where is my car going to go? There is not any room for anything now."

Alzheimer's, I remember thinking; that, and that I needed to find out where this guy lives and to somehow get him back there. "My name's Hank," I said. "Would you like a cup of tea?"

"Of course," he said, and sat down in the reading chair. He placed a hand on each knee and looked out the window while he waited for me to bring him his cup of tea.

I plugged in the kettle and went back up to ask him what his name was and all the rest of it, but the chair was empty. A few days later I ran into the landlady, who lives in one of the two apartments in the main house, working in her small garden out front and she asked me if I'd met George, that she'd seen him leaving our backyard. It turned out that he'd taken to occasionally dropping by his old house since he'd started suffering from the disease. The next time he showed up, a few months later when I was shovelling a path to the gate door, I said, "Hey, George," and he answered, "Hello," back like I was an old, if slightly boring, acquaintance.

George wordlessly watches me fill up a progressively bulging bag of dog faeces the same way that I sometimes catch Barry watching me at the park after he's had his dump, like he can't quite figure out my fascination with collecting his shit. I stand up and tie the two ends of the white plastic bag together into a knot. "It's a dog's life, George," I say. I pull a fresh bag out of my coat pocket and squat back down to business.

"The first dog in space, he was a husky named Laika," George says into my back. "The Soviets, they sent him into space on Sputnik 2 in 1957. The Soviets, they did not know how to bring him back to earth so he burned up with the ship. There is a statue of him in Leningrad with all of the other Soviet astronauts."

I keep picking up Barry's poop, keep putting it in the bag. A lot of the Poles in the neighbourhood, especially the older ones around George's age, don't like Russians for what Communism did to their homeland, don't like anything even hinting at having to do with Russia. You don't need to hate Communism to feel lousy about the idea of a dog in outer space. A cat, maybe — a cat probably wouldn't even notice that there wasn't anyone else around — but a dog drifting alone through infinity is just about as lonely as it gets. Barry gets panicky when we leave him at home by himself longer than dinner and a movie.

"Did you have a dog when you used to live here, George?" I say.

George doesn't answer. I turn around on my heels and the gate is wide open, George is gone again.

FIRST, THE ANSWERING MACHINE, a chance to say something to someone you really don't want to say it to with only the ghost of a recorded voice on the other end to spook you; now, even better, e-mail, not even the danger of a real live person picking up and making the exchange remotely human. So, instead of, say, "What's your problem, Roberts? Get off your ass and do what we pay you to do or we'll find someone else who will," such canned cyber-niceties as:

> *Mr. Roberts:*
> *Our records indicate that the manuscript of Ms. Lenore*
> *Shipely (Student # 6714256) was mailed to you over*
> *three weeks ago; may I inform her that she can expect*
> *your response soon?*

I shut down my computer, grab the manila envelope off my desk and a can of Diet Pepsi from the fridge, and head upstairs; settle down in the reading chair so I can watch the afternoon flurries provide snow-show delight during brain-breaks from being wowed by Ms. Shipely's words; crack the tab on the pop, cross my legs just so, take an inaugural sip, set the can down on the side table, and, comfy, yes, very comfy, thank you, let us begin. Now. Let us begin now. Right now. Now.

Memories….
Of Mother, Father, Frank, little Billy, Sarah,
Nanna….

The wispy spectres of myself as a child on the plains
of Regina.

But who is the memory and who is real? Who is
the dreamer and who is the dream? Might I not be
a memory myself without even knowing it? Might
not these very words I write be the real dream? Have
I become a prisoner of Western "ideas" of time,
personality and the past? These are the questions that
haunt me. These are the questions that I must ask.

It could be me. Maybe Marcel Proust is still hard at it and living in Thornhill, Ontario, and I'm too dumb to know it. Look at Van Gogh — ha ha ha until he's History, and then all of a sudden a genius nobody knew about. Look at Rebecca. Maybe that's me, too. One of the newspapers, I forget which, called her last book hauntingly lyrical and emotionally coura-geous. CBC serialized it on the radio on some book program and she flew around the country to a bunch of literary festivals to read from it. She won some award for up-and-coming writers, too, and was a finalist for a couple of others. What do I know that everybody else doesn't? All I know about literature as anything more than something you read because you like to read it I learned at Phil's elbow, for nearly fifteen years an unbroken tutorial at beer-bottle-cluttered kitchen tables, freezing all-night streetcar stops, and bars bars bars — the Duke mostly, paperbacks and library books and the ones we were going to write someday fighting for table space with glasses of warm, soapy beer and loose change for the jukebox.

Once, we — he, Phil, really, I just typed out what he said — wrote a letter to Raymond Souster — a poet, not a great one, not even a great Canadian one, but a poet — who Phil somehow found out lived in Etobicoke, just like him. *Dear Mr. Souster, we've been reading your* Collected Poems *with much pleasure and interest, and wonder about your use of ...* And goddamn if he didn't write back, an envelope in my mailbox a couple of weeks later right there along with a phone bill, a reminder of some overdue library books, and something for somebody who moved a long time ago, no forwarding address.

Among other bluster, we'd asked him about the difficult business of attempting to fuse poetry and ordinary language, and he'd suggested we get a hold of Baudelaire's *Paris Spleen* if we hadn't already. We sure as hell had. Phil read aloud from memory with closed eyes. I signaled Lenny for another pitcher of Red Baron.

"'Which one of us, in his moments of ambition, has not dreamed of the miracle of a poetic prose, musical, without rhyme and without rhythm, supple enough and rugged enough to adapt itself to the lyrical impulses of the soul, the undulations of reverie, the jibes of conscience?'"

"Fucking A," I said.

"To Mr. Charles Baudelaire," Phil said, lifting his glass.

"To Mr. Raymond Souster," I said, raising mine.

Phil stood up. Me, too.

"From Paris, France, 1855," he said, "to Etobicoke, Ontario, 1989, to the Duke of Connaught, right here, right now, at the corner of Queen Street West and Agusta Avenue. The torch has been passed."

Lenny placed our fresh pitcher of beer on the table. "That's $9.50, ladies," he said.

I go to the bookshelf and pull down Rebecca's latest, *Shadow Love*. I flip past the inscription —

For Henry and Mary,
To the start of a great new friendship.
Best,
Rebecca

— and start reading at random. A couple of minutes later I look up from the novel to find Barry sitting politely beside the chair with a yellow tennis ball stuck in his mouth. How did dogs ever manage before there were tennis balls? I pluck the thing out and toss it across the room. One of the advantages of living in a converted garage is not being overly fussy about home decor or its upkeep. Barry, born to retrieve, returns with the ball, and I take turns reading and tossing.

Dogs don't lie, not about what they want to do, not about what they don't. Barry trots back one last time and lies down at my feet; drops the ball between his paws and stares up at me, panting, the business end of his long black nose good and wet and glistening in the afternoon sunlight. I step over him to where we keep the poetry and grab *Paris Spleen*, turn to the only page marked with a paper clip.

> *Dissatisfied with everything, dissatisfied with myself, I long to redeem myself and to restore my pride in the silence and solitude of the night. Souls of those whom I have loved, souls of those whom I have sung, strengthen me, keep me from the vanities of the world and its contaminating fumes; and You, dear God! grant me grace to produce a few beautiful verses to prove to myself that I am not the lowest of men, that I am not inferior to all those whom I despise.*

I put the book on the arm of the chair and take a drink of pop; lean over and scratch Barry, lying on his side now, stretched out tail to snout as long as he can, between the ears.

"Fucking A," I say.

OWNING A CAR IN THE city is like brown-bagging it at an all-you-can eat lunch buffet. We don't need one, so we don't have one. And what excellent ecologicals are we. And if, because we want to take Barry with us when we visit my parents, there's simply no way around renting a brand new Ford Lexus equipped with computer mapping capacity, a plug-in for the cell-phone we don't own, and a surround-sound stereo with three-inch woofers front and back, who's to blame? Not me, not Mary. Let's go, let's go, and don't forget to pull over at the first Tim Horton's we see on the highway, two double-doubles and twenty assorted Timbits to go.

Mary drives and I manage the music and pump the gas. My uselessness is legit — even with my contacts lenses in I can't read the cut-off signs until we're practically on top of them, and as soon as the sun goes down anything further away than ten feet melts into the dusky fog of everything else. But I'm glad to be riding shotgun, always have.

I pull this afternoon's first selection, T. Rex's *Electric Warrior*, out of the case of used CDs I've accumulated over the years for just such cruising occasions, and set the Groover, Marc Bolan, grooving. The mambo sun is high in the clear, bright, blue sky, and though it's cold enough outside for Mary to have the defroster blasting to the max, my clan is safe and warm inside one whole ton of moving metal whizzing west down the 401. After having executed his usual bon voyage happy roll in the backseat, all four black furry legs straight up in the air and kicking while we head-butted with traffic trying to get out of town, Barry is now asleep lengthwise across the seat.

Every relationship should undertake at least one extended road trip every six months. Nowhere to go but where you are, you talk. Even for couples like Mary and me who are each other's number one listener, a speeding vehicle is the perfect place to be forced to sit still and say what you didn't know you had to say.

Mary looks great in her black Ray-Bans and with her hair pulled back into a shiny brown ponytail, and I slowly run my hand up and down her blue jeaned thigh while Marc and the boys bang a gong all in the name of getting it on. We're not old but we're not young anymore, either, and every fresh sex itch is a success. Love needs lust, too.

Eyes on the road, Mary rests her free hand on top of mine for a long moment; reaches between her seat and mine and pulls two photographs out of her bag on the floor in the back, hands them to me.

"What's this?" I say.

"What do you think of when you look at these?"

There's a picture of me taken around the time we met, trying to look cool leaning on one foot with my back against the brick front of the Duke, and another one of me throwing a ball to Barry in the park in the fall, just a couple of months back.

I scratch my head. "Fourteen years, wow. Does it feel that long to you? It doesn't to me."

"Yes and no," Mary says, turning down the heat halfway. We've both got our hats and coats off now.

"I know. It's like it seems just like yesterday, but also like I can't really remember my life before then, before me met."

She gives my thigh a quick squeeze, smiles. "Anything else?"

she says. "Anything, maybe, different between you then and you now?"

I look at the twenty-two-year-old version of me again and then the one that's me now. "I sure dress better these days," I say.

Mary hits the turn signal and pulls around a lagging transport. As kids on field trips, every time the school bus would end up beside a truck everybody would hang their arm out the window and start pumping it up and down trying to get the trucker to blow his horn. The teachers would always yell at us to keep our hands inside at all times, and we'd all sit back down in our seats. But sometimes it worked, sometimes one of the drivers would hit his horn and we'd all go nuts, yell and clap and cheer.

"Hank," Mary says, peeking in the rear-view mirror at the Saab behind us, "you know I think you're a very attractive man. You know that, right?"

"Okay."

"And that I love being with you. Being with you in bed."

"Sure." I'm getting that fluttery feeling in my stomach that comes from knowing that certain kinds of compliments are only a warm-up to something else.

"And I know that you think it's just as important as I do that we keep finding each other as attractive as we can. Like when you told me how you hated it when I wore my sweat pants around the house, even when I was painting, because that was something your mother did when you were growing up and it grossed you out. So I stopped wearing them around you, remember?"

Now my hands are starting to perspire, and the little black heat vent in front of me isn't even open. "What are you trying to say?" I say.

"Don't get mad, I'm just trying to talk to you about something that I think is important. Important to both of us."

"Well, say it, then. Whatever it is it can't be worse than this."

"Jerk," Mary says into the mirror. "If you want to pass me, pass me, just don't sit on my bumper." Turning to me, "It's not only inconsiderate to drive that close, it's dangerous."

"So I've heard," I say.

She shoots me a look that I don't require x-ray vision to see through her sunglasses to know isn't anywhere near affectionate. "You don't have to deal with assholes like this," she shoots back. "I do." She buzzes down her window and sticks her arm outside and motions for the guy to go around. Amazingly, he stays where he is.

Mary not only hates it when motorists don't keep to the prescribed distance of two car-lengths between vehicles, she also can't stand people who butt ahead in line at the grocery store or try to get away with not paying their full fare on the streetcar. Mary's parents were both public school teachers who brought her up to believe that the world is essentially a good place filled with basically nice people who usually do the right thing, and that it's up to everyone to set a good example for everyone else. Sometimes I tell her that she should sue for prolonged mental abuse.

"I don't believe this," Mary says. Now she's got her eyes on the rear-view mirror more than she does on the road ahead.

"Forget about him," I say. "If you let him get you upset, he wins." I can see she's got an answer all ready for that, so I say, "Tell me what you wanted to tell me before." At this, her face softens and I'm immediately sorry I helped let the guy in the Saab off the hook.

She caresses my thigh. Two thigh massages inside fifteen minutes are definitely not a good sign. It couldn't be cancer. I haven't been to a doctor in months.

"How come you and Phil stopped playing hockey at Scadding Court?" she says.

It's been so long, three, maybe four years, I have to think about it for a moment. "I don't know. It was just pick-up hockey. Not enough guys showed up after awhile to make a good game of it, I guess. Why?" I turn in my seat to face her. "You want to tell me what's going on?"

She looks in the mirror again; the Saab's not there anymore, there's nobody around but us. "I just think we're both getting to that age where we need to think about getting some regular exercise," she says. Tapping her washboard stomach, "I know I can stand to lose a few pounds."

"You think I'm fat," I say.

"Hank, I didn't —"

"You think I'm fucking fat." In spite of the sweater, jeans, and winter boots I'm wearing, I feel naked. I cross my arms over my chest.

"Don't get mad and don't turn this into something else," Mary says. "This is about me caring about you and how you feel and wanting you to keep feeling good and looking good."

"Or what?" I say. "Or you'll leave me for somebody who looks exactly like he did fourteen years ago? Who the hell looks like they did fourteen years ago? Who looks like they did *ten* years ago?" I glare at the first photograph, the one of me standing in front of the Duke with a stupid grin on my face, and slap it upside down on my knee. "And I do feel good, all right? I feel great, in fact. How do you know I don't feel better now than I did back then?"

In a tiny voice, "Fine," she says. "Forget I said anything."

"Fine."

When the last song on *Electric Warrior*, "Rip Off," fades to its end, I pop out the CD, click it back into its case, and don't stick in one of the other eight I've brought along for the trip. And look at all that farmland, would you? Miles and miles of hibernating southwestern Ontario farmland tucked in for the winter under a nice big white blanket of southwestern Ontario snow. Which we do, in silence.

Somewhere between London and Chatham I think about how strange it is that someone like Marc Bolan, someone who did so many drugs and drank so much alcohol, should end up dying in a car crash. And just how odd is it, too, that his girlfriend, the one who was driving, ended up walking away without a scratch.

I SUPPOSE I COULD get all sensitive about all the ways my parents let me down, never giving me the this, that, and the other thing I needed to become the fully adjusted adult that destiny so clearly intended me to be. But something happens around the time you hit the age your mum and dad were when you moved out of the house. Slowly it starts to sink in that they were probably just as messed up as you are now — more, very likely — and that they probably did as competent a job as they were ever equipped to. Thought thunk and sunk in, soon the poison from the family puss bag you've been lugging around with you your entire life long begins its slow, steady drain, never to be entirely emptied, to be sure, but a lot less heavy as time does its own dependable drip drip drip.

So, no, no home movies, no why and how of what made me me, just right here, right now; which, really right now, means everyone but me in my parents' house asleep for hours, me in my dad's spare bathrobe on the rec room couch downstairs in front of the TV with all the lights turned off and channel surfing from one coast of the satellite TV universe to the other. The rabbit ears from Radio Shack we have at home do the trick — *Hockey Night in Canada*, NFL football on Sunday afternoons, *The Simpsons* — but I don't even try to resist the remote control the first night whenever we come to visit.

It's like what they used to do with teenagers caught coming home tipsy from their first high-school dance — get the bottle down from the kitchen cupboard and get them so liqoured up and puking sick that they never want to touch the hard stuff again. By about four in the morning — after seeing every basketball and hockey highlight so many times that I'm doing my own post-game recaps in my head when it finally hits the pillow, every episode of M*A*S*H, *Barney Miller*, and

63

RAY ROBERTSON

Taxi I can luck in to, snatches of every second-rate movie I
succeeded in avoiding at the theatre when it came out, every
music video by musicians who are no way old enough to have
any idea what they're singing about, every piece of nasty news
CNN, CBC Newsworld, and City-Pulse 24 can come up
with — I've got a thumb cramp from three straight hours of
channel surfing and an excellent reminder of why relative
poverty has its upside. Cocaine and satellite dishes: life's way of
punishing people who have way too much money.

Not that my parents are rich; just the familiar formula of
saving and saving and never spending because they never do
anything because there's nothing they like to do. The old man,
fifth of nine children, a grade eight dropout to get the hell
out of the house and start making some of that good green,
running errands at an auto supply store for $1.15 an hour and
washing cars at a taxi stand at thirty cents a pop, was lucky
enough to hop aboard the last stop that the Milk Train made
at the automobile factories in the mid-sixties, when a guy
without a high-school diploma but with a strong back and a
high tolerance for mind-mushing boredom could get married,
buy a house, own his own Oldsmobile, raise a few rug rats,
and have just enough left over in his savings account to go to
Florida every year for a couple of weeks in March. Today, he'd
have to lie about his highest level of education just to cop the
midnight-to-eight shift at 7-11.

He and mum made out all right. A split-level ranch-style
prefab in a freshly bulldozed subdivision with a winterized
garage equipped with a colour TV and beer fridge for him,

wall-to-wall everything inside the house for her (pink hand towels you don't dare dirty proudly on display on the bathroom counter, a rock garden out back just like the one she saw on *Home and Garden Television*), they got the stuff they wanted. And going by the bumper sticker on the cherry-red SUV parked in the driveway of the house across the street, whoever has the most toys at the end wins.

In the dark of the basement only the television screen exists. I mute the sound but keep it turned on for light, pad across the thick carpet in my bare feet and turn the door handle of the spare bedroom where Mary and I sleep, as quietly as I can, whisper, "Barry, c'mon, let's go for a pee." With me out of the picture he's made his move, is back-to-back with Mary, his head almost as high as hers, practically resting on my pillow.

As well as suffering from a touch of arthritis in his back hips and beginning to develop cataracts, Barry's starting to lose his hearing. I come closer and give him a shake.

"Barry, let's go," I whisper again. Normally he'd be good until at least ten in the morning, but away from home he eats irregularly, pisses and shits irregularly, and generally needs twenty-four hours to get in synch with his new surroundings. Although mum gets up at around seven, an indulgence she allows herself after rising at 5:30 nearly every morning for twenty years to make breakfast for a hundred-plus residents at a senior citizens' home, I don't want him scratching at the back door at dawn, waking her or the old man up. They've earned their rest.

Barry lifts his head, jumps down from the bed without disturbing Mary, and I shut the door behind us; he following me, we creep up the stairs. It's not the same house I grew up in — mum with rheumatoid arthritis in both knees wanted a laundry room on the first floor, laundry being her number one retirement pastime, and the old man thought it was time to move up to a two-car garage although they only own one car. I still don't have a feel for where the light switches are or how the walls meet up, the general geography of groping along in the dark. Guided by the familiar grind of my father's teeth, we bump and bungle our way past my parents' closed bedroom door through to the kitchen that's Christmas-light lit by the digital green pulse of the stove clock and the steady red glow of the coffee maker waiting to percolate to life at 6:45, and into the living room and to the front door. The recently installed hardwood floors prickle my nose hairs with the residue from what must have been their lemon-scented morning chemical bath. Cleanliness is next to nothing. Not even God could make shiny things shine like my mother.

I unlock the deadbolt and open the screen door, and Barry and I both take a step back, stare at the whirling white of the snowstorm that must have whipped up after the world went to bed. Every car, truck, lawn, driveway, and rooftop is thick with the stuff, no street plow or huffing shoveller having had a chance yet to correct nature's work. Every window in every house along the street is black. The streetlight in front of my parents' house attracts snowflakes like mosquitoes to a porch light. A wind chime in someone's backyard tinkles in the pounding wind.

I give Barry's rear end a push with my bare foot. "Hurry up and piss."

He heads straight for my mother's favourite azalea bush and does his business, long black ears blowing in the wind, eyes half shut against the drifting snow. He trots right back inside as soon as he's done.

"Good boy," I say.

"YOU SURE YOU DON'T want a toasted western?"

Spoon to mouth, "Cereal is fine, mum."

"I'm making your dad one anyway."

"I know, I'm okay."

"I didn't bake because the last time I baked it all went bad after you'se left."

Chew, swallow. "I told you not to make a big deal and bake for us. We usually don't eat sweets around the house anyway."

Especially now that Mary has apparently decided that I'm obese. Even though I haven't eaten meat in six years. Even though I don't take sugar in my tea anymore. Even though I drink diet, not regular, Pepsi. I try to remember if she should be starting her period around now.

"Well, I didn't," she says. "If I bake, it'll just go to waste. Your dad and I can't eat like we used to."

Every time I come home my parents seem smaller. A little

more wrinkled, greyer, stooped over. Within half an hour they're my parents again and I'm their son, but the initial shock is always the same. When the hell did my mum and dad turn into my grandparents?

"I bought fruit," my mother says, hobbling from the stove to the overflowing bowl on the kitchen counter, "because you said to get fruit when you came to visit and not to bake. So eat it, don't let it go bad."

Everything that can be done for her arthritis — anti-inflammatory pills, cortisone shots, physical therapy — has been done. The best she can do now is stay off her feet as much as possible and stay doped on television and fresh home-improvement schemes like rewallpapering the downstairs bathroom every six months.

I look up from yesterday's *Chatham Daily News* sports page. Mary is in the shower downstairs, my dad with Barry out in the garage. Reminding him that ours is a rental car never makes any difference. By the time we roll out of bed Saturday morning not only has the tank been filled up, but the wind-shield wiper fluid has been topped off and he's washed and dried it by hand at the car wash.

"Maybe I'll have an apple after I finish my cereal," I say.

"Since when do you eat apples?"

"Since, I don't know, forever."

"Apples make your stomach upset."

"No they don't."

"Well, they did when you were growing up. You'd eat

bananas and pears and oranges, but never apples. Oranges were your favourite. I'd always pack an orange in your lunch."

"I eat apples all the time now."

Not looking at me, looking out the patio door, "Well, I didn't buy any apples," she says.

I stare into my bowl of cereal; lift a spoonful of Raisin Bran then set it back down in the milky mush. "How about a banana?" I say. "I can put a banana on my cereal."

My mother has stopped listening, is fixated on a squirrel standing upright in the middle of the backyard holding something close to its chest between its two front feet. The radio on the kitchen counter is on, is always on, and always on the same station, CFCO, Chatham's only radio station, but she's not paying attention to Karen Carpenter musing in tune about how we've only just begun any more than she'll hear the news at the top of the hour, the sports at ten past, or the weather forecast five minutes after that. But CFCO is never not on. In high school, whenever she wasn't in the kitchen, I would shut the thing off as some kind of unarticulated protest against the tyranny of the nuclear family or the insipidness of commercial radio or the self-numbing narcoticism that was the North American obsession with what Pascal identified as divertisse-ments, I forget which. She'd just click it back on when she came back into the room.

"Those damn squirrels better not be into my rose garden," she says.

I can hear Mary coming up the stairs. Reinforcements for

the troops, and not a moment too soon. "The squirrels aren't eating your roses, mum," I say. "He's probably just got a nut or something."

"Where would he get a nut? There aren't any nut trees around here."

"I don't know, maybe he buried it."

"There's two feet of snow out there, how could he dig up a nut?"

"How could he dig up one of your rose bushes?"

Mary sweeps into the room, barefoot in blue Levi cords and an oversized sweater and with a thick blue towel wrapped around her wet hair like a freshly scrubbed swami. She kisses me on the forehead and sits down across the table. "Well, what's the plan for today?" she says.

My mother finally gives up on the squirrel, pivots around to face Mary. "Well, look who's up," she says. "I've just been waiting for you, little girl. As soon as you get ready, you and I are going to Winners."

Mary is no more thrilled at being in Chatham than I am, just does a much better job of pretending like it, probably because she didn't have to grow up here. Mary does all of the things my mother wishes I would do when we visit: shop, overeat, watch too much TV. Me marrying Mary almost makes up for my wasting four years studying philosophy, not having a career yet, not wanting to have children. Never mind that Mary doesn't want any either.

"Just let me dry my hair and we'll go," Mary says, rubbing her head with the towel. "What's everybody eating?"

Before I can suck in my stomach and answer *Just cereal*, my mother lumbers to the stove and opens the oven door.

"Have all you want," she says, pulling out a cookie tray crammed with date squares, hunks of fudge, sugar cookies, and homemade Nanaimo bars. "They'll all just go bad if you don't eat them."

"DID YOU CLEAN THE filter in your dehumidifier like I said to?"

"Yep."

"Hey?"

"Yeah, yeah, I did, I did," I say.

"Did you just shake it out, or did you rinse it with warm water and a squirt of dish soap like I told you?"

"I rinsed it."

"Bullshit, you did," my father says from his easy chair, flipping the channel from the all-highlight station back to the hockey game. "I know you. If you did anything, all you did was shake it outside for a minute and then stick it back in." We're downstairs in the basement watching the Red Wings play Anaheim, my mum and Mary upstairs watching some movie. "You've got to give it a chance to do its job, boy," he says. "If you don't, you know what'll happen, don't you?"

"It won't work properly."

"It won't suck out the moisture and you'll just be wasting your time."

"All right."

"You don't want your downstairs all musty and damp, do you?"

"No."

"Okay, then, do it the way I told you to when you get home. Give the poor bastard a chance to do what it was made to do."

The Anaheim goalie — my dad and I refuse to refer to the Anaheim players as "Mighty Ducks" — kicks out a slap shot from the point, but the Red Wings' captain, Steve Yzerman, lifts the rebound high over the sprawling, helpless netkeeper for an easy goal.

"Stevie Wonder," my dad shouts, clapping his hands once, hard.

"The Captain," I say.

We both watch the replay, then another, then another one after that. Pretty, so pretty, no matter what angle you look at it from.

"I'll tell you one thing," my dad says, picking up the package of Players' Lights off the coffee table, shaking a cigarette free and stabbing it in his mouth. The table is covered in shiny black remote controls (one each for the TV, the VCR, and the stereo hooked up to the television), opened bags of Cheezies, potato chips, and Doritos, all rendered airtight with old white plastic bread tabs, a marble ashtray whose SIEMENS AUTOMOTIVE: DO WHAT YOU SAY, SAY WHAT YOU DO is half obscured with crushed butts, and a foot-long skinny metal device designed to fire up the gas barbecue but which my parents have adopted for use as the world's longest cigarette lighter. One flick of his thumb, and a six-inch flame leaps to ignite the cigarette in his mouth; he takes a deep, satisfying suck. "That son of a bitch may be skating on only one good wheel," he says, gesturing toward the TV, one eye shut and the other squinting through the smoke, "but he still knows what to do with the puck when he gets it, I'll tell you that."

"Upstairs every time."

"Nothing but net. There's no goalie that can stop that."

"What is he, thirty-eight?" I say.

"Most guys with his knee problems, I don't care what their age is, they wouldn't be out there, let alone making the plays he still does."

"What is he, thirty-eight now, thirty-nine?"

"Other guys, they panic and whack at it as soon as they get it. He takes his time and puts it where they keep the cookies. There's no way a goalie can stop that. No way."

The game goes to commercial and an ad comes on plugging the eleven o'clock Detroit news. One homicide in suburban Hamtramck and a drive-by shooting downtown, three fires raging out of control, arson suspected in each, camera crews on the scene, and Red Wings and Pistons highlights and your Channel 50 extended weather forecast right after the game. Dad punches the review button and we're back on The Score. Detroit is only fifty miles away but might as well be a thousand. Growing up an hour from the border, America was always good for a few thrills and chills, but never really seemed real, was as much make-believe as the twenty-four hours a day of fun and games on The Score, only without the feeling that on any given day anyone could end up a winner.

Settling back into his chair again, "How's that course you're teaching that your buddy got you working out?"

"Good."

"You still getting work through Mary's place?"

"It's a little slow right now, but yeah, sometimes."

We both watch some guy fly through the air and jam a basketball in a net. Basketball is better than the Meryl Streep movie playing upstairs, but it's not our game. What you never played, you can never really know.

"That thing you've been working on, that thing you started back at school, how's that going?"

A short white guy nails a three pointer. As little as I follow the game, it seems like all white guys are good for is scoring three pointers and getting beat to the basket by taller, bigger black guys.

"I'm getting there."

"And Mary?"

"What about her?"

"Things are all right there, too?"

"Sure."

"That girl is a winner, boy, hold on to her."

"Yeah, Dad, I plan to."

He aims and presses the remote. A commercial for a used car dealership featuring a guy in a cheap bear costume and a Red Wings jersey throwing fistfuls of money into a wind machine finishes up, and we're back just in time for the face-off. My dad leans forward and taps his cigarette in the ashtray, pulls a hundred dollar bill from his pants and sticks it in my shirt pocket.

"What's this," I say, pulling it out.

"What the hell does it look like."

I make a face. "I mean, why?"

"I don't need a reason to give my son some spending money."

"I said I was doing okay."

"Good, I'm glad. So take your wife out and have a nice dinner."

"Dad, I —"

"Hello!" he shouts, jamming his cigarette in his mouth, lunging forward to the edge of his chair.

I'm too late, look back at the set only in time to see the Red Wings players in front of the Anaheim net exchanging gentle head butts and swats to each other's rear ends.

"Who got it?" I say.

"These guys are no match for the big red machine tonight."

"Who scored?" I say, sticking the money in my jeans.

The old man takes a long drag on his cigarette. "These guys aren't even in the same league."

AFTER EVERYONE ELSE HAS hit the sack I call a cab and wait upstairs by the front window. In the city you put your hand in the air and get in. In a small town you have to pick up the phone and give somebody your name, address, phone number, and where you're going, then twiddle your thumbs for twenty-five minutes hoping they show up.

The cab, the only car on the street not asleep under three inches of snow, finally stops in front of my parents' house, honks. The driver probably doesn't make too many trips out to Prestancia Village so can be excused for not knowing that a single beep from a car horn at the corner of Water Crescent and Daisy Avenues during single digit a.m. hours can part an entire neighbourhood's worth of bedroom curtains.

"How's it going?" I say, sliding into the backseat. No CD player or even tape deck up front, he's got CFCO on the AM radio, the Guess Who doing "Undone," their uniquely Winnipeg take on free jazz. Middle-of-the-nighttime is Canadian content time, the same time you usually hear the public service announcements they're obligated to play.

"Car freeze up?" the driver says, checking me out in the rear-view mirror as we pull away from the curb.

"Yeah," I say, "froze right up." Why else would somebody from the suburbs call a cab? It's not worth explaining.

"Colder than a witch's tit out there tonight," he says.

Most Toronto taxi drivers are uncommunicative when they aren't busy chattering away into their cell phone headsets, but this guy is eager to get some yackety-yack going. He's wearing a Red Wings baseball cap so I ask him if he watched the game before he left for work.

"Been on since four," he says.

"That's a long day."

"A long day and a long night."

"Wings won six — two," I say.

"Oh, yeah, I know, I listened to it," he says, pointing at the radio, as if I needed proof. If you're from Chatham, you're either a Red Wings fan or a Maple Leafs fan. My dad's team is the Red Wings, so my team is the Red Wings. Real fans don't get to choose who they cheer for.

"They're going all the friggin' way again," he says. "The only one's that can stop them is themselves."

"Colorado looks good," I say. "And Vancouver scares me a little."

"*Vancouver.* I thought you said you watched the game tonight. The only one's that can stop them is themselves."

"I hope you're right," I say.

"Hoping's got nothing to do with it. All the friggin' way."

Queen Street — Burger King, McDonald's, Blockbuster Video, Taco Bell — then King Street — Kentucky Fried Chicken, Hooters, Little Caesar's — then the Thames River bridge. The British had their shot, now it's the Americans' turn to make us over in their image. At least the cold and hockey are still ours, if only because nobody else wants them. Not yet, anyway.

The Thames, our Thames, cuts Chatham in half. There's the south side, where my parents used to live and I grew up, containing what's left of the old downtown core and the first scab of suburbs encrusting it, and there's the north side, where instead of the corn fields and tomato fields and empty acres of earth of my youth, there are the new subdivisions like the one my parents live in now. We cross the bridge, and for the first time all weekend I finally feel like I'm back home.

There's Sears, where I used to work weekends in the sporting goods department during high school; there's the house where Stacy Larmner, the first girl I ever got to second base with, used to live; there's where Coles Books used to be, where I bought Tennessee Williams's *The Glass Menagerie* and *Cat on a Hot Tin Roof* on the same rainy Saturday afternoon in March when I was seventeen, the first books I ever paid for with my own money that weren't about sports or rock bands.

Warm and fuzzy are the first-evers you never get back. Where they happened to happen is just accidental geography. Chatham is my accident, the same way that the Red Wings are my team. I don't have to cheer, but I can't wear anybody else's hat, either.

"Here's good," I say, and the driver slows to a stop in front of Brad's parents' house.

In spite of themselves, all subdivisions eventually shed their stubborn sameness, decades of dedicated landscaping and home improvements slowly cracking the neighbourhood mold. Thirty years after we moved in, my parents' old place, a ten minute walk from Brad's, almost looks like it's supposed to be there. Unlike their new house, surrounded by the skeletons of half-finished homes rising out of frozen, muddy lots, and all-day-busy, beep-beeping cement trucks.

"Eight-fifty," the cabbie says, stopping the meter. He turns down the radio while I pull out my wallet. Poor Corey Hart can't even cut it keeping taxi drivers interested anymore. When Brad and I were in high school you couldn't get away from the guy, we thought he'd never go away. He did, and nobody even noticed.

I hand the driver a ten. "Thanks," I say, hand on the door handle.

"Hold on, don't forget your change," he says.

"Don't worry about it," I say. "Thanks for the lift."

"Thanks a lot," he says, saluting me with the bill before sticking it in the front pocket of his red and black-checked bush jacket. A whole loonie and two quarters to the good; back in the city, it wouldn't even rate a phony smile.

"No problem," I say, getting out.

Big, fat, slow-falling flakes are coming straight down from the sky, but it's so still in the street that the crunch of the snow under my boots is loud. I can hear the hum from the street lamp in front of Brad's house. His basketball hoop with the same torn net is still hanging over the garage door in the driveway.

The driver rolls down his window as he pulls away. "Go Wings," he says.

"Go Wings," I say.

WE LIKED THE SAME records, sat beside each other in the same classes, agreed on which girls were hot and which ones were stuck-up, stood around together at the same parties drinking beer from the same twelve-pack of Blue and making fun of the same people, and, most of all, wanted the same thing: to get out of Chatham. And we did, too, me to U of T, him to Queens, in Kingston.

Then the then. Then the unimaginable, but no less inevitable, then. We saw each other less and talked to each other less, and when we did get together, at Christmastime or during March break or the couple of times I took the train up there and visited him at school, we had less and less to say. No disagreements, no personality clashes, nothing simmering underneath the hood that needed to be cooled off if the engine wasn't going to boil over. We just had less and less to say.

Brad dropped out of Queens in the middle of his second year, moved back into the room his parents had fixed up for him in the basement the summer before we started grade thirteen and never left. Last time I was through town, near the end of summer, he'd just quit his job as the midnight-to-eight security guard at Natural Gas. After only a couple of weeks, they'd sprung some sort of electronic key on him that he had to use on his rounds so that they could keep tabs on their guards during unsupervised shifts.

"What am I, twelve?" he said. "They can't trust a thirty-seven-year-old man to do a job that any halfway intelligent chimp could do blindfolded?"

"But you weren't doing it. You told me you spent most of your shift sleeping in the cafeteria."

"That's not the point."

I walk around the side of the house and squat down beside the basement window, rap twice, once, then twice more, the same knock we used during high school when I'd have Stacy drop me off after making out in her basement rec room or I'd get tired of becoming wise gobbling up *Why I Am Not a Christian* or *The Conquest of Happiness* or whatever other Bertrand Russell book the Chatham Public Library had special ordered for me, and hoof the ten minutes over from my place. No matter how late it was, Brad would always be up.

From behind the window curtain, as if he was expecting me, "Come round back," he says.

In the thirteen years since he'd come home to stay, the downstairs bedroom has metamorphosed into a full-blown basement apartment equipped with its own bathroom, bar fridge, and private entrance. Brad still eats his meals upstairs with his mum, though, she still making him all of his favourites: Shepherd's pie, three-cheese lasagna, liver and onions, and BLTs on Wonder bread for breakfast every Friday, just like during high school. Friday was always a good day to drop by Brad's house before school.

"Hey," he says, unlocking the screen door.

"Hey."

I follow him down the carpeted stairs. He's wearing the exact same thing he wore fifteen years ago: running shoes, loose grey track pants, and a baggy white T-shirt. His blond hair still hangs almost to his shoulders, but there's a small bald spot on the top of his head that gets a little less small every time I come home. What, back in high school, was the enviable heft of the anchor of our offensive line is now about fifty pounds more than his six-foot frame should be carrying.

He leaves me my choice of the recliner parked between the

stereo speakers and the couch in front of the TV; lies down lengthwise on the bed and grabs the ashtray and package of du Maurier Lights off the side table and lights up, ashtray on his chest.

"How are your folks?" he says.

"Good. How's your mum?"

"Okay. She might have diabetes, they're not sure. They're still doing tests."

"That's a drag."

"Yeah."

"That kind of thing isn't as big a deal as it used to be," I say. "Sometimes they can treat it just by changing the person's diet."

"Yeah."

"It's still a drag, though."

He taps his cigarette on the lip of the ashtray. "Yep."

The easy chair, the couch, the mini-fridge, the stereo, the computer, the DVD player, the milk crates full of CDs where there used to be records — it's just a bigger version of his old room. Somehow, though, it feels like we've shrunken in the interim, that everything else has stayed the same.

"How's things at the university?" he says.

I never fibbed, I never willfully misled, but, no, I've never actually corrected Brad's impression that I'm a bona fide Professor Roberts either, never explained that all I really am is the custodian of a glorified correspondence course for bored housewives and even more bored middle-aged businessmen who, now that they've made all of the gold that they can eat, have finally decided to sit down and write that memoir chronicling their thirty-five fascinating years as a high-powered executive in the pig iron industry. Brad seems proud that at least one of us made it. I like the idea that one of us did too.

"Same old, same old," I say.

Brad nods.

"You working?" I say.

He sets the ashtray down on the bedspread and goes to the mini-fridge. It's crammed full of bottles of Blue and he pulls out two, handing me one on the way back to the bed.

"I've got my resume out there," he says. "Things are tough around here right now."

"What are you looking for?"

He takes a swig of beer then puts the bottle between his legs, lights up a fresh smoke. "There's this course some company is offering down at the mall that gives you your lift-truck license in ten days. Supposed to be as much or as little work out there as you want as long as you're licensed."

"Great, that sounds great."

"Once you're licensed, it's not like you've got to run out and get something full-time. You can sign on with one of these temp agencies and work for a couple weeks, put away some cash, then kick back for awhile. Sort of be your own boss."

"Sounds perfect."

Brad takes a drink. "The course costs like a thousand bucks."

"Can't your mum help you out? I mean, until you get your license and start working?"

"I guess. It's just that I'm already into her for, like, I don't even want to think about it." He shakes his head and taps his cigarette in the ashtray.

"Yeah, but in the long run ..."

"Yeah, I know."

We drink our beer in silence. Not literal silence — we don't talk, but the stereo's playing, "Light My Fire," what used to be the last song on side one of the Doors' first album but is now just the fifth track on the CD, approaching the long organ solo that precedes the long guitar solo. Brad leans his head back on the pillow, blows a smoke ring straight up in the air. I close my eyes and sip my beer.

The first time I heard the Doors was upstairs in Brad's old bedroom, him slipping their *Greatest Hits* on the turntable as casually as anybody who's ever changed somebody else's life without knowing it. Not hip enough yet for FM but too cool for the crap playing on CFCO in my mother's kitchen, Jim and the boys popped my musical cherry, until that moment in Brad's bedroom never ever anything entering my virgin ears even remotely like that nightmare soundtrack sound, circus music for the mad, Morrison screaming his head off over top of Manzarek's swirling organ sounding a hell of a lot more like what a poet was supposed to sound like than Earle Birney or James Reaney or all of the other edifying bores we were being peddled as the genuine bardic article in Mrs. Ross's grade ten English class.

I took the album home with me and didn't give it back until I could afford my own copy. Brad was always good about lending records. His older brother had left behind a mother-lode of what now would be called classic rock but back then we just called good shit — the Doors, Creedence, The Band, Jimi and Janis, plus lots of left-field stuff like Big Star, Hot Tuna, and the Velvets that we weren't going to hear even if we had been tuning into the FM stations out of Detroit, all in their original sleeves and all neatly stacked in the corner of his brother's old room, just waiting to spin to life and feed our starving suburban souls.

I'm still true to vinyl, so the CD's three-second pause between the end of "Light My Fire" and the start of "Back Door Man," the first tune on side two, bumps me out of the easy bliss that most of the band's stuff still manages to deliver, even now, after what's got to be a thousand spins since the original goosebumps Brad's brother's record let loose. I'm done my beer, so I get up to get us two more.

"I guess you heard they're back together," Brad says.

I swivel around from my squat in front of the fridge. "Fuck off."

He flicks his cigarette in the ashtray, grins. "Wait. It gets worse."

"How? Did they dig Morrison up?"

Brad sucks a long suck from his cigarette. "Get this," he says, lifting his chin, exhaling through his nostrils. "Densmore's not even playing drums, it's just Krieger and Manzarek."

"The guitar player and the organist."

"The guitar player and the organist. Unbefuckinglievable, isn't it?"

"Christ."

"Densmore's suing the other two. He says they can call themselves the Windows or the Trapdoors or even the Door Frames, anything except the Doors. He says it's a moral and musical travesty, and is suing to keep them from using the name."

I'm not exactly hip to what the kids are up to these days, but unlike Brad, I have listened to an album or two that was recorded since we graduated from high school. Brad's idea of new music is bootlegs of Neil Young shows from the early seventies and combing band Web sites for reissue information. Brad is part of a select group of individuals who can tell you what county in Ireland Noel Redding, Hendrix's ex-bass player, made his home until his recent death of natural causes, and what the odds of another John Fogerty solo album appearing before the next millennium look like.

"Good for him," I say. "Good for Densmore. At least somebody's ..."

"Yeah."

We both stare at the bottles in our hands.

"Hey, guess what?" Brad says.

I look up. "What?"

"You're not going to believe what I downloaded last month."

"What?"

"You're not going to believe it." He swings off the side of the bed and into action, gets down on his knees and starts digging through a red milk crate. I'm pretty sure they don't make them anymore, but every time I'm over he seems to have a couple more filled with even more CDs.

"Aha, gotcha," he says, holding a CD over his head. "This is going to blow your fucking mind."

He hits the eject button on the stereo, plucks out what's inside the player, slips in the new disc, and turns up the volume. Brad's dad was a contractor, did drywall and flooring and insulation and stuff before he died of prostate cancer about five years ago, and he soundproofed the entire basement after Brad moved back home. I settle back in the recliner between the speakers. Brad parks himself on the edge of the bed and pushes play with the remote control. He's watching my face to see how I'll react.

I'm ready for a jolt since he's cranked up the sound, but the high hiss and dull mono drone of what I instantly recognize as a lousy sounding live version of the Doors' song "Five to One" makes me want to tell him to turn it right back down. But as soon as Morrison slurs his way through the first verse and stops singing and starts talking about how he's not talking about a revolution, he's just talking about wanting somebody to come up there and love his ass, ain't nobody gonna love his ass tonight, I shake my head, laugh, and shake my head again, motion with my thumb for Brad to turn it up even louder. A Doors devotee's dirty wet dream: somehow, from somewhere, a bootleg of the infamous Clearwater, Florida, gig from '69 when Morrison got falling down drunk, pulled out his pecker, and was busted and eventually convicted for lewd and lascivious behaviour.

"Where the fuck —"

"Listen, listen," Brad says, raising his hand.

You're all a bunch of fucking slaves. I bet you like it, I bet you like being slaves. I bet you like having the shit pushed in your face. So what are you going to do about it? What are you going to do about it? What are you going to dooo abooouuut iiit?

Brad passes me a joint. I hadn't even seen him whip it out or light it.

I take it, toke, hand it back.

"This is incredible," I say.

Standing in the middle of the room with the joint between his lips, miming Densmore's rim shots with imaginary drum sticks, playing along with the band playing on in vain, hoping, somehow, to bring their boy back from the brink, "It really is, isn't?" he says.

"EXILE ON MAIN STREET?"

"A very strong contender."

"London Calling?"

"It's right up there."

"What about *Zen Arcade*?"

"There's filler."

"Not much," I say.

"No," Simon says, "but there's some. The acoustic songs aren't there yet, and the tape experiments just don't work."

"It's a pretty major departure from *Metal Circus*."

"We're talking about the best double album of all-time, not Hüsker Dü's best."

"Well, I say it's on the list."

Simon locks his fingers behind his head, shuts his eyes. "Fine," he says, "we'll put it on the maybe list."

"On the definitely maybe list."

"Fine, we'll put it on the definitely maybe list."

It's Monday afternoon, the first day of the rest of my life — this, following closely on the heels of Sunday, the first day of the rest of my life yesterday. Coming back to the city fresh from visiting my parents usually puts Mary and I in a productive panic, the storm after the forty-eight hour comatose calm. Today, though, instead of being at home giving Lenore Shipely and her novel-in-progress, *The Wounded Mirror*, her two-hundred dollars' worth of insightful analysis, I'm shooting the breeze with Simon. Barry welcomes the chance to have somewhere else to snooze in the sun, and there's a certain slant of light that likes to cozy up to the frayed red carpet in She Said Boom's doorway on winter afternoons that he's got a real fondness for, so the decision to do what I shouldn't isn't as hard as it should be. And Simon and I have been having this same conversation for at least six months now and still can't agree on an uncontested winner.

"I could live with *Zen Arcade* if you'd give me *Self Portrait*," he says.

"Talk to me when you're serious," I say, waving him away.

Above all else — She Said Boom's sole full-time employee,

ex-bass player in semi-legendary Toronto 80's roots-revival band The Whiffle Balls, twice-clobbered Green candidate in our Ronscesvalles-High Park riding — Simon is a Dylanophile. He steps from behind from the counter and follows me to the new arrivals table.

"When was the last time you listened to *Self Portrait* all the way through?" he says. "Without prejudice, I mean."

"The first time. Which was also the last time."

"Then how can you talk about it? You're not going to understand it by just listening to it once."

As with any other fundamentalist, you're simply wasting your time attempting to speak sense to Simon once the Spirit moves him, once Saint Bob has spread his intractable singing shadow. I flip through a hardcover first edition of *Infinite Jest*, all 1076 pages of it. The spine doesn't look as if it's been cracked. There's a bookmark stuck at page twenty-three.

"It's pop music's first postmodern record," he says.

I give *An Illustrated Guide to the Kama Sutra* a much more considered going-over. The smiling, limb-twisting man and woman in the pictures — each blond, bronzed, and of equal height and above-average level of attractiveness — look as if they've either attained such a glorious state of unimaginable ecstasy that they've transcended happiness all together or they're just plain bored.

"Dylan knew what he was doing, believe me," Simon says. "To this day, everybody still misses the point. *Self Portrait* is a metamusical soundscape. It's a collection of twenty-one songs that — precisely because they *are* so unlike Dylan — helped him redefine the possibility of who and what he was and who and what he could go on to be. Call it an attempt by Dylan to shatter the musical shackles that his audience had increasingly been binding him with."

Still looking at the book, and against my better judgment, "Call it what it really is. Call it a contractual obligation album. Call it bad music. Call it —"

"Now, hold on there, just hold on a second, you can't —"

"Excuse me, could I trouble you to let me have a listen to this?"

We both turn around. It's the woman from the park, the English woman, with a CD in her hand. Her mass of kinky strawberry-blonde hair is tied back, but only just; rings of it dangle in front of her face, a particularly long corkscrew curl bobbing over one eye.

"Oh, hello there again," she says, noticing me, fingering the ringlet behind her ear. I close the *Kama Sutra* as slowly as I can, return it to the table as casually as possible.

"Sorry to interrupt," she says. "I was just wondering if I could have a listen." She holds up the CD.

"Sorry, the machine's broken," Simon says. Turning back to me, "Look, you can't dismiss a work of art just because it doesn't fit your preconceived notion of what it should or shouldn't sound like."

"It's okay, it's not broken anymore," I say, taking the CD from the woman's hand. When Simon is arguing with his girl-friend on the phone or needs to pop outside for a butt or feels compelled to defend the aesthetic worth of the nadir of Bob

Dylan's recording catalogue, the store's listening station tends to become temporarily out of order. I hand him the empty case. "Will you get my friend her CD?"

"Oh, sorry. I didn't know you were a friend of Hank's," he says. He disappears behind the counter, searching for her CD along the bottom row. Bottom row means it's jazz.

"Well," she says, "I certainly know who I need to get to know in this neighbourhood, don't I?"

"I'm afraid that getting Simon to do his job is about as far as my influence extends."

"It's Hank, isn't it?"

"Right. And you're, uhm ..." I shake my head. "Sorry."

"It's all right," she says, smiling, offering me her hand. "It's Beverly." Her grip is strong, firm. "It's part of my job never to forget a name."

"What do you do?"

"Right now, I'm afraid not very much. Before too long, however, I hope to begin practising again."

"Practising what?"

Beverly smiles again. "Law. I'm a lawyer."

"Oh."

Simon is back. "Here you go," he says, handing over the CD. He hits the eject button on the machine and plugs in the headphones for her. "Volume's here, bass and treble and song search over here."

"Thank you, Simon," she says, throwing back her head, pulling on the headphones over her hydra of hair. She inserts the CD and pushes play, watches Barry curled up tight like a sled dog in the streak of sunlight on the carpet while she listens. Each track is given only a snippet of seconds to impress before she clicks forward to the next. She leaves her finger on the song search button.

Simon grabs his jacket and the pack of Marlboros from his pocket. After all that, he's earned himself a smoke break. I call Barry's name and clip on his leash and the three of us step outside. The 504 streetcar dings its bell at another 504 going the other way down Roncesvalles which answers the greeting with its own.

In his best bad English accent, "Who's the bird?" Simon says.

"How should I know?"

Simon eyes me, takes a puff.

"I thought you said you were friends."

"It's an expression, Simon. Like the way I tell people you and I are friends." It's cold enough out, my frozen breath makes it look like I'm smoking too. "I met her at the park."

"Walking Barry, or —"elbowing me lightly in the ribs "— walking after midnight, Guv'ner?"

"Fuck you," I say, pulling Barry's leash, hitting the sidewalk.

"Hey, Hank," Simon calls after me. "Don't think twice, it's all right."

PHIL LOCKS THE DEADBOLT, takes my coat. The ceilings of Rebecca's condo are high, the walls drip with original artwork, a large aquarium stocked with exotic-looking fish bubbles reassuringly in the middle of the room, and the air is stuffed with the smell of roasting garlic and the sound of opera softly playing on the stereo. Phil hangs my buckskin jacket in the closet at the end of the long hallway.

The jacket's got a musty smell I've never been able to get rid of since the day I bought it back in school, and Mary hates it, but Rebecca hates it more. She's never said she doesn't like it, but that doesn't matter. Every event has a cause and Rebecca James hates buckskin jackets. Sometimes a priori knowledge can be a beautiful thing. I always make a point of wearing it whenever I know I'll be seeing her and Phil.

"Where's Rebecca?" I say, flopping onto the black leather couch. I say it like I'm wondering what's robbing me of the opportunity of seeing her, and not who or what I should be thankful to for the unexpected holiday.

"At her agent's. They're trying to figure out the best strategy for breaking her into the States."

"That's great," I say. It's only fair. After all, they've dumped acid rain, Britney Spears, and George W. on us.

From the kitchen, "You want a beer?"

"Are you having one?"

"It's a little early for me."

"But it's not for me?"

"Do you want one or not?" Something metal and not small crashes to the kitchen floor. "Shit," Phil says. I can't see it from where I'm sitting in the other room, but I know he's on his knees.

"Don't bother," I yell. "Sounds like you've got your hands full."

"Hold on, Henry, I've got an incident in here."

I get up and go to the window. The toy cars along King Street do what the traffic lights tell them to, stop and start just as they've been instructed. None of the black dots inching along the sidewalks stand in rags on street corners begging for spare change for something to eat from people with cell phones stuck to their ears and oversized paper cups of coffee attached to their fists. No one bumps into anyone else at the crosswalks, no one in a hurry to get to the other side to get nowhere before everyone else. Things make sense from a tenth story window. Plato must have mapped out the *Republic* on a mountaintop.

Phil steps into the kitchen doorway with a damp white dishtowel hanging over one of his shoulders. "Sorry about that. Knocked over the lamb I've been marinating all afternoon."

"God, I hate it when that happens."

Phil frowns. "Did you want a beer, I forget."

"It's too early for me, but you go right ahead."

He frowns again. "Sit down and behave yourself, I'll be right back."

I wander over to the stereo instead.

It's the real deal — Yamaha receiver and compact disc player, 100 watt Mission speakers, cordless Sennheiser headphones — but it's like a Corvette with an empty gas tank. The adjoining custom-built, walnut CD shelf is crammed floor-to-ceiling with Puccini, Verdi, Purcell, Wagner, Rossini and, on the bottom right hand corner of the bottom shelf, the seven lonely compact discs that comprise Rebecca's pop music ghetto: best-of collections from U2, Talking Heads, UB40, and a few other 80s once-weres, emotional keepsakes from her wild and crazy college years, no doubt, aural souvenirs from a kinder, more existentially innocent time. I switch the stereo from radio to CD and pop in the Heads disc. A little art-school rock band cleverness goes a long way with me, but "Psycho Killer" beats out a fat woman shrieking in a language I don't understand every time.

"Jesus, Henry, what did I say?" I turn around. Phil, with a bottle of Heineken in each hand, is standing in the middle of the room.

"What?"

"I was taping that."

"Taping what?"

"What was on the radio."

I look at the stereo. "How was I supposed to know you've started taping opera off the radio?"

"It was for Rebecca. She asked me to record it for her while she was out. It's a rare performance of Virgil Thomson's *Four Saints in Three Acts* by Gertrude Stein that she doesn't own."

"Sorry," I say. I click the stereo back to FM. "There."

"Great. I'm sure with all the over voices, she won't notice David Bryne's thrown into the mix."

"Look, I said I was sorry. Tell her I did it, tell her I —"

"Just forget it," he says, handing me a beer, sitting down on the couch. Phil still has his place in the Annex, but spends most of his time at Rebecca's now. Every time I'm over I'll spot another one of his books or coats or, this trip, his laptop and printer.

He takes a drink of beer and stares out the window; I sit down at the other end of the couch and do the same. From where we're sitting sunk deep in our seats, all you can see is a generous chunk of ice blue sky and a few lolling-by dirty white clouds, mother nature screensaver #7. The Heineken is ice cold and slightly bitter, exactly like it's supposed to be, the leather of the couch pleasantly cool in contrast to the overheated room, itself not unwelcome after the icy streetcar ride over. It's been awhile since Phil and I stoked an afternoon buzz. And if Rebecca's oversized stainless steel refrigerator and three-hundred thousand dollar vista make the job a little easier, well, that's all right too.

"How are you doing?" Phil says.

"Slow down, Lambchop, I'm not even halfway done this one." I take a gulp to help catch up.

"No," he says, holding up his three-quarters full bottle, "I mean, how are *you* doing?"

Thou Shall Not Make Small Talk While Getting Tipsy During Daylight Hours. One of afternoon drinking's sacred commandments has been broken and a price must be paid. What's worse, I've got a bad feeling that it's going to end up coming out of my pocket.

"What do you mean, how am *I* doing?"

"Relax. You're among all your friends here, remember?"

I lift my bottle and drink. "Fine. So what's with the shrink act, then? Friend."

"No act," Phil says, looking out the window, not at me. "We're simply concerned about young Henry, that's all. His grades are down, you see, and he hasn't been doing his chores and doesn't even appear all that interested in extracurricular activities anymore. And such a promising lad, too. Quite frankly, we're at a loss."

"Ah, yes, master Henry. And a fine-looking boy, isn't he? A real hit with the young ladies, I'm told."

"I hadn't heard that."

"Oh, yes, apparently the girls can't get enough of him."

"No, I most definitely have not heard that."

"Yes, well, as I say, I'm led to believe that he has that certain special something that the fairer sex simply cannot resist."

"How odd that I've never heard anything of the sort."

"It's actually quite common knowledge, it seems."

"Odd. Not a word I've heard of it."

"Common knowledge, apparently."

"Not a peep even."

"Yes, common knowledge."

"Not even a whisper."

"Huh."

"Hmm."

By now I actually do need another beer. "I better make sure that dead animal of yours in the kitchen isn't moving around again." As I pass his chair, Phil places his empty green bottle in my hand like a relay runner a baton. You don't get coordination like that without years of practice.

Everything in the refrigerator looks like it's either from a specialty shop or been ordered directly from the back pages of *The New Yorker.* To get to the Heinekens I have to reach over five different kinds of cheeses, each one opened but neatly resealed with a thin red elastic band in its original Dutch or French or German wrapper, and a small, single piece of pink meat the size of a hockey puck in a clear plastic pouch with the name of a Vermont farm and a Web site address stenciled onto it. I set the beers down on the counter beside a bottle of balsamic vinegar that could, in a pinch, pass for a handsome vase, and three perfectly round hothouse tomatoes in a white bowl that look so red they don't look real, like they've been spray-painted. I crack open the Heinekens and palm pass Phil one on my way back to my end of the couch.

Before I've taken my first sip, "You want a job?" Phil says.

"I already have a job. You got it for me, remember?"

"I mean a good job, a real job."

"Oh, a *real* job. Why didn't you say so."

I get up and go to the wall of bookshelves. *The Portable Joseph Campbell. Ten Secrets of Ten Successful People. The Norton Anthology of English Literature. Harry Potter. The Prophet.* Pound's *Cantos. A Dummy's Guide to Jewish Mysticism. Selected Poems of Erica Jong.* Yep, just like my mother used to say: You are what you eat.

"It'd be for about a year, it pays okay considering it'd be

part-time, and the work itself would be pretty interesting."

Still scanning book spines, "It sounds wonderful, but I'm afraid that my gigoloing days are over. Don't get me wrong — I love the idea of making people happy — but it just wouldn't be fair to Mary. I'm a one woman man, Phil, you know that."

I can hear him take a long swallow from his beer. I pull down the only book on the shelf that I also own, Kierkegaard's *Journals*. Probably left over from a class she had to take.

"Rebecca's working on a non-fiction book now, a book about nightmares."

"Neat," I say. I turn the page.

"It's going to be part history, part personal testimony. She's been keeping a dream journal since she was a teenager, so that's not a problem. It's just the other end of it, sifting through 2,500 years of nightmare literature."

"Sounds great."

> *The difference between men is simply a question of how they say stupid things; the universally human is to say them.*

Ah, Søren, old pal, no wonder the Copenhagen pretty people ended up calling whoever passed for a freaknick a *Søren*. Nobody can swallow that much truth in one mouthful, not without more spoonfuls of sugar than you were ever packing in your hump.

"So what do you think?" Phil says.

"About what?"

"Christ, Henry, have you heard a word I've said?"

"Don't get your knickers in a knot, I was listening." I shove the book back in place and turn around. "Rebecca's writing a new book. A non-fiction book about nightmares. It's going to take a lot of work. Don't worry, I'm sure it'll turn out great."

"Are you interested?"

"Sure, I'd buy it. I bet lots of people will." Who better to chronicle twenty-five centuries of bad dreams?

"Interested in helping her. Are you interested in being her research assistant?"

My face feels hot, like someone has just slapped me. I feel like a drowning man who's just been tossed a concrete life preserver. I feel like I need a drink.

"What are you trying to say to me?" I say.

"I'm not trying to say anything, I'm trying to help you. *We're* trying to help you."

"By making me your girlfriend's lackey."

"You wouldn't be anybody's lackey. It's a legitimate, Canada Council-funded research assistantship. And here's what else we were thinking. When this job is over, what's to stop you from printing up some business cards and getting a killer letter of recommendation from Rebecca and letting her spread the word around about what a great job you did? Who knows? It could turn into something permanent."

I lift my beer and drink what's left in three long swallows.

"Whose idea was this?" I say.

"What are you so pissed off about?"

"Whose idea was this?"

"Ours, Rebecca's and mine. If you're not interested, fine, just say so, just don't have a fucking hissy fit."

"Rebecca's and yours. But mostly hers, right?"

"Like I said, we both thought —"

"But it was her idea, right? She suggested it to you."

"I don't know. What does it matter who —"

"She's the one who brought it up first, right?"

"If I think about it, maybe, I don't know, I guess, yeah. And so what if she did? She was just trying to help you out."

"Help me out. Right."

I brush past Phil into the kitchen, grab another two beers from the fridge, pop them open with the IKEA bottle opener on the counter, and drink from mine like I'm actually thirsty. I wipe my mouth on the back of my sleeve and come back into the living room.

Handing Phil his, "As long as this wasn't your idea, fine, let's just forget it." I crouch down in front of the CD rack and start rummaging for something that isn't entirely terrible. "I should have brought a tape with me," I say. "I just got a copy of this bootlegged Doors concert a friend of mine from high school made for me from '69 where —"

"What do you mean as long as it wasn't my idea?"

"Like I said, forget it, it's nothing between us. Drink your Heiny. It's never a good idea to show up at the Duke sober."

Bingo! A CD of a fraction of Dylan's finest that someone had put together for her. I stand up and slip in the disc.

"Meaning what?" Phil says. "That there's something between

you and Rebecca? Because she went out of her way to try and help you?"

Dylan's doing his thing, delivering the news that the times they are a changin', but the sound is too soft, the strumming too measured, the rhythm too slow. I ride the song search until I hit the sweet electric guitar screech that ignites "Subterranean Homesick Blues." Psychobilly ventilator for a wheezing, wearied soul. I lean into the beat. I begin to feel like I can breathe.

"You know, you've made it pretty clear from day one that you don't like Rebecca," Phil says.

"I don't not like Rebecca."

"Fine, whatever you say, Henry. Either way, it's your loss. Just don't talk about things you don't know about, okay? In spite of whatever you think of her, Rebecca thinks you're a good guy who could use a break. And that's the only reason she offered you the job. End of story."

I'm still standing in front of the stereo, bottle of Heineken hanging from my hand. Phil's got his back to me looking out the window. His beer is on the coffee table, sweat-beaded, untouched.

I know I should just go, but I stay where I am anyway. The snare shot heard around the rock and roll world that kicks off "Like a Rolling Stone" sends Phil into the kitchen, presumably to check on dinner. As though I'm just killing time, just waiting around waiting for him to grab his coat and take a final piss before we pop into a cab and head for the Duke like we've done a hundred times before, I wander over to the other side of the room and pull the Kierkegaard back down from the shelf, flip it open.

> *Job endured everything — until his friends came to comfort him, then he grew impatient.*

Kierkegaard. What a fucking *Søren*.

I'M ON MY KNEES drinking a can of Bud and pulling records off the shelves, trying to put together a pile of get-rid-ofs. Because I can use the money. Because one record album takes up the space of approximately four CDs. Because albums are difficult to find. Because a good record needle is even harder to locate, and criminally expensive, besides. Because albums scratch. Because CDs hold more minutes of music and often come with bonus tracks, impossible-to-locate curiosities you simply can't acquire anywhere else.

But records feel right. Getting rid of even one of your old albums is like putting your grandfather's pocket watch out on the curb because your brand new Timex keeps better time and you can wear it in the shower. Doing what's smart isn't always what makes sense.

I stand up to stretch my legs and give my nose a rest from the reek of the rug. We must keep Loblaws in the black with the amount of carpet deodorizer we buy, but no amount of sprinkle-and-wait-fifteen-minutes-for-hard-to-get-out-smells vacuuming is ever going to make this room daisy fresh again, no matter how pretty the floral picture on the package looks. The people who lived here before us had cats who weren't crazy about litter boxes, Barry smells like a wet goat on the best of days, and the baseboard heater and single space heater we've got rigged up upstairs are just TLC to the mildew and mustiness we do daily battle with with enough incense that we get it at a bulk discount from She Said Boom.

Barry doesn't care. He's stretched out on the floor beside me with his entire furry front facing the wall unit, every hairy black inch of him soaking up as much of the thin electric heat struggling to fill up the damp room as it can. I consider watering the few potted plants not yet crusty brown, still fighting the good fight despite the lack of light, but decide against it. I haven't got time. I've got a job to do.

The records are ours, Mary's and mine, but unlike the books covering the other two walls, they're really mine. Mary joined the other side when we moved in here, a small CD boombox in her basement studio helping to make up in extra space what she's lacking in light and proper ventilation. Besides, she likes to drink wine and listen to mostly wordless music while she works, and the contemporary composers she's partial to aren't the kind that tend to turn up in Goodwill bins or at garage sales or in second-hand record shops, where I get most of my new sounds. Of course, my new sounds aren't actually new, just new to me. But dusty doesn't have to mean dead. Just ask anybody who's ever discovered Etta James by way of an original Chess recording of *Tell Mama* or lucked into a first pressing of *Sticky Fingers*, the one with the Warhol-designed working zipper on the front.

So far I've managed to weed out Alex Chilton's *Flies on Sherbet*, the Doors' *Weird Scenes Inside the Goldmine*, and the Strangler's *Feline*. *Flies on Sherbert* is one of those works of art that's more fun to talk about than actually experience, the gleefully off-key, inebriated vocals and willfully incompetent playing placing it just a notch below Syd Barrett's two solo albums for the title of Best Job of Capturing a Career Suicide on Tape. But the only thing everybody loves better than a parade is a car crash, the bloodier the better. I slide the Chilton back in place beside *The Best of The Chocolate Watchband*.

The Doors' compilation is simply redundant and should be a no-brainer, every tune but one on one or another of their six studio albums. And the single extra ditty is no great shakes, doesn't even feature Morrison on vocals, but Manzarek. Still, "You Need Meat" *is* one of my all-time favourite song titles, right up there with Jimmy Buffett's "My Head Hurts, My Feet Stink, and I Don't Love Jesus" and the Meat Puppets' "Enchanted Porkfist." It's also a double album. I check out the kaleidoscope of band photos inside before refiling it away.

Feline is simply crap. Snyth-slop candy-floss fluff masquerading as jazz pop or New Romantic rock or New Wave torch balladry, I don't know what and I definitely don't care which. The summer of '84, though, it *was* the Stacy Larmner-supplied soundtrack — that, along with fellow English fakes Fun Boy Three and Orchestral Manoeuvres in the Dark — to my nearly nightly quest to round third and make it home before I had to have the Buick Skylark back in my parents' driveway before one a.m.

The smack of the backyard gate turns my head but not Barry's. If he sees you coming he's still a first-rate watchdog, still flashes his whites and snarls with the best of them, but preventative security is pretty much a thing of the past since his hearing has started to fade. Dogs need their dignity as much as the two-legged animals they live with, though, so I give him the heads-up whenever I can.

"Barry, what's that?"

He lifts his head an inch off the carpet; blinks a couple of times.

"Barry, what's that?"

This time he delivers the deepest chest growl he can and charges to the window with tail lowered and ready to go the distance with whomever might be thinking of messing around with his pack. Then he realizes it's Mary. He wags his tail and runs to the door and turns around in circles, whimpering while he waits for her to come in.

I don't whimper, but I do go to the door and unlock it and hold it open so she can bring her bike inside without having to dig her keys out of her bag. If possible, I'm even happier Mary's home than Barry. He's delirious anytime either of us comes through the door. After my afternoon with Phil, I'm in special need of being in the same space as someone sane. I'm also out of beer and two dollars short of the price of a six-pack.

"Hi, guys," she says, undoing the chin strap of her helmet.

"Hi, kiddo," I say.

A kiss for me and a scratch between the ears for Barry. We watch her take off her helmet and coat and hang them on the back of the door and put her bag on the arm of the couch and pick up her bike and hoist it onto the black metal hooks above the stairs. It's the same show we've both seen a couple of thousand times before but today is like a rerun you're happy to tune into at two o'clock in the morning when you're all alone at home, a liturgy of flickering familiarity to beat back the empty night.

I go to her and hug her. She feels like a set of training wheels I took off too soon. I close my eyes and rest my chin on her shoulder.

"Whew," she says, waving her hand in front of her face. "What's the occasion?"

I let her go. "What do you mean?"

"You smell like a brewery."

"I had couple beers at Phil's. At Rebecca's, I mean. I mean, with Phil at her place."

"And decided to keep the party going, I see," she says, smiling, picking up the can of Bud from the record shelf and drinking.

"I thought it'd be a good time to go through the albums again."

She takes the copy of *Feline* that's still in my hand. "Well, I won't miss this. I didn't even know we had it."

"I'm actually going to hold onto that one," I say, taking it back and sticking it into the wall of records. "There's some interesting early post-punk stuff on there."

"Whatever you say, you're the music man." She lifts the Bud to her lips. "Whoops, looks like I finished your beer. Sorry." She hands me the empty can. "Has the Bubs eaten dinner yet?"

At this, Barry tilts his head to one side. *Dinner* is one of his favourite words, right up there with *walk, treat,* and *good boy.*

"Not yet. I was just going to feed him."

"Well, you feed him and I'll get supper started. Did you get the tempeh and the stuff for the salad and the other stuff on the list?" Mary cooks and I do the dishes, clean the house, do the laundry, and pick up the groceries. Usually.

"I didn't get a chance to go to the store yet."

Mary's face falls. Not because she's pissed off. Not even because she's disappointed, although coming home to an empty vegetable crisper while the man of her dreams sucks on a can of Budweiser and contemplates the lasting worth of a poofter punk band isn't anyone's notion of an ideal end-of-the-day greeting. It's just that, because I didn't do the shopping, one or both of us will now have to, which means that we won't be able to eat until after eight, which means that by the time we clean up and one or both of us walks the dog it'll be nearly nine, which means that Mary won't make it into her studio until she's probably too tired to put in a good night's work.

Maybe she is pissed off. Maybe she's pissed off *and* disappointed. Maybe she should be.

"I've had a bad day," I say.

Mary's face changes again. Her brow becomes furrowed, her eyes still soft but intent, focused only on me and what's wrong. "What happened," she says. "What is it?"

So I tell her about Phil sucker-punching me with Rebecca's scheme to make me her errand boy. Tell her that I know it's not really Phil's fault but that he should have nipped the thing in the bud, should never have let it get as far as it did. Tell her that I can forgive him because he's hopelessly pussy-whipped, but that there's no way I can be in the same room as her for a long, long time.

Mary crosses her arms, looks at her shoes. "Do you really think she offered you the job just to make you upset?"

"Why else would she do it?"

"Maybe she really wanted to help you."

"Yeah, just because she likes me so much."

"No. Because you're her partner's best friend." She looks up. "And it does sound kind of neat, don't you think?"

I go to the door and unlock it for Barry although he's lying on the floor between us, waiting for all this talk about dinner to finally turn to action. "This is great," I say, "this is just great. First I have to deal with those two, then I have to come home to this."

"Come home to what? Hank, we're just talking. If you don't want to take the job, fine. I just wonder if you're —"

"Okay," I say, holding the door open, "now I see what you're saying. You think I should kiss Rebecca's ass because I don't make enough money. Because I don't make as much money as you do."

"Hank, what are you talking about?"

"C'mon, Barry, in or out, it's cold enough already in this fucking morgue."

"Close the door, Hank, the dog doesn't want out."

"How do you know what he wants? Oh, I forgot. You know what everybody wants. Or is supposed to want."

Mary picks her bag up off the couch. "After I feed Barry, we're going to go for a walk and get what we need for dinner. If you can talk about this sensibly and without raising your voice, we'd like you to come with us." She starts down the stairs, Barry right behind her.

I stand there alone in the middle of the living room. The sound of nothing feels like it's going to burst my eardrums.

"Maybe I don't feel like eating right now," I shout downstairs. "Just because you feel like eating doesn't mean that everybody else does."

Mary doesn't answer. I can hear her pour Barry's food into his bowl. I can hear him begin crunching away.

A BIG FIGHT WITH the wife is usually like a good puke — days, sometimes weeks, of bubbling guts and an overheated brain having very little to do with her, and then the familiar finger down one's throat of a much-needed marital screaming match to bring on a good groaning upchuck containing all of that bad stuff boiling your innards alive, pure barfing relief. Love means never having to look too far for someone to take out all your shit on.

Tonight, though, I still feel full of poison, as if our spat has only made things worse, as if our arguing has only served to lodge in my throat whatever it is that's festering deep down there inside me. I come downstairs with my coat on and my eyes on the floor to let Mary know that I'm going out for a walk. She says okay and to be careful. I say I'm sorry, and she says just be careful.

I've raided the junk drawer for the empty film canister we keep our laundry money in, and am now eleven loonies and several quarters to the good. I don't know where I'm going, but that's okay because any place I could come up with wouldn't be anywhere I'd feel like being right now anyway. This probably isn't what Aristotle meant when he wrote that *All imperfect things must travel.*

It's only a little after seven but already dark. Three grade-school girls in toques and scarves are sitting in a row on the curb of the sidewalk underneath a streetlight. There's about a five second lag between what each of them is singing, but they're all singing the exact same thing.

> "Row row row your boat
> Gently down the stream
> Merrily, merrily, merrily, merrily
> Life is but a dream."

Easy for you to say, I think.

"THIS BAY STREET BIG shot, he wants to quit the rat race, junk the whole thing, so he sells his company and everything he's got and moves up north and gets himself a cabin as far away from everybody and everything as he can. A couple months later, there's a knock on his door and this big lumberjack-looking guy is standing there.

"'I'm your closest neighbour from down the road,' the lumberjack guy says, 'and I'm havin' a party at my place and want to invite you.'

"The guy, the business guy, he says, 'You know, two months ago, I would've had to say no, but you're the first person I've set eyes on since I left the city. Thank you, I'd love to come to your party.'

"So the lumberjack guy, he gives him directions to his house and is going down the steps when he remembers something.

"'One thing you oughta know,' he says. 'There's gonna be some loud music at this party.'

"'I don't have a phone, let alone a stereo or even a radio,' the businessman says. 'I'm looking forward to hearing some music.'

"So the lumberjack guy, he nods, and is going down the walkway when he remembers something else.

"'One more thing,' he says. 'I gotta tell you, there's gonna be a lot of drinkin' at this party.'

"The businessman, he says, 'I haven't had any alcohol in months. I believe I'm about ready for a drink or two.'

"The lumberjack says okay and is almost at the end of the path when he stops and turns around again. 'I guess I might as well tell you right now,' he says, 'there's more than likely gonna be some fightin' at this party.'

"The businessman laughs. 'I'm a pretty easy guy to get

along with,' he says. 'I don't think anyone's going to encounter any problems with me.'

"The lumberjack, he nods again and is on his way back home when the businessman shouts out after him, 'Oh, I almost forgot. Is this going to be formal or should I just dress casual?'

"The lumberjack stops and turns around. 'Whatever you want,' he says. 'It's just gonna be the two of us.'"

Julio shakes with silent laughter, struggles to keep his lips around his mouthful of beer. Lenny refills his pint from the tap. Frank allows himself a small smile and shifts in his table seat away from the bar toward the TV. Sam grins into his nearly empty glass. Mission accomplished, having left the world a happier place than the way he found it, he drains his drink and steps down from his stool and goes behind the bar to mix himself another Special Sam.

For a guy who has access to as much booze as he wants anytime he wants it, Sam only really lets loose about once a month. Even then, except for a little more colour in his face, Sam messed up isn't all that much different from when he's riding his usual two or three beer buzz, the only real telltale sign being his pint glass full of a single twelve ounce bottle of Mike's Hard Lemonade fortified with three generous shots of Smirnoff Vodka and a splash of creme de menthe, a handful of maraschino cherries bobbing for their lives on top. It's the kind of recipe for a hangover that only a person who owns their own bar could come up with.

I manufacture a smile and take a sip from my glass of draft. Not used to light-to-night drinking anymore, I need more beer in my belly like I need another bag of salt and vinegar potato chips or one more pickled egg. Taking a leak at the urinal earlier, the washroom mirror caught me with my pants down and my stomach unsucked, usually an instinctual reaction whenever it's in the vicinity of any reflective surface. In front of me on the bar, the ripped-open, grease-glistening silver carcasses of several empty chip bags dare me to look down. I take another drink, take up the challenge, get what I deserve. Welcome to the not-so-fun house. Obese and oily, octopus-armed with a drink in each hand — any objects in the mirror are precisely what they seem.

"Hey, Hank," Lenny says, followed by something I don't hear.

"What's that?"

Catching Sam's, then Julio's eye, "I said, 'All cocksuckers are deaf.'"

This time Julio loses the battle with his beer, sprays a fine Molson Dry mist all over the bar. Lenny waddles over to the tap like a pudgy peacock and rewards himself for his rare wit with a fresh half-pint. Sam, smirking, nods to Len to set Julio up with another beer on the house, Julio the only paying customer in the place besides me and Frank and a guy asleep with his head resting on his red Adidas gym bag at a corner table. When I was twelve, the best you could do was get some other kid laughing so hard that his milk would run out of his nose. But that was a long, long time ago, before I started hanging around adults.

I stand up and stick my hand in my pants pocket. I put what

I've got left on the bar, fifty-six cents. Jukeboxes don't barter, so I count what's there again, this time sliding the dimes through Julio's wet mess to sit with the other dimes, the nickels with the nickels, the pennies with the pennies. It's still fifty-six cents. I wipe my hand on my jeans.

"Shit, Hank, I almost forgot," Sam says, plucking a cherry from his drink, popping it into his mouth. "Mary called."

"Oh, yeah?" I say.

"Yeah. She said she wants you to stay away from home for another hour or so. She said she's only blown about half of the Raptors, and that she needs a little more time to finish the job right."

Frank takes his bookmark out of his book. I pocket my coins and pull on my scarf. Sometimes drunken imbecility just isn't enough.

NOT WANTING TO GO home and having nowhere else to go — the metaphysical weather report of every great country-and-western tune and the theme song of nine out of ten decisions that you just know you're going to regret later.

It's just after eleven, but judging by my internal inebriation clock it feels more like four. I stand on the sidewalk in front of the Gladstone Hotel's big picture window trying to figure out the duet that the man and the woman on stage are doing. He's skinny but with a pot-belly poking through his untucked white shirt and with his tie jammed inside his suit-jacket pocket, the knotted part hanging out. She's wearing oversized red plastic-frame glasses and is short and fat with feet that seem even fatter for resembling Porky Pig's girlfriend's when she'd get all dolled up and stuff her fleshy hooves inside a tiny pair of high heels.

I finally decipher the tune they're singing — "Islands in the Stream," the Kenny Rogers-Dolly Parton duet — and if the song itself is woeful, their interpretation of it is even worse. They're worse than worse. They're horrible. If they didn't look like what they are, a couple of white-collar slaves trying to wake up from the nightmare of the office with a loud night out, they could pass for clever deconstructionists attempting to illustrate the fundamental hollowness of romantic love as axiomatic of late-capitalistic Western society as expressed in terms of contemporary popular music. Except irony isn't on the dance card tonight. They're terrible but sincere. That might not be saying much, but that's not saying nothing, either.

I find an empty table up front, right near the stage. Between being drunk and staring at the singers having such a swell time struggling through their song, it takes me a moment to realize that my ass is wet and that I'd better change chairs. A puddle of spilt beer follows me everywhere I go.

When the song's over the crowd erupts with applause. He gives her a peck on her chubby cheek, she waves to someone out in the audience, and each of them returns their respective microphone to one of the two mic stands and strolls back to their table crowded with a bunch of different versions of themselves.

"April and Peter, ladies and gentlemen," the karaoke guy

says, followed by a second, fresh set of cheers. Except for the droopy moustache and birdhouse haircut — it looks like a brown Jell-O mold held in place with half a can of hairspray — he's every guy who's thirty-nine and holding and who thinks le château is high fashion and that Elvis's Las Vegas period was when the King finally got it right.

"Next up," he says, "let's hear it for Billy. Billy, ladies and gentlemen."

And here comes Billy. Jogging up to the stage, bottle of beer in hand, sharing an aside and a laugh with the karaoke guy and waiting for his tune to come up on the monitor. He's wearing his Dunlop Home Heating insulated vest with his name stitched over the right-hand breast pocket and has got that work-day-done bounce that can only come from doing what has to be done and knowing that you did it well; that, or from two fat lines of good coke. But Billy is Labbatt Blue Light and Tim Horton's double-double and Don Cherry for Prime Minister all the way. The pounding guitar riff to "Born to Be Wild" leaps from the speakers and fills up the room and Billy loses his easy smile, stiffens to attention, shifts the microphone from his left hand to his right. Puts his voice where Mr. Steppenwolf's, John Kay's, used to be.

He's not good, he's not bad, but that's not the point. His eyes are shut while he sings, both hands gripped tight around the microphone, and he bends over at the waist and squeezes the mic even tighter every time he gets to the tune's title line. He won't be wild when he punches the clock tomorrow morning at eight a.m. for Mr. Dunlop, but he sure as hell was born to be. And right here, right now, he is. We all are.

When the song finally fades to its end, everybody stands up and claps their hands and stomps their feet and whistles if they can. It's only when I stop applauding that I realize I'm the only one standing. I don't care. There's already somebody else up on stage, and he looks like he's a real rock and roller too.

I'M UP AT SEVEN and out the door with Barry by 7:20. Technically, I should be post-plastered groggy gloomy, but I don't feel it. Hangovers are dangerous, and not just for the obvious reasons. Hangovers are easy progress. Getting rid of a headache or a sour stomach has a way of becoming a day well spent, reason enough to believe that one's done more than just punch the cosmic clock. But not me. Not this morning.

The park is busier than I remembered it being this early, almost as much sniffing and squatting going on as in the evening. I recognize Casey and his mum and Fraser and his dad outfitted for work in his cop uniform, but most of the dogs and their people don't register. The women are all freshly painted and wear skirts with knee-high leather boots underneath their winter jackets, most of the men in trenchcoats and black dress shoes, all of them pink-skinned and clean-shaven.

The sky reminds me of summertimes in high school when you'd stay out all night; between the guy before you getting dropped off at his house and the car pulling up in front of yours, the entire hockey-puck black sky suddenly streaked with pink light, the chirpy trees full of busy grey birds, dewdrops on your father's perfect lawn like a bumper crop of sunrise just waiting to be picked.

I steer Barry to the outside of the track. Once he lowers his nose to the ground and starts his Sherlock routine — scratching and sniffing inspecting the same three square feet of earth, doggie magnifying glass on the trail of the ideal place to deposit this morning's delivery — I pull out my plastic bag and hold it open at each end. When I see his anus begin to pucker, that's my cue, I move right in. Other people wait until their dog is done his business to clean up the mess; Barry and I have learned to eliminate the need for stooping and scooping by my placing the bag directly underneath his rear end and letting what's left of yesterday's dinner drop harmlessly inside. I look like a quarterback hunched underneath his canine centre. When he's done, when he rises from his squat, I jump to the left to avoid the chunks of wet earth he lets fly with each celebratory kick.

"Go for the bomb, Bubs," I yell, and Barry takes off on a long fly route, his normal stool-clearing sprint.

I tie the bag with a quick knot, fake the handoff to the running-back, and pitch the warm sack underhand into the garbage can by the baseball backstop. Barry has stopped running and is standing in the middle of the field smiling, panting, whatever you want to call it. The steam coming from his nostrils in the cold morning air proves that he's alive. I can see it, so I must be alive too.

I feel good but I can't remember why. Before I can, "I'm gonna get you, Barry," I shout, and charge after him. Barry loves to be chased. I run after him until we stop. Who caught who, I really couldn't tell you.

IT'S ONLY THE FIRST week of December and already I'm starting to hate Jesus. It's nothing personal — one Sky God is no worse than the rest — but when the coloured lights come out, no storefront window is complete without a sign demanding Peace on Earth, and the guy with the Rottweiller in the stud collar in front of the beer store can't beg for change without wishing you a Merry Christmas. In the mail today, an X-mas card from our dentist reminding Mary that her next teeth cleaning is in five weeks and declaring Good Will Among Men and Have a Happy New Year, in that order.

But a cheque with my name on it, too, so Joy to the World. It's only for 150 bucks, but that's 150 more than I had when I woke up this morning. Back in the fall, Phil hooked me up with a friend of Rebecca's at *Books in Canada* and I penned my first and only book review. Six hundred and thirty-eight pages of the life and times of a very important person no one has ever heard of, and half way through all I could think was, *Die, you boring sonofabitch, die.* All biographies are the same, no one has ever been happy, but some people do suffer with more style than others. I earned my hundred and a half.

On our way to the bank machine to deposit the cheque Barry and I pass two young men standing in front of the butcher shop handing out Church of the Latter Day Saints literature. If it's only old ladies, I let it go, let them have their

RAY ROBERTSON

unearthly wisdom in lieu of children who visit and a life that hasn't come down to this, seventy-three years old and standing on a freezing street corner making a public nuisance of oneself. Young guys in cheap suits with bowl haircuts who make no smirking secret about feeling sorry for you because of all the neato stuff you're going to miss out on once the lights go out and the Big Guy starts handing out His final grades make it a little harder to be good. Reason's no use — that'll only get you a smug headshake. Logic they can ignore, but somebody as loony as they are doesn't compute. Fanatics hate fanatics. Doing unto others as they've done unto you is the only thing that works.

One of them sticks their pink pamphlet at me.

"Praise Mohammed," I say, stopping.

The one looks at the other. "Praise Jesus," he says.

"Praise the Holy Koran," I say.

"Have you read the New Testament, friend?" the other one says.

"Don't have to," I say, "I've read the Holy Koran. It's the Last Testament, brother." I leave them looking at each other and move down Roncesvalles.

I tie Barry to a parking meter in front of the bank. When I come back out, my hand's in my pocket, fingers curled around the bills inside. When we get home I give Barry a dog treat and call Mary at work.

"Creative Services."

"Hey, kiddo."

"Hey, you."

122

"How's it going?"

"Oh, the usual. My computer crashed again this morning. Haven't been able to get my stuff to the printer yet and it was supposed to be there yesterday. How's my dog?"

"My dog just got back from his walk."

"Did you guys meet anybody?" Dogs, she means, did we meet any other dogs. Mary loves to hear about any new mutts that we've met on our wanderings.

"Nope, just some nice young fellas wanting to save our souls."

"I hope you were nice."

"More than nice. I put them on the road to Allah."

"*Hank.*" She says it like she's disappointed, but we both know she's glad I do my bit to help keep the neigbourhood honest. I can hear her tapping computer keys.

"You sound busy, I'll let you go," I say. "Just wanted to let you know I finally got paid for that book review thing."

"Great. Want to meet me after work? We can eat at Buddha Gardens and I'll leave my bike in my office and we can walk home together and then we can vote at the high school on our way to taking the Bubs to High Park."

"Can't."

"Can't which part?"

"All of the above."

"What's wrong, don't love me anymore?"

"If I loved you any more, it'd be against the law. I have to meet Phil."

"You guys are talking again?"

"Of course we're talking again."

"Since when?"

"Since ... always."

"Okay, if you say so." Semi-silence. "But you're going to vote before you go, right?"

One hundred percent silence.

"Hank, you promised."

"I promised I'd think about it."

"And?"

"And, so, I thought about it. And decided against it."

"Because the system's broke and voting isn't going to fix it."

"Something like that."

"But, Hank, if you're going to complain about how things are run, you've got to at least try to make a difference. If you're —"

"— not part of the solution, you're part of the problem, yeah, I know."

Mary and I have been having one or another version of this argument since practically date number one. By now, she knows my clichés and I know hers, and neither of us is afraid to throw them in the face of the other. This is love, too.

"Look," I say, "you and I both know that that clown is going to get elected again no matter what box I fill in, so what's the point?"

"The point is that you'll know that you didn't just lie down and accept it, that you made your voice heard."

"Gee, I get tingly all over just thinking about it."

"It's something."

"It's not enough."

"It's better than nothing."

"We want the world and we want it now."

"Okay," Mary says, "that's enough."

When I start quoting Jim Morrison lyrics, Mary knows it's time to change the subject. I'm the expert at starting arguments, she's the champ at short-circuiting them. Each partner brings their own unique talents to their relationship.

"You going to be late?" she says.

"Don't know," I say. "Maybe."

"If you two are going to talk, it might be late, I won't wait up."

"Yeah, you better not, it might be late."

"Okay."

"All right."

"Hank?"

"Yeah?"

"Listen to what he has to say. Try to understand where he's coming from."

"Understand where who's coming from?"

"Phil, you dummy."

"Oh, right. Yeah, I will."

I hear her stop hitting keys. "Are you all right?"

"Never better. I'll try not to wake you when I get home."

"Are you sure you're okay?"

"Don't forget to walk my dog when you get home."

"He's my dog, and I wouldn't."

"Bye."

"Bye."

I pull the fold of bills from my jeans and count out what I've kept for myself. Ten, twenty, forty, fifty. I look at the clock. Only five more hours until showtime.

AFTER ENOUGH DRAFT BEER anything is possible.

Well, almost anything. I didn't actually make it up on stage and belt out the Georgia Satellites' "Keep Your Hands to Yourself" better than the guy in the backwards baseball cap and the GIVE ME HEAD 'TIL I'M DEAD t-shirt like I knew I could have, but I did manage to scribble my name and the title of the tune on one of the little white slips of paper you're supposed to fill out and hand over to the karaoke M.C. when you're ready to sing. I was ready, but not able. Or able, but not ready. If you don't think there's a difference, you've never sat alone for three hours trying to drink yourself into being brave. Or stupid. The distinction between these two isn't quite as clear.

On the walk home, trying to figure out why I'd thought it necessary to lie to Mary about meeting Phil, I run into Frank. He's out of his neighbourhood, lives just around the corner from the Duke, but walks Queen Street the nights he's trying not to drink. Chain-smoking hand-rolled hemp cigarettes, a paperback swelling his back pocket, he'll cover four, five miles over the course of an evening's hard-earned sobriety.

"Hey, Frank."

"Hank, how are you?"

We shake hands.

He looks surprised, pleased, but nervous. Staying out of the bars is supposed to keep him from temptations like this, deliver him from the evils of bumping into booze buddies like me.

"You and Mary, you live around here, don't you?" he says. He unzips his jacket and pulls out a ready-rolled cigarette from inside his shirt pocket, zips back up.

"Near here, further west, Roncesvalles."

Frank lights his smoke with his Zippo, inhales hard, nods. I can tell he can smell beer on my breath. He takes a step back from me on the sidewalk by pretending to get a better look at the moon half-hidden behind a billboard advertising push-up bras.

"Supposed to be a full moon tonight," Frank says.

"Oh, yeah?" I look up. "Maybe that explains it."

"What's that?"

"Nothing," I say, shaking my head.

Last call at the Gladstone is one a.m., an hour earlier than most everywhere else, so I've got time for one more if I don't dawdle. I don't particularly want another beer, but feel like I've got to do something since I didn't do what I promised myself ten times tonight that I would.

Frank tugs the paperback from his pocket, pulls off one of his gloves. "While I've got you here, let me ask you something, Hank."

It's a fat copy of Sartre's *Being and Nothingness* with a Book City bookmark sticking out three-quarters of the way through, its bright yellow end flapping in the cold street-corner wind. Only a restless autodidact living off his accumulated dope-smuggling money would actually read *Being and Nothingness* like an actual book. *Being and Nothingness* is the sort of book you buy in order to put on your shelf to impress people who come over to the house. No one actually *reads* *Being and Nothingness*. Frank does. He retrieves his black reading glasses from the same pocket as his cigarettes and thumbs the pages until he finds the one he wants.

"I realize I haven't finished the entire book yet, so maybe I'm jumping the gun a little bit here, but ..."

But Frank launches into a spirited critique of Sartre's conception of Bad Faith anyway, complete with two lengthy, apparently self-contradictory quotations right from Jean-Paul's mouth. He closes the book but doesn't return it to his pocket, holds it in front of him with one bare bony hand folded over the gloved other like an end-of-service minister his Bible. His reading glasses are still hanging off the end of his nose.

"Well, that sounds about right to me, Frank," I say.

Frank nods, pulls his toque down a little further on his forehead, awaits the arrival of even further profundities.

"I mean, like you say, you should probably get through to the end before you reach any definite conclusion, but, yeah, I think you're on to something there." If I didn't feel like having a beer before, I do now.

Mercifully, Frank squeezes the book back in his pocket. "Thanks, Hank," he says, "thanks a lot. You know I appreciate our little chats."

"No problem," I say. We shake hands again.

"See you, Hank."

"See you, Frank."

On the walk home I try to remember what the hell Bad Faith is. I had to have known once. I mean, I must have.

IN THE MORNING THERE'S a note from Mary on the kitchen table saying there's a message from Phil on the answering machine saying for me to call him when I get a chance. But I'm a busy man, was up just after Mary left for work, and spent what was left of the morning and most of the afternoon slicing and dicing two out of three of my delinquent Independent Writers' Classroom manuscripts — Lenore Shipely's brave "journey into the heart of loss, the memory of loss, the unquenchable, never satiable quest to remember that which can never be forgotten" the undone exception to my sudden industriousness — and now need to hustle to the Continuing Studies office downtown so I can hand them in and get paid. All I've eaten all day is the apple I munched while walking Barry, plus seven Fig Newtons washed down with about half a litre of Diet Pepsi while I worked, so the grumble in my gut and slight shake in my hands that I notice while shutting down my computer and packing everything up aren't cause for worry, aren't even surprising, even if I hadn't spent my last six dollars the night before on an overpriced imported beer at some loud, neon nightmare on the way home that had nothing more to recommend it other than it was still open.

Alcohol always ends up a draw. Last night's exaltation always equals out to this morning's melancholy. It's only physiological, sure, just altered brain chemistry and next-day dehydration, but put aside the science and there's a dialectic tied up with tying one on. Whatever nature gives, it takes back. Hangovers are the coins you feed the happiness machine.

This morning, though, in the shower as soon as I got up, I sang "Keep Your Hands to Yourself" just like I would have if I'd had a microphone in my hand and a pre-recorded musical track backing me up. I was right. I *was* better than the guy in the backwards baseball cap. I was at my desk half an hour later. Sometimes the machine coughs up a free game.

There's a coffee shop I eat at sometimes near the subway that's run by a Cantonese woman named Jenny. The filthy yellow canopy hanging over the door reads JENNY'S COFFEE SHOP, so everyone calls the woman Jenny. I used to feel sorry for her for having to answer to such a dumb honky name as Jenny just because we're all too lazy to get to know her by her real name, but then I thought that maybe she was actually lucky. Almost everyone is doomed to piss away the majority of their days doing something they'd really rather not do, but at least Jenny has an alias, a word to hide behind when she's up to her knuckles in mayonnaise or dishing out day-old walnut crullers and crappy coffee. Whoever she really is she can save up for when she gets home.

The coffee shop is part of a decaying mini-mall that must have seemed real spiffy around the same time I was bugging my parents for a pet rock, and sits between a doctor's office specializing in human prosthetics and a hairdresser who caters to old women who haven't given up on the joy of sitting underneath those mammoth hair dryers you usually only see at unsuccessful yard sales. Once in a while a guy with a plastic arm or a woman with a missing hand or a just-coifed old lady, tentative touch to her newly tinted hair every thirty seconds, will sit amidst the rest of us. Us being me and a roomful of people I don't know. Mary is a by-the-book vegan without her husband's weakness for white-trash sugar treasures like bear claws and jelly-filled donuts, and has never deigned to join me and experience for herself all that is chez Jenny.

I haven't got time for sitting today, so I ask Jenny for my usual, an egg salad sandwich on wheat and a can of Diet Pepsi, to go. I grab one of several discarded copies of the Toronto *Sun* sitting on the counter and flip it open to the sports section. I don't buy the *Sun*, don't approve of the *Sun*, and never read the *Sun*. Except when I'm at Jenny's and no one I know can catch me reading it. Everybody needs a few dirty little secrets they can only share with strangers.

"Let me guess. You know the help here, too."

I want to say, *We've got to stop meeting like this*, but am afraid it'll come across less like a cliché than a come-on; instead, say, "Hey, Buh ..."

"Beverly," Beverly says.

"Beverly, right, sorry."

Smiling, "I can see I've made quite an impression on you, haven't I?"

I shake my head. "I'm not very —"

"Good with names, I know. We've established that. So," she says, looking at the chalkboard menu on the wall behind the counter, "what *are* you good at, then?" She's smiling while she says this, too, so I know she's not being nasty, although I'm not so sure she isn't being flirty. Which makes me feel guilty. Which compels me to remind myself that as long as you're on the receiving end of a come-on, not the giving part, you've got nothing to feel guilty about. Which makes me feel better, if not any less guilty.

"Four dollar, please," Jenny says, placing my paper-bagged sandwich and my pop on the counter by the cash register.

"That's disappointing," Beverly says as I pull out my wallet.

"What's that?" I say, handing Jenny a five.

"When I saw you through the window as I was passing by I thought we might have a proper talk over lunch, we only seem to speak to one other whenever we're in a park or a bookstore. But it appears as if you have other plans."

"Thank you very much, see you next time," Jenny says, handing me my change.

"That would be great," I say, "but I've got to meet my wife." I hold up the brown paper bag. Sometimes telling a lie is the most moral thing you can do.

"You're married?" she says, raising an eyebrow.

"Almost seven years."

"I hadn't noticed a ring." We both look down at my naked fingers.

"Oh, I just don't like jewellry. Not so much jewellry, really, as having to wear it. I feel like I'm being weighed down."

"And how does your wife feel about you feeling weighed down by a wedding ring?"

"Yes, please, next?" Jenny says to Beverly.

"No, Jenny, she's with me, she doesn't want anything," I say. Beverly steps in front of me.

"Yes, Jenny, I'd like a Coca-Cola — not diet — and ..." She scans the two rows of donuts. "... one of those lovely choco-late eclairs, please. For here, please, Jenny."

"You're eating here?" I say. Black skirt, black pumps, black sheer hose, white blouse, single string of pearls — she looks like she's just come from either an exclusive dinner party or the opera. Court, I suppose, remembering she's a lawyer.

Beverly snaps opens her purse. "That's what people ordin-arily do in restaurants, isn't it?" she says. "Or is that just an English convention?"

"No, no, I just thought, I don't know —"

"Two dollar twenty-five, please," Jenny says, Beverly's can of Coke, her donut, and a napkin on a orange plastic tray on the counter before her.

Beverly pays and picks up the eclair without the benefit of the napkin, doesn't wait until she sits down to take a first bite. Cream oozes out of each side of the donut, a smear of choco-late sticking to her upper lip.

"Sorry," she says, licking off the chocolate. "I'm afraid I have the most terrible failing for sweets."

"Thank you very much, see you next time," Jenny says, placing Beverly's change in her other hand.

Beverly takes another big bite. This time, a white dollop of cream drops from the eclair onto the plastic tray.

"If you're going to have something bad for you," she says, "have something bad for you, that's what I say."

SECOND VERSE SAME AS the first: the Gladstone Hotel, Just-Do-It Round Two, just a sticky tabletop littered with several small pieces of paper neatly filled out with all of the songs I didn't get my ass out of my chair and sing by the time the M.C. announced last call for alcohol. I get to my feet and stick the white slips of paper in my coat pocket so no one will find any evidence of what a big karaoke coward I really am. I exit through the side door, the one that leads into the actual hotel lobby, so I don't have to walk in front of the stage.

Doing up the buttons of my coat, I read the handwritten sign posted on the wall beside the front desk. A bald man with large, woolly black eyebrows sitting in an old swivel desk chair reads a racing form with one hand while eating what's left of a submarine sandwich with the other, his brown carpet slippers up on the desk. The sign is written with a thick black magic marker.

WANTED:

DOOR MAN

INQUIRE AT DESK

"Pays eight bucks an hour," the man says.

I turn away from the sign. "Oh," I say. He's still reading his racing form.

"Tuesday through Saturday, seven until around two. It's on account of the karaoke. We're making it a five-night-a-week thing. On account of how popular it's getting."

"Right," I say. I look back at the sign, read all six words all over again.

"You want an application?" the bald man says. This time he is looking at me, the racing form face down on one of his thighs. He takes a bite out of his sandwich. His bushy eyebrows wiggle up and down in unison while he chews, as if a caterpillar has wandered onto his forehead and decided to stay. The more I don't answer, the more he keeps looking at me.

"Okay," I say.

He doesn't move, keeps on looking at me, keeps on chewing.

"I mean, sure, if it's ..."

The bald man slowly slides his feet off the desk, lets the soles of his slippers fall flat to the cement floor with a sticky smack. He puts the racing form and the sandwich on the desktop and pulls a single sheet of paper out of a drawer.

"You got a pen?" he says.

I'm mute again. He's holding out the application for me to take. "I thought maybe I'd fill it out at home," I say.

"I've got a pen," he says, hand in the same drawer. He puts a capless Bic pen and the sheet of paper on the desk. He goes back to the racing form, takes another bite of his sandwich.

I fill out the application as quickly as I can, leaving any

section I don't absolutely have to answer blank, not taking the time to lie wherever I'm expected to. When I'm finished, I place the pen on top of the piece of paper and wait. When the bald man doesn't look up, I push both toward him across the desk.

"Thanks," I say, nodding goodbye, pulling up the collar of my coat as I turn toward the door.

"Just give me a second," he says, taking one last look at the racing form before he picks up my application. He rubs his brow with his fingertips while he reads like he's trying to massage away a migraine or erase a stubborn spot. A minute later, maybe less, "Can you start tomorrow?" he says.

I'm not quite sure what he's asking me. "Tomorrow. That's ..."

"Thursday," he says. "Are you able to start working tomorrow night, Thursday night?"

"I guess," I say.

"Good," he says, "welcome aboard." He puts out his hand. "How you doin', Hank, my name's Sid." Sid and I shake hands.

My new employer slips my application and the pen back into the drawer underneath the desk. "Be here tomorrow at 6:30 so I can show you around and run through what you'll be doing."

"Uhm ..."

"Don't worry," Sid says, putting his feet back up on the desk. "I can tell just by looking at you you're gonna work out just fine."

ALL THE LIGHTS ARE on when I get home. Mary must have caught a second wind and still be at it at her easel. I'm glad she's up, so I can tell her the good news. If that's what it is. I'm glad she's still up so she can help me figure out what kind of news it actually is.

"Hey," I say, putting my key back in my pocket, Mary hurdling up the stairs two at a time to greet me, Barry coming on strong right behind her. When she reaches me she throws her arms around my neck and plants a wet kiss on my right ear. The saliva from her mouth on my earlobe warms me, makes me slightly shiver at the same time. Hot and cold running love.

"What did I do to deserve this?" I say.

"You didn't do anything," she says, "Barry did. You're just cashing in on the interest." She wraps her arms around me and gives me a big squeeze.

Barry puts his paw up on Mary's thigh and lifts his snout as high as he can, motioning with it upward, upward, as if to say, *Hey, gang, I want in on the action, too.* No dog can stand to sit still when there's this much loving and hugging and sweet talk going on. I get down on my knees and give Barry the business, rub him hard between the ears.

"So, what did the wonder dog do today?" I say.

"Nothing but be the sweet thing he always is," Mary says, joining me on the floor. She pats the carpet, Barry lays down, and she carefully flips him over on his back, proceeds to scratch his belly while I concentrate on scrubbing him underneath his chin. Dogs aren't particular where their pleasure comes from. The more the merrier, as far as they're concerned.

"Guess who's moving?" Mary says.

"Don't know, who?"

I'm having such a fine, family-time time I don't really care, either. When merriment comes calling you don't ask where it's been hiding or how long it plans on sticking around. You just keep on scratching and scrubbing.

"Rover and his parents. Remember we were wondering if they had children or not?"

"Um hm." I knead the left side of Barry's face, just above his upper jawbone, forcing the skin that is his top lip to involuntarily lift above a row of exposed white teeth. It looks like he's talking out of the side of his mouth. It looks like he's saying, *Keep it coming, pal, if you know what's good for you.*

"Well, they do, a son, a dentist, who lives in Scottsdale, as in Arizona, and Tom and Lynn —"

"Who?"

"Rover's parents."

"Oh."

"They're moving down there in the spring to be near him and his wife and their kids. They're both pretty creaky looking, so it's probably just as much for their health."

"And Rover's."

"And Rover's," Mary says, laughing, tickling Barry's back feet sticking straight up in the air, one hand for each foot.

"So they actually stooped to speak with you long enough for you to find all of this out, huh?"

"More than that. I saw their house."

"The *inside* of their house?"

"Yep."

"Unbelievable. What'd you do, promise to help them move?"

"Not even. Somehow we got talking about Barry and pet insurance — Rover, of course, is fully insured."

"Of course."

"And I said that maybe we should start thinking about it for the Bubs, but that right now we're sort of saving to buy our own place."

"We are?"

"Without trying, sort of."

"Yeah, I guess."

"Anyway, that's when they — her mostly, he was pretty much his usual grouchy self — told me that they're moving to Arizona and how they've lived in that same little house since 1966 and that they want to avoid using a real-estate agent and having people coming and going through their house for months on end and that it'd be nice if someone already from the neighbourhood bought it."

"So how come you went and looked at it?"

"Because I think we should buy it."

I stop rubbing Barry's stomach. He doesn't mind. He's been asleep for a couple of minutes now.

"You're serious," I say.

Mary smiles and takes me by the hand like she wants to hit the sheets, but leads me downstairs instead. Her studio is dark, but the kitchen is fully lit and alive, the tea pot, calculator, and several pages of my printer paper crammed top to bottom with numbers, inexplicable abbreviations, and rows and rows of columns with underlined headings, all conspiring to cover the tabletop. Mary's been busy. It's what she does best.

"Look," she says. "We can do it."

Mary sits me down — I've still got my coat on, although I have managed to unbutton it — and walks me through the labyrinth of her evening's labour. I get lost a couple of times, but eventually we surface at the same exit at the same time. The fact that I can continue to be roughly the same economic underachiever I have been and still not sink the deal is noted in typical, matter-of-fact, reproof-free Mary fashion: *Hank = $13,000/year (approx.) O.K.*

"I don't get it," I say. "How can this make sense?"

"I know," Mary says, "but there it is."

We both survey the paper-strewn table. Barry has joined us downstairs and drinks from his water bowl.

"If the bank gives us a loan," I say.

"They will. The amount of money they make off the interest on a mortgage, we're doing them a favour, not the other way around."

"And if Rover's parents sell us their house this cheap. I still don't get that."

"Like I said, they want to do a private sale — that saves them a ton of money right there since they don't have to pay an agent. And the place is tiny. How they raised a child there, I don't know. And they want to sell it to someone from the neighbourhood."

"Yeah, but why us?"

"Lynn said we remind her of them when they were starting out. Did I tell you that Tom is a retired linguistics prof at U of T?"

"I'm not a professor of linguistics," I say. "Or of anything."

"No," Mary says, "but when I told her that you did your B.A. in philosophy, even he couldn't help looking pleased. Sort of." Mary laughs.

I look at her. She looks the same way she did the night we decided to move in together. The day she found out that York had accepted her into their M.F.A. program and awarded her their biggest incoming scholarship. The day we brought Barry home from the Humane Society.

"You really like this place?" I say.

Still sitting in her chair beside me, Mary leans over and drapes her arms around my shoulders, keeps herself up by holding onto me tight. Her face is maybe three inches from mine.

"Wait until you see it, Hank. It's like it was meant for us. It's like it already *is* us. There are old hardwood floors everywhere, and all the fixtures are the original, beat-up ones. We'd finally have our own bedroom, too, on the second floor, looking onto a big elm tree on the north side of the house. And there's even a nice little backyard for the Bubs."

"And for your garden," I say.

"A garden would be nice." Mary rests her chin on my shoulder.

"You deserve a garden," I say.

"But you need to like it, too," she says, lifting her head. "This

is a big commitment. For both of us. You need to feel like
this is what you want to do, too. They said we could come by
and look at it together tomorrow night."

"I can't," I say.

"I think they want us to decide soon. I don't think they're
big on social visits. Can't you postpone whatever it is?"

"No, I can't."

"Hank, this is important."

"Well, how would it look if I called in sick my first night
on the job?"

"What job?" she says.

"The one I got tonight."

Mary pulls me closer and squeezes me harder, enough so
that I tumble off my chair, taking her, laughing, down to the
floor with me. When Barry wakes up to what's going on he
leaps up off the carpet and charges over, big fat juicy face licks
for the whole gang.

"Ah! Dog slobber!" Mary shouts, pushing him away.

"Barry alert!" I yell, joining in.

The more we scream and shove him back, the more Barry
keeps right on coming. Just like we know he will.

FREEDOM IS GREAT, JUST not too much of it. It's even better
when there's something keeping you from enjoying it. It's the
same as being healthy or having enough money in your pocket
or getting laid regularly — they're all easier to appreciate if
you've done without them for awhile.

These days, I get up around eleven, take Barry for his walk and buy a newspaper, and finish eating my cereal and reading the sports page by about 12:30. I wash my bowl and spoon and set them out to dry on the counter, put the sports section with the rest of the unopened paper in the recycling bin, and do whatever the day requires. Maybe it's grocery shopping, it could be waiting around for the plumber to come and fix the dripping kitchen faucet, it might be carting our dirty clothes to the laundromat a block and a half away. Today it's taking Barry to the vet for his annual check-up and overdue booster shots. Whatever it is, I've got to be done by four-thirty, five at the latest. After making and brown-bagging my supper and taking a quick shower, I like to sit in the silence of the living room and read for half an hour or so before I go to work, poetry usually, nothing in particular.

Before I had to be somewhere five nights a week I could have snuck in *War and Peace* between chapters of *Decline and Fall of the Roman Empire* and still had time left over for rereading *The Brothers Karamazov* before bed. Could have, would have, should have. Now I like to read poetry for half an hour or so before I go to work. Like to, so do.

The quiet time is nice — is necessary, even — since I spend most of my nights at the Gladstone parked beside one of the two mammoth speakers that the karaoke guy — Bob, actually — uses to blast out his black plastic binder full of singalong songs. Once the requests really start rolling in I'm in for several hours of 300-watt amplified shrieking, warbling, moaning, shouting, and even occasionally something not unlike

143

actual singing. Not that hitting all the high notes is the point. Karaoke is about a lot of things, but sounding just like the record isn't one of them.

I don't do much, but what I do needs to be done. I check IDs. I turn away the odd drunk (being drunk is okay, being a drunk is not). Mostly I just stand around with my arms folded across my chest and try to look tough and keep an eye out for anything I don't think I can handle and need to let Sid know about so that he can call the cops. So far I've only had to bother him once. Two clowns going nose-to-nose near the bar had, in spite of my calm counsel to *Take it outside, guys*, graduated from finger-jabbing each other in the chest to open-palmed shoving. I sprinted for the lobby.

"Two assholes who won't leave look like they're going to go at it," I said.

"Anybody bleeding yet?" Sid said, studying his race form.

I stuck my head back outside the lobby door. "No."

Sid picked up the phone, punched 911, and told the cop shop what was what without once interrupting his scouring of the race form. He put the phone back down and finally looked at me.

"It's okay to get the police involved if it's nothing serious, but anything that reflects bad on us, it's better we take care of it ourselves, understand?"

I nodded.

"Good boy. Now go wait out front for the police. Bob can handle the door."

For a guy who believes that every woman he meets either

wants to sleep with him or is a lesbian, Bob's all right. The only woman who probably does think of him as anything more than a Wal-Mart Romeo with a beer belly and a ninety-nine-dollar hair weave is Sarah, his shack job. Sarah's an M.C., too, works part-time at a place called Joe Mercury's in the east end, and I've never asked, but I'm pretty sure that she and Bob hooked up somewhere along the karaoke circuit. Karaoke masters of ceremonies are musical mercenaries, tin-eared troubadours, zig-zagging across the city in their rusted-out station wagons and lease-by-the-month vans and hiring out their time and equipment and expertise to the highest bidder. Bob's gear is bigger and louder, his song selection more diverse and deeper, but Sarah has her own sound system and songbook as well. I've never seen her in action, have only met her once, when Bob's van was in the shop and she'd had to haul him and his equipment to and from work, but Bob says she's good. They're both good at what they do.

One of the things they're good at is getting people up on stage who might not otherwise have the guts to be there. This is the true litmus test of a top-shelf M.C. Every karaoke bar has its regulars, the same characters who always show up at the same time on the same nights to do the same numbers, and we've got our own fair share of what Bob calls Karaoke Cowboys and Cowgirls.

There's Miss Pamela, a grandmother of five who always wears the same sequined red dress, elbow-length white gloves, and black feathered boa and who specializes in '40s show tunes. There's Michael, a huge, mentally-retarded guy in his early twenties who nurses a glass of Coke all night and who only does John Denver songs. There's Pistol Pete, a gay black guy decked out in army fatigues and a tight, white T-shirt who wears a plastic pistol and holster set on his hip and who always shoots his cap gun over his head a few times at the end of every one of the campy old country songs he's partial to, coolly blowing its smoking end when he's done.

Most people are built to watch the show, though, not be in it, and that's where an experienced karaoke M.C. comes in. Bob, for instance, will hold up a large cardboard sign that simply reads APPLAUSE! whenever anybody's struggling up on stage, giving whoever's clamming up or tripping over the lyrics on the teleprompter or all at once realizing what a lousy voice they've got a helpful blast of hooting and hollering and handclapping to help pull them through, telling the rest of the room in the process that we're all on the same team, folks, everybody here goes home a winner. Sometimes the push is a little more personal.

Every night at around eleven Bob'll watch the door for me while I pop across the street to get him a meatball sub and a large double-double at Country Style. I don't mind, the new guy always ends up being the gopher, it's one of the things that helps him not be the new guy anymore. One night I came back with his sub and his coffee, handed him his change, and he pushed a hole in the white plastic lid, blew away the steam, and said, "You want to go up tonight, Big Guy?"

Big Guy is one of those names that can go either way. I choose to believe that Bob is simply able to see why I was a natural fit to play outside linebacker for the Chatham Collegiate Institute Cougars nineteen years ago and am still more than capable of taking care of myself if the situation demands it.

"What do you mean?" I said. Bob keeps his chair close to the black railing that runs around the edge of the stage, nearest to the door, so neither of us usually has to shout over the music.

Bob unwrapped his sub. "What do you think I mean? It's like a fucking tomb in here tonight, I need some fresh voices to shake things up." Miss Pamela was on stage doing her thing, belting out "There's No Business Like Show Business," so he didn't have to worry about working the applause sign. Everybody loves Miss Pamela, almost as much as she does.

"If I hear Michael do 'Sunshine on My Shoulder' once more this week I swear to God I'm gonna fucking kill myself," he said. "Hey, speaking of fresh, did you check out that number in the blue T-shirt? The one who did 'Heat Wave' about half an hour ago with a bunch of her little college buddies? Christ, talk about obvious. I'm just glad Sarah didn't decide to drop by tonight."

The room erupted and we looked up. Miss Pamela had tossed one of her white gloves into the crowd and began tugging off the other. She does the same thing at least once every night. Whoever ends up with them just hands them back when she sits back down.

Bob took another big bite of his sub. Tomato sauce and bits of chewed meat splattered his tongue, a string of congealed cheese hung from the roof of his mouth while he spoke.

"Anyway, do me a favour, get up and do a tune. That way I can say, 'Ladies and Gentleman, Hank, the doorman.' Everybody'll love it." He took another bite. "And, hey, how about this: you get up and do a Doors tune, that'd be great, that'd be perfect. Hank the doorman does the Doors. People'll eat it up."

"I'm working," I said.

"Yeah, sure you are. What I do is working. What you do is stand around with your thumb up your ass all night." He sipped from his paper cup of coffee. "I'll call you up right after Pistol Pete."

"I don't know."

"Relax. You're doing me a favour, that's all. I'll owe you one."

"Yeah, but —"

"Just be ready."

I wasn't, but Bob called my name anyway. I also wasn't drunk. The Gladstone isn't the Duke, the staff isn't encouraged to sample the merchandise. Like everything, nothing ever happens the way you think it will. As long as it happens, though, there's not much point in complaining. Some of my best friends were unplanned pregnancies.

I picked up the microphone from its stand. And whispered my way through the first two verses of "Love Me Two Times." And kept right on talking until Bob held up his APPLAUSE! sign and eventually I started singing. And then the song was over. Then Bob asked the crowd for a big hand for Hank the doorman and announced that it was time for two more first-timers, Tracy and Tim, doing "Summer Love."

Standing back in my usual spot beside the door, "Hey, Bob," I called out over the music.

Bob looked up from the pile of CDs he was sorting through on the table in front of him.

"When can I go again?" I said.

BARRY LOVES GOING TO the vet. He forgets all of the bad stuff, like submitting to the ordeal of getting his nails clipped or the time when he was a puppy and the doctor had to give him an anal probe because he'd swallowed one of my house keys, and has a perfect memory for everything he likes about the place, stuff like the dog treats the receptionist feeds him out of the barking cookie jar on her desk and the section of High Park we don't usually get to that we always end up hiking through on the way to our appointments. There's a truth here, and you don't need to know how a syllogism works to figure it out.

The last time we were at the vet was eight months ago, but Barry pulls toward the frosted glass door that has McFarlane Animal Clinic stencilled across it like it's a part of our regular route. After we check in, after Barry gets weighed, and after I leaf through a couple of dog magazines intended to make you feel like a horrible pet owner — the food you buy not rich enough in iron, protein, and energy-boosting vitamins, the toys your dog plays with not safe or stimulating enough, the lack of consideration you've given to his or her final resting place not just thoughtless but downright irresponsible —

the veterinarian steps into the waiting room in his white lab coat and salt-and-pepper beard.

"Barry?" he says.

"That's us," I say, standing up. Barry and I follow him into one of the examination rooms.

"And how's Barry doing today?" the doctor says.

"He's good," I say, taking the liberty of answering for him. Barry's too busy attempting to sniff the accumulated dog and cat history of the room to bother replying.

"Let's get him up on the table, if we can," the doctor says.

"I think I can handle it," I say.

Dogs are stiff-limbed, are day-old cadavers still very much alive, and big dogs like Barry tend to get a little panicky when someone they don't know attempts to pick them up and haul them around. Barry knows me. I hoist him on top of the metal table with one clean lift. He surveys the room like a billy goat standing on a mountaintop.

"Okay, let's have a look at you, Barry," the doctor says, pulling back his patient's eyelids, opening up his mouth, looking inside his ears. I hold onto Barry's collar with one hand and place my other hand on the middle of his back while the vet goes about his business. Whenever Barry feels like the vet is stepping over the line of doctor-patient familiarity, I stroke him the length of his long black back a few times and tell him that he's a good boy. He always settles right down and lets the doctor do his thing. He's never told me, but I know that he knows that I know what's best for him and would never let anyone do anything to him that wasn't.

"Hmm," the doctor says, running his hand along the underside of Barry's belly.

"What is it?" I say.

"Hmm," he says again, massaging the same spot. "How long has he had this lump?"

"I didn't know he had one."

"Here, feel," the doctor says, placing my hand on a mass of flesh the size of a golf ball.

"Christ, how did I not notice that?" I suddenly feel very hot and the room smells like rotting animal corpses and I wish that someone would pet me and tell me what a good boy I am. "It isn't a tumour, is it?"

"Probably not," the doctor says.

"Probably? Isn't there any way of knowing for sure?"

"Not without surgery. Besides, feel it again." I put my hand back. "Feel how it moves around? How it almost rolls?"

I nod.

"That means it's not attached to the bone and is probably just a fatty deposit. It's very common with retrievers as they get older."

"So it's not a tumour or anything bad?" I keep moving the lump left and right, up and down. Barry keeps looking around the room, doesn't even seem to notice.

"As I said, it's very unlikely, he's more than likely just fine."

"But you're not sure."

Probably. Very unlikely. More than likely. Skepticism is a dandy philosophy for doubting the existence of tables and chairs and even other human beings, but it just doesn't cut it when it comes to things like potentially cancerous lumps that may or may not go bump in the long night.

The doctor goes to a computer in the corner and rat-tats at the keyboard. "Unless we remove the growth and send it to the lab for analysis, no, we can't be completely sure. But aside from the cost to find out something we're already fairly sure of — an operation of this nature is going to be around $600 — I don't recommend older dogs like Barry having non-emergency surgery. Besides, as I said, because of the constitution of the growth, I don't think we have anything to worry about. Just check for lumps regularly — whenever you comb him, for example — and if they feel like the one that's there now, he's more than likely fine. Otherwise, bring him in and we'll have a look."

The doctor takes some blood and sticks Barry with a couple more needles to keep him safe from a bunch of other things he'll probably never get, and I put the bill on our VISA card but don't stick around long enough for the receptionist to refill her battery-operated barking cookie jar with more dog treats. Barry knows what's going on, doesn't want to leave until he gets his customary cookie, but I don't feel like staying any longer than we absolutely have to.

Once we're outside in the cold afternoon air I begin to feel better. It's not the wind on my face that begins to cool me off, but the people on the sidewalk, the cars and trucks and buses in the street, the restaurants and banks and shops with even more people milling around inside or passing in and out. A world this busy doesn't have time for death.

Barry's confused when we don't turn into the park where we're supposed to, but I keep us walking in the opposite direction of home until we hit the Pet Value store on Bloor. Barry's getting a bone. And maybe some dog treats, too, although there's already a nearly full box of them at home.

A cherry red Lexus being dragged backwards down the street by a tow truck whines away helplessly, the useless screaming of its car alarm not turning anybody's head. We step up to the door of the pet store and it opens for us on its own. As soon as we're inside, the noise is gone.

WE'RE JUST OUR PARENTS with better haircuts.

Talking to my old man on the phone, imagining him pacing up and down the kitchen floor with his phone in one hand and a cigarette in the other, I'm downstairs in the kitchen with my phone stuck between my shoulder and my ear while I wash and rack the dishes. I wipe a hand on my jeans and turn down the radio to better hear what he's saying about the cost of replacing knob and tube wiring in old houses. Now that Mary and I are prospective home owners, my dad and I have more to talk about than just hockey; my mum and I more than the weather and who in Chatham is recently dead, dying, or definitely getting there.

"It's all gonna have to go," my dad says. "The insurance companies these days, they've got guys like me and you by the balls and they aren't about to let go. Unless you get that knob and tube out of there pronto, they'll gouge you like you wouldn't believe on your rate."

"That's what the inspector said," I say.

"Well, he knew what he was talking about. What did he say about your amp service?"

"I don't remember."

"Is it sixty or a hundred?"

"I don't know, he talked about a lot of things. We were over there for over two hours."

"Well, you better find out. A lot of those old houses are only rigged up with sixty amps. Most companies today won't even sell you insurance unless you've changed over to a hundred."

"Hold on a second, the report's on the kitchen table." I put the last dish in the drying rack and shut off the tap.

Knob and tube wiring, house inspectors, amp upgrades — buying your first home is like learning a new language. Every time you congratulate yourself on adding a fresh noun to your vocabulary, up pops an adjective, a verb, and a pronoun that have got to be mastered if the noun is going to make any sense. Who knew being a petite bourgeois was so much hard work?

Mary was right, though. Rover's parents' house is great, is perfect for us, already is so much us. The handmade bookshelves. The overgrown garden in the back. The dulled-down, scuffed-up hardwood floors that Lynn was quick to apologize for not waxing enough over the years and that we said we'd restore ASAP but know very well that we won't. It's Hank and Mary's very own Platonic form of Houseness. All we need to do is move in and grow old and dotty together.

"What am I looking for?" I say, flipping through the green plastic binder we got in return for our $325.00 inspection fee plus $22.75 GST.

"Something that says something about your electricity."

"Hold on, let me look." I sneeze, look. "Electrical Service slash Panel?"

"That's probably it. What does it say underneath that?"

I sneeze again and read what it says. *Recommend upgrading and installing new circuit breaker panel. This is an outdated sixty amp service — recommend upgrading to one hundred amps.*

"There you go," my dad says. "So you've got to budget for that too."

"Budget how much?"

"I'm not an electrician, but not less than a thousand, anyway."

"Christ," I say, tossing the binder back on the table and grabbing the dish towel from the refrigerator door handle. I start in on drying the dishes with the phone stuck back between my shoulder and my ear. I can hear the ice cubes in the old man's rye and coke tinkling against the sides of his glass as he stalks around the room. I can hear CFCO faintly playing in the background, a Bryan Adams power ballad, I think.

"Hey, better you know about it now than get knocked for a loop later," he says.

"Yeah, well, getting knocked for a loop now doesn't feel so great either." For some silly reason I'd thought that borrowing $150,000 from a bank was terrifying enough economic news for one lifetime.

"Hey," my dad says, "this is big-time stuff, boy, you're buy-ing a house here, not a new pair of sneakers. This is grown-up stuff."

I'm pretty sure that this is the old man's way of compliment-ing me on finally making the screaming leap to adulthood, so I resist the urge to tell him to can the coming-of-age bromos as I feel nervous enough every time I tally up all those accounts-payable zeros in my head all on my own. I also don't tell him that they call them running shoes now, not sneakers, but do let him know that there's somebody at the door. Barry, the walking, barking doorbell, is howling his windpipe raw upstairs.

"I've got to go," I say.

"I'll check with a guy I know about prices for amp upgrades."

"Tell mum I said hi," I say.

I jog up the stairs to find Phil with his nose pressed to the glass of the big picture window, his face framed on each side by a hand to help cut the glare. Barry, growling now more than howling, is jumping up against the door, his long nails carving fresh scratches into its already scarred surface with every angry lunge.

"It's all right, Barry," I say, "it's just Phil, it's all right."

When he calms down enough to hear the assurance in my voice, he stops barking and starts wagging his tail. From fero-cious attack dog to expectant host in less than ten seconds: dogs don't hold grudges. I unlock the door and let Phil in.

"Well, that's some way to treat your old Uncle Phil," Phil

says, bending down and massaging Barry's rear end, sending him spinning in slow circles while Phil continues to rub his rump. There's probably some sound physiological reason why Black Labs are given to executing 360-degree pirouettes while getting their ass ends stroked, but there are some mysteries that are simply better left unsolved.

"You'd think this mutt of yours would know me by now," Phil says, straightening up, taking off his black leather gloves.

"He knows you," I say. "With the door and the window closed he couldn't hear your voice. Dogs don't trust sight as much as they do smell and sounds."

"Ah, picky little empiricist, aren't you?" Phil says, leaning over again and petting Barry between the ears. It's only a head pat so Barry stays where he is.

"How're you doing?" Phil says.

"Good. How about you?"

"Good."

Phil nods, looks around the room. "You're going to need a lot of boxes just for your records and books," he says.

"I don't even want to think about it," I say.

Technically, we haven't talked since the blow-out at Rebecca's place. But voice mail messages have been left and returned, e-mails have been sent and replied to, information has been exchanged on both sides. If you try hard enough or not at all, it is possible to conduct an entire relationship without ever speaking directly to the other person.

"Any word on the mortgage?" Phil says.

"We're still waiting."

"What's taking so long?"

"You don't want to know," I say. "The things that a bank can ask you to verify that you wouldn't tell your best friend ..."

Phil looks around the room again. I rub Barry's head.

"Banks," he finally says.

"Yeah," I say. "Banks."

It's only a bit past four in the afternoon, but the week before Christmas in Toronto means that the little light that does visit our apartment via the front window is already retreating for the day, a few thin shafts of dusty sunshine all that's left of our daily dose of sky-sent Vitamin D. It's too early to turn on a light and too dark not to.

"How's the bouncing business?" Phil says. "Have a chance to kick anyone's ass yet?"

Smiling, "Actually, doorman is the preferred professional term," I say.

"Sorry about that. How's the doormanning business, then?"

"Not bad. No actual ass-kickings so far, but I did have to refuse admission the other evening to a gentleman who desired to bring a mannequin into the bar with him."

"That seems rather unfair of you, if you don't mind me saying so. Perhaps he was just lonely."

"Did I neglect to mention that he was also covered in dried blood?"

"His own or someone else's?"

"That's really beside the point, isn't it?"

"Perhaps he'd been having a particularly rough day."

"And did I say that the clothes the dummy was wearing still had price tags hanging from them?"

Phil laughs. "We did worse," he says.

"When?"

"How about the time you stole that huge glass jar of mustard from the hot dog salesman?"

"Only after you took the ketchup."

"Remind me again why we did that?"

"Boilermakers, I think."

Phil is sitting on the arm of the couch with his coat still on. I'm sitting on the arm of the easy chair.

"Hey," I blurt. "Remember the time we took —"

"The wheelchair?"

"From the hospital."

"After visiting Scotty."

"Oh, Christ."

"Oh, man."

Scotty was one of the few Duke regulars who didn't give us the cold shoulder early on just because we weren't old, alcoholic, and pissed off to be alive. He had to have been over seventy when we met him and definitely did know how to juice it, but he was anything but angry. Every day he'd shave, put on the same shabby suit, buy all three local dailies as well as the *New York Times*, and take possession of the seat nearest to the pool table that gave him the best vantage point of the front door, usually by no later than three in the afternoon. Here, as day turned to evening to night, he'd sip draft beer, read about what kind of nonsense the world was up to, and keep an eye on who came and went. I think he liked Phil and me because we always seemed to be carting around our own pile of reading material and because we weren't adverse to singing along with the jukebox if the song at hand deserved it or shouting out lines of poetry at each other if the words themselves demanded it. Scotty liked action.

One week he wasn't at his usual table, and the next week he wasn't either. Lenny told us he'd had a stroke and which hospital he was in and that he couldn't talk or move and that he wasn't supposed to make it. He didn't. His watery blue eyes were the only thing about him that were still him the evening we made it to Toronto General the week before he gave it up. We took turns reading to him, Phil from *A Season in Hell*, in the original because Scotty always used to get a kick out of Phil speaking French at the Duke, me fragments from the Stoics — in English — because it seemed to make sense. I don't think he heard a word we said. For his sake, I hope that he didn't. We'd made sure to get good and loaded beforehand because we knew from Lenny what to expect, so stealing the wheelchair from the hospital lobby on our way out the door was the only sensible thing to do. Scotty would have loved it.

"Remember when you fell out of the chair when we were crossing at Queen and Bathurst?" Phil says. After we'd left the hospital we went bar-hopping with the wheelchair, each taking his turn pushing the other one around.

"And that Goth guy and his girlfriend who freaked out and came running over and helped get me back in the chair?"

"Never have two so cool ever looked so dumb."

"Beelzebub was surely watching over us that night."

"Man," Phil says, laughing.

"Yeah," I say.

My legs are hanging over the arm of the chair now, my back nesting in the seat, my head resting on the other arm. Phil is lying on the couch looking up at the ceiling, his legs dangling over the arm where he was perched.

"Look, I didn't mean to get in your face about that job with Rebecca," he says. "My mum's been sick and I haven't been the best company with anybody lately."

"Is she okay?" Phil never says anything about his family, never has. I know he's got a brother and a sister who lives somewhere out east, and that his parents still live in the same Etobicoke house he grew up in, but that's about it.

"Now she is. She had a mastectomy, but the doctors say it was a clean cut, everything looks good. It was pretty scary there for awhile though."

"That's great," I say, "that's great news."

"It's not any reason for me to make waves with you though."

"Don't worry about it," I say.

"We just thought — I mean, *I* just thought — that if I could help, why not, you know?'

"No problem," I say. "Besides, I've got a job now, so no worries. Let's just forget it, all right?"

"Done."

"Good."

The room is almost entirely dark now. I know I should probably get up and turn on a light. I know I should probably be getting ready for work.

"*Queen's Quarterly* has asked me to edit one of their special issues," Phil says. "The title they came up with is sort of lame — "Earth and/or Art: Ecology in the 21ˢᵗ century" — but they want edgy, interesting stuff, not just stuff written by activists or politicians. And I know you've said that there's something in your book about Heidegger that has got an environmental slant to it, so I want you to let me print whatever you think would work, however much of it you want."

"Which book of mine?" I say.

"*Your* book," Phil says. "*Work in Progress.*"

It's so dark, Phil is just a voice.

"Right," I say.

He's sitting up on the couch now. I can just make him out. "This isn't me meddling," he says, "and I don't want to hear about how the book's not done yet. It'll just be an excerpt — say, three thousand, four thousand words — and to have a section of it published in a legit journal would go a long way toward getting somebody interested in publishing the entire thing eventually."

"Great," I say. "Thanks."

"Fantastic." He slaps his palms on his knees. "You want to take a look at what you might want to use right now? I can even read it over if you want. Are you hungry? Is that Thai place that's got take-out still around the corner? Let's surprise

Mary and get enough for all of us. It's been ages since we all chowed down together."

"I've got to go to work," I say.

"Oh," Phil says. "What time? I mean, you've still got to eat, right?"

"I usually bring my supper with me. In fact, I better get making it or I'll end up starving tonight."

"Oh. Okay. What time do you get done?"

"Around two."

"In the morning?"

"It's a bar. What time did you think I got off?"

"I don't know, I guess I never thought about it."

I reach up and pull the chain of the floor lamp, shut my eyes against the explosion of light. When I open them, Phil's are still closed.

"Just promise me you'll give me the excerpt," he says.

"Sure," I say.

"HEY, HANK."

"Yeah?"

"There's a guy in the washroom with his dick hanging out."

"So?"

"So, he's standing in the middle of the room with his eyes closed and his hands behind his head and he's talking to himself."

"What do you want me to do about it?"

"You're security, deal with it."

"I'm the doorman."

"You're everyman," Bob says. "And this job's got your name all over it."

Ordinarily, drunken subnormals with their pants wrapped around their ankles giving speeches to themselves don't unduly concern me. Crazy people aren't the ones you have to worry about — they're usually too busy scaring themselves to bother anybody else. But the sneezing I'd started at home has graduated to a runny nose and a low-grade fever, so I'd rather sit, not stand, beside the door and hope that it's a slow night than escort a drooling, speech-sprouting madman from the men's room. This is what I get, I guess, for not listening to Phil and not going on to get a Ph.D.

"I'll make you a deal," I say, standing up from my chair. "I'll clear the john if you watch the door for me when I get back so I can get some aspirin from the 7-11."

"Late night last night?" Bob says, winking.

He's standing beside me by the door, both of us as far away from the speakers as we can get while Michael screams his way through "Thank God I'm a Country Boy." Michael has the body of an overfed offensive lineman, the mind of a slow eleven-year-old, and the enthusiasm of every devoted amateur. He's loud. He's very loud.

I shake my head. "I think I'm coming down with something," I say over the music.

"Sudafed," Bob shouts, nodding.

"What?"

"Don't waste your time with aspirin, get some Sudafed. Take care of your symptoms and get you feeling better in no time."

"Thanks for the tip," I say, and make for the washroom.

As expected, the guy in the can is more of a threat to himself than others — keeps muttering, "Bob Loblaw, Bob Loblaw, Bob Loblaw," over and over as I coax him into pulling up his pants and taking his troubles home — and as soon as he's weaving down Queen Street I call Bob down from the stage to cover for me.

"Sudafed," he says over Miss Pamela chirping away at "Jingle Bell Rock." Bob has an entire sheet of seasonal karaoke tunes at the back of his binder for the Christmas-conscious.

"Right."

"And hey, since you're heading out ..."

I wait with my hand on the door for Bob to pull out his wallet. "Foot-long or six-inch?" I say.

Bob hands me a ten dollar bill. "C'mon, Hank," he says, "you know I'm a twelve-inch man all the way around."

I sneeze, push open the door. "I'm sure you are," I say.

I take Bob's advice and buy the Sudafed, and along with his meatball sub and coffee, get my own large double-double minus the double-double. I try not to drink coffee at work since it's already a tough enough sell convincing my body to go to sleep after eight straight hours of people and noise and loud music. Even after winding down for awhile listening to the Fan in the kitchen over a bowl or two of Mini-Wheats, it's never a sure bet that I'll nod off without a half an hour or so of preliminary tossing and turning. More and more, I've taken to crashing on the couch in my room downstairs.

I do it for Mary's sake, so she won't get woken up, even though it means that it feels as if we hardly see each other anymore, me long gone to the Gladstone by the time she bikes home from work, she usually hard at it on a new series of paintings for a solo show out west in the spring when we are both there, both of us more often than not run-around busy with this or that house-buying duty. Our main mode of communication these days seems like the notes we leave for each other on the kitchen counter. *Msg. from bank on machine, need letter by Monday from U of T proving you work there, call me, M. XXOO*, they'll say, or, *1. Barry needs food. 2. Lynn called and said it's O.K. to come by and measure windows Thursday night after seven. Love, Hank.*

Tonight, though, I need a caffeine kick, and quick, or else I'm afraid I'll drop off in my chair in spite of Michael's and Pistol Pete's and everybody else's best efforts at making the audience's eardrums bleed. I wash down the Sudafed while I wait for Bob's food. By the time I hand him his dinner and his change and settle down in my seat, I can't stay sitting, I've got to get up and move around.

"See, what did I tell you?" Bob says after I've returned from patrolling the entire room for the second time. "You're feeling better already, aren't you?"

Bob's sitting behind his table stuffing his mouth with a handful of sub, his other hand happily doing its own thing, busily pulling out and putting away CDs. A guy in his twenties with rockabilly sideburns, a Green Day T-shirt, and those baggy-ass pants that middle-class white kids wear to look like poor black kids, is mumbling the words to "Because the Night" into his chest. When he does manage to raise his eyes over the microphone, he's sneering into every corner of the room in the hope that everyone will think that he thinks that the whole thing is just a clever joke, but which only succeeds in making him appear even more terrified than he probably actually is.

"I guess," I say. "I'm feeling something, anyway." Sitting again, I cross my legs, uncross them, then recross them. I drain what's left in my cup of coffee.

"Whoa. You don't want to be doing that, Big Guy," Bob says, pointing to my cup.

"What do you mean?"

"I mean," he says, shaking his finger, "caffeine and Sudafed are a definite no-no."

"Really?"

"Shit, yeah, really. Don't you know that that's what all the hockey players these days are taking?"

"Cold medicine and coffee?" I say, pulling the package out of my shirt pocket, scanning the tiny black fine print on the side of the box.

"Sure. Gets them right fucking cranked up and ready to go, apparently."

"Get out of here," I say, looking up.

"Don't believe me, then," Bob says. He reaches over and picks up the APPLAUSE! sign with both hands, holds it high over his head. The audience cheers, the kid on stage smiles a real smile for the first time, and Bob sets the sign back down.

Cramming what's left of his sub into his mouth, "Just don't say I didn't warn you if you start laying body checks on the old lady when you get home," he says.

I DON'T BODY-CHECK Mary when I get home, just like I don't hip-check her, slew-foot her, or even wake her up. Mary never wakes up no matter how late I make it back from the Gladstone. She did in the beginning — the house key scraping for the click of the keyhole, Barry barking at what he can't see, me shhhing him and shutting and locking the door behind me and care-fulling down the stairs past the head of our bed as quiet as I can — but now she's used to it.

What else I didn't do but I wish that I had was sing my usual Doors' number, if only to help douse the remaining flames still flickering in my gut and elsewhere that I'd cooked up with my cold medicine and black coffee cocktail. I'd begged off when Bob had asked me if I was feeling better enough to take a crack at "Break on Through," one of the few Doors' songs left in his binder that I hadn't tackled yet, but between the sniffles I was still stifling and the sour stomach and brain buzz I was nursing, I'd thought it best to sit tonight's performance out. I should have known better. Rock and roll, even the canned karaoke kind, is the best mind medicine you can score without a doc-tor's prescription. Good vibration self-medication.

I do manage to execute my usual after-work drill — shut the basement door tight once Barry has head-butted it open less than a minute after I've gotten settled (dogs always loyal to the last pack member still awake), turn on the radio, pour myself a bowl of Mini-Wheats, and get ready to get good and dulled down.

But there's not enough Soya milk left for my cereal, the overnight host on the Fan is blathering on not about who came out on top tonight and how come but, instead, the importance of tax cuts for professional sports franchises, and there's a note from Mary on the table letting me know that Phil called to remind me about some excerpt for some magazine he says I'll know about, and that we need to decide if we want to keep Tom and Lynn's stove even though something's wrong with the oven, or if we want it written into the Agreement of Purchase that they have to have it removed before we take possession of the house. *I Love You, Mary*, it says at the bottom of the piece of scrap paper. *I Love You, Mary*, with plenty of hugs and kisses.

I redo everything I've just done, only in reverse: take my coat and toque down from the rack hanging on the back of the bathroom door and put them on again, empty my milkless bowl of cereal back into the box, put my hand to the ON/OFF knob on the radio.

Sports isn't supposed to make you think — sports, even talking about sports, is all about doing, thinking's number one nemesis — so a loud rant by some misinformed yahoo about all those poor, overtaxed multimillionaires out there who need a bigger slice of our take-home pay to subsidize their rinks and stadiums, the same ones that most of us will never be able to

afford to attend, isn't the agreeable lobotomy I'd been looking
for. I wait for the quarter-hour update to get my guaranteed
fact fix, but only make it halfway through the Leafs recap,
when the beat reporter asks Mats Sundin how he feels about
getting his historic one-thousandth point in tonight's game.

"*Everything* is historic," I say to the radio, snapping it off. "If
it fucking happened, it's fucking history, therefore, it's fucking
historic. Jesus Fucking Christ."

"Hank?" I hear Mary say through the still-closed door. I
open it, and nearly trip over Barry who slips around and ahead
of me up the stairs. Dogs don't have manners. Frequently, this
is their appeal.

"Sorry," I say. "I'm just trying to get ready to take Barry for
a walk. He's got ants in his pants."

Mary yawns. "Are you alone?" she says.

"Of course I'm alone. Now go back to sleep, we're going
out now."

"I thought I heard you talking."

"Go back to sleep."

"Kiss me goodnight."

I'm standing by the front door now, Barry sitting beside me.
"I've already got my coat on and it's still wet."

"I don't care, come kiss me anyway."

"I'll just get you and the sheets all wet. I'll kiss you before
I go to bed."

"Sleep up here tonight," Mary says. "I'm tired of waking up
and finding you downstairs. I want both my boys with me
when I wake up."

"I only do it for you."

"I know, but promise me you'll sleep with me tonight."

I unlock the deadbolt. "Go back to sleep," I say.

"Promise me, Hank."

"Okay, I promise, now go back to sleep."

"Now I will."

The slow, heavy flakes of snow that had looked so melan-cholically lovely through the backseat window of the cab I'd taken home just feel cold and wet on my face as we walk down the alleyway toward the street. Midway, Barry stops, turns around, tugs in the direction of the park. I could probably use a few laps around the frozen track myself, but I steer us back toward the street, and then Roncesvalles, instead.

I try not to think about Phil's message. But between my Sudafed espresso and the meditative clickity-clack of Barry's nails on the snow-dusted deserted sidewalk, I don't do so well at making my mind do what I tell it to, can't help but feel clammy in spite of the icy wind on my face at the thought of what he wants from me

I thought he wanted to be a poet. Rimbaud never would have edited a special issue of *Queen's Quarterly* called "Earth and/or Art: Ecology in the 21st century." Neither, before he became Philip, would Phil.

A house three doors down from Roncesvalles on Garden Avenue wrenches me back to right now. Not only is every inch of the eavestroughs and the outline of all of the windows and the entire perimeter of the house plastered with flashing red and blue and yellow and green Christmas lights, but every tree and bush and hedge are draped in blinking good cheer as well, an enormous, kilowatt-sucking MERRY CHRISTMAS arrangement standing to attention on what has to be a six-foot-by-six-foot wooden background in the middle of the yard giving off just that little bit more of throbbing joy to the world gleam that is needed. Barry and I stand there on the sidewalk in front of the house, bathed in the electric glow.

I look to see if anyone's watching. I let go of Barry's leash and creep up to the house. Jesus was born in a barn and there are only four more shopping days left until Christmas. I tear the set of lights off one of the pine trees. They're still flashing when I finally wrestle them to the ground, but at least they're off the tree. Barry and I beat it back down to Roncesvalles, take a left at Grenadier, and then sprint all the way home.

There's your ecology in the 21st century, pal.

II

MARY NEVER SEES JANUARY coming. I can spot the signs that a swoon is sneaking up a mile away, but invalids can't take their own temperature. They can, but all they end up feeling is what they are, heat on heat.

It's not post-Yuletide letdown. It's not the weather. It's not getting another year older. It's not anything to do with us, her job, her art, or the new house. It's not anything that is a thing. It's the blues, the blahs, the downs, the glooms. The first time I was around when it happened, the first full year we shared an apartment, I thought I'd done something wrong and made her even more miserable by making her talk about it until something actually was wrong, me making her talk about it.

Whatever it is, I know that it's back because when I come home from work at night the entertainment section of the *Star* is on top of the recycling bin, not the sports page the way

I left it. The entertainment section contains that evening's TV listings. Eleven months out of twelve, you'd have a better chance of hearing me do a Michael Jackson tune at the Gladstone than you would of finding Mary under the covers in bed with all of her clothes on staring at the television. Eleven months, I said. Not having to be there because I'm at work most evenings yet knowing that somebody, Barry, is, curled up at the end of the bed with his head resting on her feet for as long as she needs him to, makes me feel better. A coward's comforts aren't any less comforting.

After I've packed up my dinner and brushed my teeth and refilled Barry's water bowl, I scribble a short note to Mary reminding her about getting time off from work tomorrow so we can meet up at the bank to sign the mortgage papers. Not even our loan officially coming through seems to have made much of an impression. Just a couple of weeks ago, finding out that Tom and Lynn's place had a small attic was enough to get her excited.

"Do you think it's big enough for us to use it?" she'd said. I adjusted the phone to my ear. It was only a little after ten and I'd been sleeping when she called; she couldn't have been in her office for more than five minutes.

"Didn't they say they never go up there?" I said.

"But that's probably just because they're old and couldn't get up there even if they wanted to. I bet we could fix it up and use it."

"For what?"

"I don't know — a sitting room or something."

"Who wants to sit in an attic? Especially in the summer. It'd be like a hundred degrees up there."

"Okay, well, *something*. Anyway, it's like we've discovered a brand new room, isn't it?"

I write the note, tell her that I love her, and resist the reflex to add a concerned P.S. counselling her to hang in there, to hang tough, to not forget that spring and the new house are just around the corner. I leave it at *I love you* and place the piece of paper in the middle of the kitchen table beside her mail, an invitation to subscribe to *Maclean's*, and a fundraising letter from the York University Alumni office. Even Mary's mail is depressed.

Normally I take the Dundas streetcar to Gladstone Avenue and hike to work from there. Today, though, I've got time to walk so I do, make a fresh path of footprints through the tundra that's Sorauren Park in January as a short cut to Queen Street. It's deep freeze time, even the sound of the wind shoving the bare branches of the trees around is cold, but a kid and his dad with their toboggan are out here in the fading sunlight anyway, giving Old Man Winter their firmest middle finger. The boy rides the thing down a small hill of snow and the man hauls it back up by a short rope. The kid walks right beside him the entire return trip, never stopping talking, probably about what had just happened in case his dad didn't catch every instant of his wild four-second ride.

When I was a kid, my dad and I played this game where I'd try to uncoil his fist with both of my hands. I'd yank and pull at his fingers but they'd never peel apart. Sometimes I'd ask him to drive with no hands on the steering wheel and he'd do it. When I was really young, five or six, I told Eddie Webster that my dad could pick up the world.

"No he can't."

"Yes he can."

We were sitting on the curb in front of my house staring at the lawn across the street. It was hot, it was July, there was nothing to do as usual.

Eddie turned to me. "If he can lift the world then he can lift himself. How can he do that?"

I thought about it for a moment.

"He just can," I said.

Later on, when I was maybe eight, I figured out a way to get his hand open. Getting a good grip on his thumb, I'd tug it backward until he'd yell and then laugh and spread his fingers wide and say that I'd won. I thought it would feel better to finally hear him say it. After that, we didn't play that game anymore.

EIGHT HOURS OF DOING my job, of keeping the peace, of making sure that the show goes on as smoothly as possible, and it's my turn to get my ya-ya's out. It's also my cue to trot across the street and score a jumbo coffee and wash back a couple of Sudafeds. I haven't been sick in weeks, and that's not even half of it. Actually, that's not even any of it.

"You must be some kind of heavy sleeper, Big Guy," Bob says from behind his table.

I take a sip from my steaming paper cup. "How's that?"

"If I drank what you drink every night at this hour I'd be walking the floor until tomorrow."

"I never really thought about it," I say. "Maybe."

"No maybe about. Unless —" Bob's eyebrows lift "— the old lady's tiring you out with some welcome-home nooky every night."

I don't say a thing, just semi-smile and take another scalding sip.

"Whew!" Bob says, clapping his hands; he shakes his head a few times as he fades out the woman on stage finishing up "What the World Needs Now is Love."

Wire-rim round glasses, Cotton Ginny blue skirt, long brown ponytail; she looks like an elementary school teacher up here on a dare. She'd carefully set her can of Sprite down on a paper napkin on Bob's table before she'd picked up the mic, had laughed at herself and put her hand to her mouth when she'd messed up coming in where she was supposed to, and had winced before anyone else could at her off-key attempts at hitting the high notes. Song done, she covers her face with both hands and smiles like the good sport she undoubtedly is, scurries down the steps of the stage and back to her table. I respect people who don't need to get drunk or high or lie to themselves to have a good time. Don't understand it, but I do respect it.

"Lori, Ladies and Gentlemen," Bob says, "Lori."

Bob gives me a nod, my nightly nod, and I step away from my spot by the door; by the time he announces, "And now,

Ladies and Gentlemen, you're in for a very special treat," I've bypassed the steps and leapt up on stage and am adjusting the microphone stand. I like the mic right at mouth level when I sing. I like to grip it hard with my left hand, like to let my other hand hang at my side. Right now, it shakes, like it's fallen asleep, like an antsy sprinter's hand a second before the pop of the starting pistol.

I've learned how to mix my medicines. The caffeine and the Sudafed are done dancing around each other in my gut, have gotten down to the serious business of fucking up my head. One more minute of just standing here and not doing anything and I'll have to hit the floor and do fifty push-ups or else start a fight just so that I can stop it. And to think that chemistry was always my worst subject in high school.

"Let's give a big Gladstone Hotel welcome, everyone, to Hank the Doorman doing a little something called 'Break on Through' by ... the Doooors." Bob makes his voice deep, stretches out the word like a spooky secret until the song's first notes explode out of the speakers.

Music's always too loud when it's somebody else's. When it's yours, it can never be loud enough. I bring my lips tight to the microphone and inhale, fill my lungs with air; I wet my lips with my tongue, swallow. My mouth tastes like cold metal. I close my eyes and sing.

For two minutes and twenty-five seconds I don't see a thing. Don't need to. Everything I need to know, I can hear.

NOT EVERYONE IS FORTUNATE enough to be their very own opening act. I know I'm a lucky guy. I only wish there was somebody I could share with just how lucky I really am.

I hum what I'd just sung at the Gladstone the entire cab ride home, rat tat tat keep time with two busy forefingers on either side of me on the plastic lip of the greasy backseat, pay the fare, and am in and out of the house without waking up Mary and with Barry on his leash inside of five minutes. I've changed into the green army parka I picked up last week at Hercules Army Surplus on Yonge Street. I check the inside pockets to make sure I've got what I need.

Barry and I head for the section of Roncesvalles where the houses are older and bigger and more expensive, ditto the automobiles parked on the street. There's no one else on the sidewalk, we're the only ones out this late in this cold, but I keep my ears and eyes open anyway. Having a job to do is no reason to be careless. Whether in matters of the heart or ecological espionage, getting too comfortable is never a good habit to fall into.

Barry stops to sniff a tree and I let him. It's my walk, not his, but wintertime is not a dog's best friend, ice and snow and freezing temperatures meaning that most of the choicest smells a neighbourhood has to offer are under wintry wraps. I give him long enough to finish sniffing, and we move on.

We walk far enough that we end up in front of the Catholic church, Our Lady of the Blessed Sacrament. I'm about as big on churches as I am on what goes on inside them, but this one's an exception. The entire seven or eight blocks surrounding it is residential, houses and backyards and garages and driveways, yet here it is looking just like what it probably once actually was a hundred years ago, the spiritual and social ground zero of an entire duped community. Moonless nights like this, it's easy to forget that it's not 1912 and that the milkman won't be driving his horse and wagon past in the morning wondering how much he can get away with not telling the priest at confession on Sunday. Only the glowing red EXIT signs on each dark floor argue that it isn't.

Barry tugs me off the sidewalk and onto the snow-covered lawn. He finds what he's looking for, some frozen yellow urine, and I almost bump into a signboard on rollers that's decorated with flimsy black plastic letters I can just make out.

COMING THIS SPRING!
THE "LEGACY LOFTS"!
LUXURY LIVING STARTING AT $389,000
IN A UNIQUE 19TH CENTURY SETTING!
CHECK US OUT AT: WWW.LEGACYLOFTS.COM

The clever thing would be to rearrange the letters to say something sufficiently smart-alecky, but these are not clever times. I pull the can of spray paint from inside my jacket and shake it from side to side. The crunch of Barry's feet cracking through the lawn's thin crust of frozen snow can't cover up the *ping ping ping* that the can makes. I take a step back from the sign and aim, push the button on top.

THERE IS NO
AIR-CONDITIONING IN HELL

Barry and I start toward the sidewalk, but he digs in, leans with all of his weight the other way. I do a double take left and right, then let him do what he wants. He takes a few steps in the direction of the sign and raises his leg where the other dog has left his mark. I look around, unzip, join him. Two separate streams hit the same spot. Our piss turns to steam as soon as it hits the snow.

"LET'S WALK BY THE house," I say.

"If you want," Mary says.

"You don't want to?"

"I said all right."

"You said if *I* want to."

Mary pulls Barry's leash from her coat pocket. "Come here, Barry," she says. He walks over, tail wagging. "Good boy," she says, clipping it on. "Let's go and look at our new house."

Friday still potentially tallies up to a long High Park romp with the Bubs followed by a lazy lunch at Easy or Mitzi's and, later, maybe a shared nap and who knows where that will lead, but these days I've got to be sure to set the alarm before we lay down. Karaoke doesn't take holidays. At least not on weekends at the Gladstone, where lately we've really started to pull them in. Most of the new voices belong to the packs of university students who've begun to swarm the place on Saturday night and who take turns proudly butchering the dumbest tunes Bob's songbook has to offer. Someone who doesn't have to listen to them might call it playful kitsch. I call it a long night's work.

"Let's cross, Bubs," Mary says, looking both ways for all three of us, eight legs moving across Sorauren toward the sidewalk on the other side. I'd just assumed that we'd be heading for bigger, better High Park when we'd started out from home, but Mary had Barry hooked up to his leash by the time I locked the door and led us in the direction of Sorauren Park instead. Between last night's late-night rendezvous and the ordinary amount of stiffness that comes with it being as cold and damp as it is today, Barry's dragging his ass more than arthritically usual, so no big deal, whatever makes the pack happy.

"Less than three months from now we'll be going this way for real," I say. We're walking toward Wright Avenue, home of our April first home. "Barry Boy and I will be kicking back on the front porch and you'll be out back working in your garden just like you've always wanted to. It's kind of hard to believe, isn't it?"

"My God," Mary says, "is it really that soon?" She says it like that's when we're scheduled to be evicted, not when she'll finally be allowed to move into her dream house. I slip my arm around her waist, give her a hip-to-hip, sideways hug.

"C'mon," I say, "what could be better than moving in in the spring? You'll have your garden, Bubbaloo will have a porch to lay in the sun on *and* a big backyard to roam around in, and we'll finally have a bathroom with a window and a bedroom without a front door attached to it." I give her another squeeze. "Don't worry, kiddo, it's going to be great. It can't happen soon enough."

I can hear that extra-careful tone of too-tender concern creeping into my voice that tends to make Mary only feel worse, but it's hard to be cool to be kind when the face frowning in front of you is the one you want to see smiling more than any other. I decide to change tactics, to give her mind something to chew on besides itself.

"Hey, what do you think about what I was saying the other day about the knob and tube removal? If we get a crew in there ASAP, while we're still unpacking our stuff and before we've painted and put everything where we want it, it won't be nearly as bad as if we did everything and then hired somebody to start tearing the place apart. My dad says it can be a pretty nasty job, that on top of everything else there's a huge amount of drywall work that has to get done once they've finished disconnecting all the old stuff and put the new wiring in."

Mary stops walking. "Hank, do we really need to talk about this right now? I really can't deal with thinking about anything that major right now."

"It's not major, it's just something we've got to eventually deal with, that's all."

"Well, I've got the Vancouver show coming up around the same time as we move to deal with, and there are things at work that I'm trying to get done so I can take some time off to have more time to paint that are taking a lot longer than they should, and ..."

And nothing. Mary can, and will, deal with whatever needs to be dealt with — is the best dealer in doing what has to be done that I've ever known. It's nothing that she needs help with. The January nothing of everything. I put my arms around her and give her a long, silent hug. Mary quietly cries and I keep holding her. Within two minutes we're walking again.

"I'm sorry, I don't know what's wrong with me," she says, wiping away her tears with her glove.

"Nothing's wrong with you," I say. "Moving is stressful. So is everything else you've got on the go. Something would be wrong with you if you *weren't* stressed out."

She sniffles, smiles, reaches for and squeezes my hand. "Thanks," she says.

"For what?" I say, oblivious as I can.

"Thanks," she says.

Nearing 11 1/2 Wright we instinctively do what we always do — slow down without entirely stopping, gawk and gape without too obviously staring. We don't want Tom and Lynn to think we're stalking them, but we always manage to shuffle by and have a long enough look that's there's usually something new to ooh and ahh about.

"You know, I think that's the original door," I say.

"It could be."

"I bet it is. Do you know how old that bell probably is? Somebody probably rang that bell on that door eighty years ago. The person who rang it, the person who answered the door, both of them are probably long gone, dead and buried and forgotten, but that bell is still here. The one that's going to ring on our front door on our house for another fifty years, for as long as we live there."

"Wow."

I stop while I'm ahead, don't say a thing about the time-worn mail slot built into the door that decades and decades of letters and postcards and junk mail circulars have buffed smooth all the way around. Give us each day our daily Wow and let us give thanks every day we actually get it.

At Roncesvalles, where we're supposed to turn left to go home, I think I see what's-her-name with her accent walking our way with what's-his-name, her dog. I think that she thinks she sees me, too.

"Let's go one street further and circle back," I say, taking Barry's leash from Mary's hand, leading us into the middle of the road.

"I don't know, he seems pretty tired, Hank, look at him. I think his hips are bothering him."

I wait for a Range Rover to go by before pulling Barry — a little gimpy, it's true, but good-boy game all the same — across the street, Mary tagging along behind us.

"He's all right," I say. "This way you won't have to take him very far tonight."

We go up and over and are home twenty minutes later. Mary kicks one boot against the other trying to knock off some snow while I dig for my key without taking off my glove.

The door is as blankly, metallic white as the day the landlady brought it home from Wal-Mart last winter because the old one was letting in an enormous draft that no number of rolled-up bath towels stuffed along the bottom could manage to keep out. There isn't a bell you can ring by hand and there isn't any mail slot, either.

I turn around and face Mary without managing to retrieve the key.

"Don't worry," I say, "April first will be here soon."

"What?" she says, still thumping her boots.

"Don't worry, we're going to be home for good real soon."

YOU KNOW WHEN SOMEONE is watching you even when you don't know it. I look up from my knees and see George with his hands buried in his coat pockets staring at me through the living room window. It's too cold out to give Barry a proper hose-and-bucket bath, so I'm squirting him head to tail with this spray I bought that's supposed to not just cover dog odours but actually get rid of them, although I'd settle for just keeping them under control until I can get him outside and give him a serious soap and water scrub down.

I motion for George to come in, shout, "It's unlocked," but he stays where he is, keeps staring at Barry and me. Barry finally sees the stranger standing in our backyard and lunges toward the window with a baritone snarl, but I get my hand underneath his collar and hold him back and tell him that it's all right, that it's just George. I get up and open the door.

"Hey, George, do you want to come in?"

"Of course."

George sits down in the reading chair without taking off his coat or even unbuttoning it. Barry's wagging his tail now and plants himself down at George's feet. George scratches him between the ears without taking his eyes off the window. Barry's head is still wet from his spray bath, but George doesn't seem to mind. You're supposed to rub the spray right into the dog's fur and let it sit for a couple of minutes before you comb it out, so I get back down on my knees and start rubbing.

I'm not sure if George'll understand what I'm about to tell him, and I'm almost positive that even if he does he won't remember it tomorrow, but I feel like I've got to tell him anyway. "Just so you'll know, we're going to be moving soon, George," I say.

George doesn't say anything, keeps looking at the backyard and rubbing Barry's head with just the tips of his fingers, like he's giving him a delicate scalp massage.

"I'm going to tell whoever the landlady gets to move in here that you used to live here, too, though, and I'm sure it'll be fine if you want to drop by once in a while for old time's sake."

What I'm actually going to do is warn them about who George is and tell them that they shouldn't panic the first time they see him peeping through their window, that they shouldn't call the cops or chase after him with a baseball bat or worse. I rub the spray, which smells pretty good actually, kind of like Aloe Vera mixed with Lemon Pledge, deep into

Barry's coat with both hands.

"This place we're moving to, it's our first real place that'll be all ours," I say. "I guess it's kind of like this place must have been for you and your family. I bet you've got a lot of good memories about this place, don't you, George?"

George stops rubbing Barry's head. "This dog, he smells badly," he says.

I stop my rubbing. "Well, that's why I'm washing him," I say.

George stands up from his chair. "This dog, he stinks."

I PULL A STOOL up to the bar, sit down. "You look like you got some sun, Sam, did you go south?"

Sam carefully inserts a single potato chip in his mouth. "High blood pressure," he says.

I lift my forearms from the bar top; they momentarily resist, remain sticky stuck, arm hairs gently tugging at flesh. Liberated, I swivel on my stool, have a look around.

"Where is everybody?" I say, everybody meaning Lenny standing behind the bar and Julio sitting at one or the other end of it. Frank's off by himself, self-marooned in the middle of the room, drinking and smoking and staring straight ahead at nothing like he does whenever he's on a binge. Tonight, he doesn't even bother having an unopened book on the table in front of him. He'd managed a silent nod when I came through the door, then got right back down to business drinking, smoking, and staring straight ahead at nothing. He looks even frailer than usual, like the skull underneath his blotchy skin is only a single loud laugh or one honest scream away from tearing through his flesh.

Sam places another solitary chip on his tongue; it disappears back inside his mouth like a bored lizard's. "Jules is in detox again, Len's downtown getting his Social Insurance Number."

"I thought everybody had a SIN."

Sam shrugs. "He said he had one back in Alberta but he lost it. He's getting his health card too."

"His health card? What did he do when he was sick before now?"

"He didn't."

"He didn't what?"

"Get sick."

Sam sticks the last potato chip in his mouth and crushes the empty bag with his other hand, lets it drop to the bar. Together we watch it slowly unravel back to its original, if crinkled, shape and size. Sam stands up and places both palms on the small of his back, rocks back a couple of groaning inches, then forward; does this again, then again.

"What's wrong with you?" I say.

He shakes his head, grabs a pint glass and pours me a draft. "Just tired," he says.

"You need a holiday."

The Duke's a money pit, has to be the world's most squalid tax write-off, but Sam's old man ran the place for years and years before him, bought the building and the land it stands on

outright thirty-five years ago, so Sam's not hurting, owns a
year-old Beemer and a motorcycle he never drives and goes to
Cuba or the Bahamas or the Gulf Coast every year for a couple
of weeks with his ex-brother-in-law.

"I need something," he says.

What the Duke needs is Lenny power-pouring himself a
few half-pints, Julio giggling and dribbling over Sam calling
into question my masculinity because I've shaved and trimmed
my sideburns for work and am wearing a clean shirt that isn't
missing any buttons, and for somebody to cough up a couple
of loonies to feed the jukebox to shut up the blah blah blah of
the television set that no one's paying any attention to. Silence
plus sobriety is entropy just waiting to happen.

The beep-beep of either the Roadrunner or a car horn,
plus the sizzle of sleet hitting the sidewalk, and I know it must
be Phil coming through the door. I sip from my beer and
look at the clock. 6:40, good. Ten minutes late and I already
told him I have to leave for the Gladstone by seven, so twenty
minutes to kill, tops, before I have to start lying. Boy Scouts
and successful procrastinators are always prepared.

"Sorry I'm late," Phil says, standing beside my stool. His
leather briefcase is in one hand and a clear plastic baggy with
a single black fish swimming around in it is in the other.
Unmelted pellets of sleet dot the shoulders of his black overcoat like icy dandruff.

"I just got here," I say.

"Can we sit at a table? I want to put this thing down." He
holds up the baggy with the fish in it.

"Sure." I pick up my coat and glass and start toward our table by the jukebox.

"Do you mind if we sit over here?" Phil says. "It's closer to the heat vent. I want to keep the fish as warm as possible."

"Okay," I say.

We sit down at the table nearest to the bar. The phone rings, and Sam steps into the backroom. Phil sets the plastic bag down in the middle of the table, keeps it upright by the knot tied at the top. The phone stops ringing.

"See that spot on its side?" Phil says, his finger smudging the baggy. "Does that look red or orange to you? I left my reading glasses at Rebecca's."

I give it a look. "Hard to say," I say, picking up my glass, taking a drink.

"Well, say anyway. This is important."

"Important? How is —"

"Just look at the fucking fish, would you?"

I hold up both hands. "Okay, okay," I say. I lean in closer, take a second look.

"Well?" Phil says.

I lean back in my chair. "Definitely reddish orange."

"Thanks, you're a big help, Henry, you know that? A real big help." Phil plops the baggy down on his lap, glances over at the abandoned bar. "You'd think with three customers in here you'd be able to get a drink," he says.

"Sam must be on the phone."

"So where's Len?"

"Out joining the human race."

"Really. In what capacity, team mascot?"

"Full-fledged membership, by the sounds of it. He's getting his SIN and a health card."

"Jesus — what was he doing without them?"

"I don't know," I say. "Being Len, I guess."

Phil looks at Frank looking at the pitcher of beer on his table like he's trying not to be bored with someone telling him a story he's already heard ten times before. "You forget how lonely this place is when you're not half in the bag," he says.

"Frank's all right, he's not like this all the time."

"You know that guy?"

I take a drink. "Yeah, I know him."

The cowbell and bass-drum clink-clink-and-boom that are the slow-dragging first great eight seconds of "Honky Tonk Women" clank and kick out of the speakers. The jukebox is programmed to pick and play a tune at random if it's been silent for more than fifteen minutes, a built-in self-assertion mechanism meant to remind everybody in the bar that it's still alive and well and happy to be asked to do the thing it was put on earth to do. Jukeboxes need to be needed, too.

"Okay," Phil says, motioning with two impatient fingers, "give me the excerpt. I've got to get this —" he lifts the baggy off his lap "— to Rebecca's before its oxygen runs out."

"What's with Moby Dick?" I say.

"Nothing, it's just a fish. For Rebecca's tank."

"So what's the big deal about whether it's got a red or an orange spot?"

I know I'm grasping, but I need to eat up at least five more minutes before I can realize that I'm late for work and bolt for the door and in the panicked process forget to give Phil the essay for *Queen's Quarterly* that we'd arranged for me to finally hand over.

"C'mon, just give me the piece," Phil says.

"You c'mon. You can't just walk into a bar with a fish in a bag and grill a guy over its colour composition and not offer any explanation. That'd be just be rude. That would be bordering on the downright ungentlemanly."

I cross my arms and slide down in my seat. Phil checks out the still-abandoned bar, looks back at me. I haven't moved, and he can tell that I'm not going to until I get what I want. He grabs my pint glass off the table and takes a drink. "You'll just think it's stupid," he says, "but fine, you want to know, fine." He lifts the glass, drinks again.

"Rebecca's mum died when she was like, six or seven or something, leukemia — real, real ugly stuff, apparently — and then, about five years later, her old man drank himself to death. Because he was some hot-shot Toronto architect the obituary in the *Globe* said heart attack, but basically everybody knew he did himself in. Rebecca ended up getting passed around from in-law to in-law until she eventually moved in with her mother's parents for good. When she was in university, first one, then the other one of them, they ended up dying too."

"That's rough," I say, taking the glass, taking a sip, sliding it back toward Phil. And it is rough, even if it's impossible for me to imagine Rebecca as a ten-year-old. No it's not. Rebecca was the eighth-grade class president who everybody voted for but no one really liked, the kid with the best, most expensive bicycle who never let anyone else ride it, the best-looking girl in the entire school who never talked to kids whose fathers weren't doctors, dentists, or lawyers.

"So obviously she's been dealt a pretty tough hand, she gets a little spooked by death," Phil says. "Anybody's death."

"Sure."

"So —" Phil picks up the glass and drains almost all that's left of it, leaves me a fingertip's worth of warm beer "— whenever one of her stupid fish goes belly up, I flush it down to the big aquarium in the sky and go out and get another one just like it before she finds out."

It takes me a moment to process this. "And she never has?"

"Not yet."

"How many times have you had to do this?"

"Counting this one?" He lifts the bag above the edge of the table.

I nod.

"Four."

"You've replaced four of her dead fish and she's never caught on."

"You say it like you don't believe it."

"No, I just ..."

Just can't believe that the boyfriend of the courageous author of two critically acclaimed novels and a manuscript-in progress about the dark psychological underside of nightmares has to hide her dead fishies from her, that's all.

"So there's your explanation," Phil says. "Now give me your

essay. You said you had to be out of here by seven, right?"

I look at the clock. "Holy shit, it is seven, isn't it?"

"Yeah, so give me the damn essay."

I manage to push my hands through the arms of my coat hanging on the back of my chair and stand straight up in one clean motion. "I've got to go," I say, marching backwards, toward the door. "I'll call you."

"You don't have it, do you?" Phil says, voice rising, standing up until he realizes that he's still got the fish on his lap, bouncing the baggy in the air like a slightly deflated basketball. "Damn." He catches it, keeps both hands around the thing to stop the sloshing storm inside.

"I've got it, I've got it, I'll call you and we'll hook up later," I say, still walking backward, walking right past both the television set playing the national anthem before the start of the Maple Leafs game and heavy-lidded Frank watching me walk out the door ass-end first like I've never exited the Duke any other way.

"You don't have it," Phil says. His voice isn't angry this time.

"I'll call you," I say, and turn around on the sidewalk and sprint for a streetcar that isn't there. When one does roll by a couple of minutes later, I stop running, but let it go.

When I was six, in 1972, after Paul Henderson scored the goal for Team Canada that proved to the Russians once and for all who was best, after a few beers my old man would get me to sing "O Canada" for him while we'd be waiting for the intermission during *Hockey Night in Canada* to be over. We sang it every morning before school and I knew all the words. My dad would sit back in his easy chair with his eyes closed and I'd sing him our national anthem.

When I was done, he'd say, "There'll never be anything like that again for a long, long time." Pointing his beer bottle at the television screen, "Hockey's hockey, but something like that, that's a once in a lifetime thing, boy."

"YOU HAVE TO INCLUDE Kiss's *Alive!* album. You have to. It's not only one of the biggest-selling live LPs of all time, it also legit-imized hard rock in the eyes of the record companies. On those terms alone you haven't got any choice *but* to give it serious consideration."

Case made, Simon sweeps a greasy bang of hair off his fore-head, folds his arms across his chest — thumbs tucked in tight under his armpits — and waits for my response. A stack of Green Party election signs with Simon's name on them sit neatly bundled and tied up with white string beside a pile of newspapers waiting to be recycled.

"Kiss's *Alive!*," I say, scanning the spines of She Said Boom's poetry section. "What's next, The Monkees' *Live on Tour '67*?"

Whether Kiss's *Alive!* is eventually dubbed Hank and Simon's coveted Greatest Live Album of All Time really isn't worth the breath it takes to argue either for or against, but sometimes I think that the part Simon likes best, the whole point of us talking at all, is me disagreeing with him. Simon happiest is Simon going against the grain. Turbulence can make you sick, but at least you know you're still moving.

"You know what I think about the Monkees," he says, "so don't even go there. Especially Nesmith's country-rock stuff from *Headquarters* on. Absolutely pioneering material. Predates what the Byrds and even Dylan were up to by months."

A pear-shaped woman in a form-fitting white Ski-doo suit waddles up to the counter and in a heavy Polish accent asks Simon if he has any — she lifts the piece of paper in her hand closer to her wet, snow-smudged glasses — Justin Timberlake. Thankfully, Simon elects to neither sniff one of the thumbs he removes from his armpits nor roll his eyes in plain view of the woman, probably just somebody's birthday-gift-buying mum, after all, who Simon can find it in his heart to forgive for she knows not what she buys. He leads her off to the store's boy-toy CD section, giving me time to get back to my poetry search.

I can't remember the last time I bought a book. For years, it seems, the shelves of unread and unfinished titles at home have more than sufficed whenever I've felt the need to be reminded of just how lazy and ignorant I am. I don't know what I'm looking for, but that's half the appeal of browsing a good second-hand bookstore, not knowing who you might end up going home with.

Right, then, left to right: Randall Jarrell's *Collected Poems, Be Angry at the Sun* by Robinson Jeffers, *Lovers and Lesser Men* by Irving Layton, *The Collected Sonnets* of Edna St. Vincent Millay. I decide on the Jeffers only because it's the smallest so probably the cheapest. An hour to kill before work — showered, shaved, a mug of green tea cooling on the arm of the chair — you pull down a book of poetry, any book of poetry, open it up, open it up anywhere, and be a good boy and take your recommended dosage of one-or-more-poems-a-day for an occasional dryness of spirit or a painful, persistent lack of worldly wonder.

I wait for Simon to scan the woman's credit card and ring up her CD. He asks her if she would like a bag, and when she says no, hands her her purchase and wishes her a nice afternoon. He must be having a good day. I put my book on the counter.

"Two bucks," he says, without bothering to look inside for a price. I slide a toonie across the counter and he doesn't ask me if I want a bag. I'd be insulted if he did. We passed that point in our retail relationship a long time ago.

"A technical question," he says, raising a forefinger. "Although everybody discovered Dylan's '66 show with the Hawks in Manchester as a bootleg, Columbia did finally bring it out in '98 as a legitimate release."

"So."

"So, does it qualify for consideration or not?"

I pick up the Jeffers. "Even if it does, it's still a pretty big long shot."

"That's the tour when Dylan went electric."

I do up my coat buttons. "That doesn't mean he did it well."

"I'm talking about the show where the crowd boos him for playing with a band, the one where the guy yells out *Judas* right before 'Like a Rolling Stone.'" Simon looks a little pale. He looks like he's not sure I haven't lost the ability to comprehend English. "That's when Dylan turns around to the band and says *Play it really fucking loud.*"

"Thanks for the book," I say, opening the door.

I put my hands in my pockets, don't bother with my gloves since I'm only going a few doors down to Home Hardware. I'm almost out of spray paint. And I think it's about time I got around to checking out what they've got in the way of wire cutters.

"IS IT SNOWING DOWN there?"

"Yeah, mum, it's snowing. Is it snowing down there too?" Everywhere that isn't Chatham is *down there* to my mother.

"Don't be smart, you know what I mean."

I finish peanut-buttering four slices of bread, lick the knife clean because Mary isn't here, dip it into the jar of jam.

"Hey, mum?"

"Yes, son."

The two hundred miles between us give us both the chance to say *I love you* at the end of every phone call and my mother a way to call me *son* without either of us feeling like bad actors in a made-for-TV movie. Distance is a good truth serum.

"What should we do with the hardwood floors once we move in? Does it matter that they're so old? They look kind of brittle." I'm pretty sure I know what she's going to tell me, but I ask anyway. The new house is the grandchildren my mum's never going to get to talk about.

"First you clean them, then you can wax them. But don't use too much soap and water when you do, you can ruin them that way. You think you're doing good, but you're not. Make sure you wring out your mop real good before you clean them."

"What kind of soap? Any kind?" I crown the peanut-butter slices of bread with the jam slices.

"I use Murphy's. You can buy all kinds of expensive ones, but Murphy's is just as good as any of them."

"How much do I use?" I pull a clear plastic bag out of the stash of Barry-bags underneath the sink and pack up the sandwiches.

"Just put in a capful for every room you do. So if you're doing your kitchen, just put a capful into a pail of hot water. Have you got a pail?"

"Not yet."

"Well, you're going to need a pail. And you're going to need a mop, too. Have you got a mop?"

"I thought I'd wait until we moved into the house, mum. So we wouldn't have more stuff to move."

"Well, you better start making a list, April first is going to be here before you know it. Have you started getting boxes yet?"

"We're still two months away, there's lots of time to get boxes."

"Just start picking up one or two every time you go to the grocery store. That way you won't have to worry about not having enough later. Did you reserve a truck yet? Those things go quick at the first of the month. You don't want to call and them not have one."

A sharp, welcome-home Barry yelp from upstairs. "That must be Mary coming in the door, mum, I better go." Saved by the bark.

"Don't forget about getting those boxes."

"A couple at a time, I know."

"And don't wait until the last minute to rent that truck, either."

"I've got to go, I'll call about it today."

"Just don't wait until the last minute."

"I won't. Bye, mum."

"Bye, son, I love you."

"I love you too, mum."

I set the phone down on top of the fridge and take an apple from the crisper inside and place it beside the sandwiches on the kitchen table. My box of Sudafed and all of my instruments of night are already tucked away in my army parka for when I get home from the Gladstone. I've shaved, showered, and read seven poems, two of them twice. I've got an hour before I have to be at work and here comes my girl.

"Hi, little one," I say.

"Hi."

There's a white plastic grocery bag hanging from each hand, hunching her over. "Let me grab one of those," I say.

She lifts the bags onto the countertop before I can help. I hug her with her coat still on. She feels like I grabbed her just in time, that she'd fall over if I let go.

"How are you doing, kiddo?" I say.

"Fine."

"Let me help you put this stuff away and then you can take a nap with the Bubs."

She pulls away, goes to the bags, begins unpacking one of them. "I don't want to take a nap. Why don't you take a nap?"

"Because I'm not tired. And I've got to go to work."

She pulls cans of black beans, one after another, from the bag, a grocery store Houdini. "Well, I'm not tired either, and I've got work to do too."

"But you can take a nice long nap and get up and paint all night."

"That's what I was going to do. I don't need you to tell me when to work, Hank."

"But ..." I stop myself. I can see the potato chips and the package of Twizzlers and the large bottle of root beer in the other bag, somnambulism comfort food.

Mary turns around from the counter. "But what?"

"Look, I just care, all right?"

She puts her hand on her hip. "About what?"

"You."

"You care about what about me?"

I look at the floor, at Barry lying on the floor between us. He knows when things aren't right. His vocabulary might be only so-so, but he understands pitch. Sometimes he knows a fight is brewing between Mary and me before we do. When he was a puppy, he would tremble and sometimes even pee himself when we'd yell at each other. You learn what's worth fighting about after witnessing something like that.

"You're still wearing your coat," I say.

"So?"

"So ... Look, you just seemed tired and —"

"I'll tell you what I am tired of, Hank, I'm tired of you telling me that I look tired all of the time."

"I don't tell you that, I don't."

"Yes, you do. It's like you want me to be tired and cranky and sad."

"Now, why the hell would I want that?"

"I don't know, Hank, why would you?"

"This is ridiculous," I say. "I just want you to be happy."

"You think being like this is making me happy?"

"I just ..." I take my coat down from the back of the bathroom door and do it up with one quick zip. "Fine, be miserable," I say. "Watch TV all fucking night for all I care. I was only trying to help." I grab my sandwiches and apple off the counter and march past her up the stairs, careful not to look at Barry as I do.

When I get to the front door I take my time unlocking it, check twice to see if I have my wallet and my keys. I stand still and listen for the silence that means Mary is getting her bearings, getting ready to be bigger than me and come upstairs and say the right thing and send me off to work knowing that everything is okay. I stare at a row of old philosophy textbooks while I wait.

I hear her tear open the bag of potato chips. The sound the pop bottle makes when she twists off its top is like someone letting the air out of a tire.

I NEVER LIED TO Mary about not caring about art. It could have been a date-one deal-breaker, but we had lust and then love and before we knew it, a life. Much is forgiven the man who carts your dirty clothes to the laundromat without being asked. Besides, she knew that I knew she was the real deal, wasn't just pushing paint around and wearing too much black. My eyes may be tone-deaf, but my nose knows spirit rot when it smells it, has rarely sniffed me wrong.

I sit on Mary's stool in front of an empty easel. I hardly ever come in here, even when she's at home. Paintings a little smaller than album covers sit in long rows on Mary-made drying racks running head high around the entire circumference of the room, some of them signed and ready to be framed, some of them still shiny wet and drying. Little silver tubes of paint and big and bigger jars of turpentine and varnish and linseed oil crowd cardboard shoeboxes and white wooden orange crates and an ancient black metal tackle box that used to belong to Mary's grandfather. Paintbrushes skinny and fat, their bristles thin and thick, and palette knives and exacto blades and yellow pencils and black magic markers and dirty rags and clean rags bump up against each other all around the studio. Freshly prepared canvases lean against the walls, all gessoed up and ready to go. In the corner there's a small desk buried somewhere underneath an avalanche of grant applications, photocopied magazine articles, yellow Post-it notes, hardbacked sketch pads, glossy art magazines, coiled notebooks, a ball of string, a calculator, two fat stacks of photographs, a pair of gardening scissors, hair ties, dirty wine glasses, and a bunch of dusty, orphaned CDs. A boom box and a blue plastic fan share the single window sill with a small decaying plant, species unidentifiable. Four tall floor lamps positioned around the room oversee the entire proceedings.

Messiness gives me the creeps, even when it serves inner order. Mary's studio is as chaotic as her life isn't. The one she had before this one, the one she was renting in a crumbling former candy factory when we first met, was smaller but about the same. After a couple of weeks of screwing and drinking and getting around to figuring out we weren't going to screw anyone else, she invited me to make the trip over with her one night.

"What'll I do while you paint?" I said.

"You can work on your thesis," she said. "There's a desk someone left behind and I'll hook up a standing lamp so you'll have plenty of light."

I packed up what there was of my manuscript, plus Gabriel Marcel's *Homo Viator*, Martin Buber's *I and Thou*, and the one-two postrationalist punch of Kant's *Critique of Pure Reason* and *Prolegomena to Any Future Metaphysics*. When attempting to formulate an experientially based foundation for possible modes of nontheistic metaphysical affirmation, you don't want to be caught walking around without your Kant. I slipped a couple of lubricated condoms between the soft-back covers of Mr. Buber's finest and snapped my briefcase shut.

Mary's studio was on the third floor. It was a tired old cement-brick building just a couple of years away from reincarnation as a ten-storey condominium, and the elevator wasn't working. So much the better for sucking face and glad-handed groping on every available stairway landing. Part of the appeal of tagging along was the idea of getting it on in an honest-to-goodness artist's space. Maybe I didn't understand Mary's paintings so well, but I had read *Tropic of Cancer* when I was eighteen.

We fucked, on the desk, Mary's legs locked around my back like a giant cricket's embrace, before my books were out of my briefcase and Mary had put brush to canvas. Done, she pulled down her shirt and pulled up her panties and black tights, kissed me on the lips, and got down on her knees and got busy mixing her paints. I still hadn't unpacked my briefcase although it was now on the desk, unopened, in front of me.

"Why do you have to mix them?" I said. "Why don't you just buy the colours you want in the first place?"

Supporting herself on one arm with her legs tucked underneath her, she used her free hand to massage a dot of green into a glob of yellow. Without looking up, "This way I can get the exact tone I want." I could see all ten of her toes through the worn black sheer of her tights. They wiggled, they wiggled, while she worked.

I pulled my papers and different coloured pens and the books from my briefcase and placed them on the desk, the long pad of legal paper directly in front of me, the pens in a neat red, blue, and yellow-highlighter row to my left, the books stacked biggest to smallest to my right. I read over the last thing I'd written a few days before.

> *The question arises, however, whether these "Ideas"*
> *possess more than a regulative function. Can they be*
> *the source of a theoretical knowledge of corresponding*
> *values? It is Kant's conviction that they cannot. In his*
> *view any attempt to use these "Ideas" as the basis for*
> *metaphysics as a science is foredoomed to failure. If we*
> *do so, we shall find ourselves involved in logical fallacies*
> *and antinomies.*

I looked up from the pad. Mary was still gently rubbing a brand new colour to life. The two colours were one now, to my eye just a dull yellowish green, but she kept on kneading the widening circle of paint. She looked as though if I called her name she might not hear me.

I picked up my red editing pen and reread the same paragraph. Before I got to the end of the second sentence, I realized that the words weren't mine, were Frederick Copleston's, from his *History of Philosophy*, which I'd forgotten to enclose in quotation marks. I set down my pen. I put its red cap back on and lined it up beside the others. I turned in my seat, watched Mary make her new colour.

I close the door to Mary's studio and go upstairs and dial her work number. I sit on the arm of the chair that Barry is snoozing in and rub him between the ears while I wait for her to pick up. I get her voice mail instead.

*Hi, you've reached Mary Calder in Creative Services,
please leave a message after the beep and I'll get back
to you as soon as possible.*

I don't know what I want to say, but I don't hang up. I keep on not saying anything until there's another beep, then the line goes dead.

I WANT TO EAT up the night, swallow down the stars, pluck out every streetlight I see on the cab ride home and gobble them down raw, high voltage oysters on the half shell, night bright gut lights.

I'm only home long enough to change into my parka and put Barry on his leash and knock back a couple of post-work Sudafed with a long pull from the bottle of Diet Pepsi in the fridge. Fortified, refreshed, we're out the door and on the sidewalk and headed for trouble in less than five minutes.

First stop is the closest, a streetcar shelter advertisement near our place on Dundas, which I'd spotted for the first time the other day on the way to work. The entire ad consists of a mammoth blue SUV bursting out of a brilliant orange sunset and barrelling through an untouched field of otherwise undisturbed bucolic grandeur — all soft-focus photography leafy green trees and bright batches of yellow flowers and wide-open earthy vistas all points poster — with the slogan IF YOU WANT IT, YOU NEED IT big and black underneath. I wait for the traffic light to turn green and for the two idling cars to be on their way before pulling out my can of spray paint and shaking it ready.

This isn't the only ad of its kind, I know. All over the city and thousands of other cities a thousand different signs making it daily apparent that we haven't got a fucking chance. I'm not naive, just self-righteous and self-medicated enough to do something about it. I crane my neck left then right before spray-painting *You're An Idiot* over YOU NEED IT. You can still read what's underneath the Plexiglas if you look hard enough, but I'm only one man with one dog. I put away the can and we start walking toward what's next.

In no particular order of principled defilement: two central air-conditioning units wire-cutter clipped at their source; a Toronto *Sun* newspaper box with a leftover copy of today's edition proclaiming on its cover BUSH SAYS IRAQ MUST BE FREE spray-painted with *LIES*; and a long, graceful scratch down the entire length of a white sport-utility vehicle, as good a reason as any why God gave all of his children house keys. By the time we're finished, Barry is limping, either from ice between his toes or the arthritis in his hips or both, and I've walked most of the caffeine and Sudafed out of my system.

It's got to be after three by now, and the flurries have turned into a hard, steady blast of ice and snow. I'm leaning into the wind with a lowered head as we move down Roncesvalles toward home, but I pick out someone moving toward us on the sidewalk maybe a couple hundred feet away. I'm loaded down with enough supplies to open up my own hardware store, but I act like you're supposed to act at the border with a trunkful of cheap American beer and half-price stereo equipment. I lift my eyes and keep them on the figure coming our way, a fat guy in knee-high white snowmobile boots, and am ready to say the first word just to show him how cool and confident I am that I've done absolutely nothing wrong. He beats me to it.

"Where'd this come from, eh?" he says, one hand on his toque, the other holding onto a vanilla ice cream cone.

"I don't know," I say, and the guy takes a lick of his ice cream and is past us.

"YOU MIGHT WANT TO think about putting another hall light switch in at the top of the stairs," Tom, Tom of 11 1/2 Wright Avenue, Rover's dad Tom, says.

"My dad says when we get the knob and tube guys in here we can tell them where we want any extra outlets and switches."

Tom moves his chin just enough to indicate that he's listening. We're standing inside the front door of their old house, our soon-to-be new one, just him and me. After all the papers had been signed and lawyer-approved, after the final move-in date had been set, reset, then set again for a week later, after the home inspector had filed his report with the insurance company, Lynn suggested that we drop by sometime before April and get the real rundown on the place. It's a friendly gesture, not something they're obligated to do, but not any less unsettling for being an act of compassionate *caveat emptor*, particularly since somehow it's worked out that only Mr. Monosyllabic and me will be taking today's tour.

"You might want them to install the bathroom light switch on the outside. If you're thinking of putting in a shower."

Tom is dressed the same way he always is: grey slacks, black dress shoes, light brown cardigan over a white dress shirt buttoned but for one to the top. He looks like what he is, a retired university professor. His eyes are blue and clear, though, his body lean, his posture straight. His hair has gone entirely white, but it's all still there, still combed straight back in the manner of a leading man movie star from the forties.

"Yeah, the inspector said that that was one of the things that would have to get done right away. He said it hasn't been to code for years. Decades, actually."

Tom sticks his hands in his pants pockets. "Let's look at the kitchen," he says, marching off without me. Christ, I wish Mary was here. Or Lynn. Or even Rover.

The living room is like ours, except in lieu of albums and books there are only books. I scan the shelves as I follow Tom through to the kitchen, expecting to find only fat linguistics textbooks with titles as long as their spines, but Spanish history, a complete set of hardbound Dickens, and a whole shelf of oversized art books, French Impressionists mostly, dominate.

"Your wife said you wanted to keep the refrigerator and stove."

I nod.

"Here's what you want to watch out for, then." Tom opens the freezer door and it comes off its hinges in his hand. "The freezer works, just be aware that this isn't attached anymore. Maybe you can fix it. I couldn't."

I nod again.

Tom moves to the stove, switches on the oven. The sound of steadily lapped water, and I turn around to find Rover drinking from his bowl by the back door. I hadn't heard him come into the room, and as soon as he's done drinking he gives me only the slightest sideways glance before scuttling back out. Tom opens the oven door.

"Feel this?" he says, putting his hand inside. I bend over and do the same.

"Feel how hot it is?"

"Right," I say.

"Now look at the knob." The knob is turned as low as it can go and still be on. "The oven works, but it's always this hot no matter what you set it at." Tom stands up, turns the oven back off. "Let's go downstairs," he says.

Compared to a typical suburban basement this one seems tiny, barely able to contain the furnace and its attendant oil tank, the hot water tank, a bunch of boxes pushed up against one of the walls, and assorted this and thats, most prominently several pieces of camping equipment and a red racing bike. Mary's done most of the necessary one-on-one footwork regarding the sale, and passes on to me whatever gossip she manages to pick up. When she told me she found out that for several years Tom spent two weeks every summer vacationing by himself on bicycling tours of Europe, I had a hard time believing it.

The cast-iron furnace dominates the room, looks like an antique from a museum of turn-of-the-century appliances, and there are three swooping octopus arm heat vents that lower the ceiling level by a good two feet. The rest of the room isn't that bad, maybe six feet and a bit, only a little lower than our entire downstairs at home. Tom crouches toward the furnace with hunched shoulders and a lowered head, instinctive in his stooping. "This is something else you want to watch out for," he says, motioning me to follow.

"See this?" he says, pointing to a dirty metal pie plate sitting on top of the pot-bellied furnace.

"Yeah?"

"Don't ever take it away."

"Why not?"

He pauses, pushes a handful of silver hair that had fallen onto his forehead back into place. "To be honest, I don't really know. The man who comes and fills the tank every fall tried to explain it to me once, but I'm afraid I didn't really follow. All I know is, if you don't want to have any problems with the furnace, don't take this away."

I nod slowly a couple of times, feel like I've been initiated into an exclusive, slightly illicit society. We're still stooped over looking at the plate when the furnace comes on; first, with a sharp click, like a ten-speed bicycle changing gears, then with a deep boom quickly followed by the sound of hot air rushing through the vents above our heads. The damp basement feels immediately dryer, milder. It sounds like we're in the bowels of an enormous, warmth-giving machine.

"It's a good furnace, though," Tom says, still bent over. "It might not look like it, but it's reliable, has never given us any problems."

"How old do you think it is?" I say.

"It was here when we moved in and it was old then. See this door?" Tom points to the front of the furnace.

"Yeah?"

Embossed across it, *C.Williams Heating Co., Montreal, Quebec.*

"It's soldered shut now, but that's where the coal used to go. They did this with a lot of these old furnaces back then apparently, converted them from coal to oil."

I touch a tentative finger to the iron door. It's warm but not hot. My finger where another finger was eighty, ninety, a hundred years before.

"The inspection guy," I say, "he said that we'd have to switch over to gas someday because a lot of the insurance companies don't want to insure places with oil furnaces anymore."

"I've heard that."

"Will they convert this one to gas like they did to oil?"

"From what I understand, they take these old ones right out, take it and the oil tank and all of these big vents right out of here and put in a brand new gas furnace that's no bigger than a couple of large suitcases."

"So there'll be nothing left of this at all?"

Tom runs his own finger over *C.Williams Heating.* "A couple with children could probably turn a basement like this into a nice little family room. There's no room down here the way it is now. The way it is now, it's not good for very much at all."

"Your son, he grew up in this house, didn't he?" I say.

"Yes, he did," Tom says. "He was born and raised here."

I GO TO LOBLAWS about every other day to check underneath the fruit bins for more empty cardboard boxes. We're scheduled to move in less than four weeks and have divided up most of the packing duties since we're hardly home at the same time anymore. When we are, we're as nice to each other as any two civilized people sharing a seat on the bus.

March hasn't taken away yet what January and February have brought. Filthy snow drifts don't torrent out of sight down thirsty sewers. Winter hats and gloves aren't experimentally left behind at home at the front door. Late-afternoon dusk hasn't merged into early evening yet. Today, I pull books from the shelves and pack them into sturdy, waxy Andy Boy Apples boxes. I'm getting about half of the packing done that I should because every other book I take down I end up skimming its back, flipping through its pages, remembering without trying to where I bought it and why. Spengler's *Decline of the West*. Both volumes of Wells's *The Outline of History*. Shaw's *Complete Plays and Prefaces*. It's too much work to pretend that the pompous ninny who lugged home these still-unread must-reads ten, fifteen years ago isn't me, so I smile instead as I lay them away. Hopelessly overreaching but sincere. There are, I suppose, worse ways of wasting one's youth.

I load a box as full as I can and seal it shut with clear packing tape. Hoisting it on top of a stack of others, the hernia I narrowly avoid tells me I did exactly what Mary said that I shouldn't, filled it exclusively with hardcovers and didn't mix up the heavy books with paperbacks to make it more manageable. I look around for the scissors to slice it back open that I know are around here somewhere, that we had out and were using last night, Sunday night, a rare evening of both of us in the same place at the same time.

I had Tim Hardin strumming away on the turntable because Mary's not big on straight-up rock, particularly when she's still riding out her seasonal slide. I lit a stick of incense more for mood enhancement than for odour control, and convinced her to open up a bottle of wine even though we can't afford it. I wouldn't let her get up to let Barry out even though she was the one nearest to the door and I didn't once ask her how she was feeling. I wanted normal like I wanted a miracle.

When we were standing side by side pulling books from the bookcase, I took her firmly but gently in my arms and kissed her softly on the mouth. She didn't kiss me back so much as purse her lips every few seconds, but I didn't give up. I slid my hand slowly underneath her sweater and cupped a warm, firm breast. She let me, which was exactly what it felt like. My hand retreated, and we went back to work.

Ten minutes later, "Do you have the tape?" I said.

Mary looked up from the box she was packing. She peeked into mine. "You're done with that one?"

"Yeah, I just can't find the tape."

"Oh." She was still looking inside my box.

"What did I do wrong?" I said. Mary knows how to do things. It doesn't matter what the thing is, Mary probably knows how to do it.

"You didn't do anything *wrong*, Hank. But if you just ..." She pulled my box closer and grabbed two fistfuls of paperbacks from the floor; jammed one down here, wedged another one there, shoved and crammed and made room for at least ten more before she was finished.

"See?" she said, looking up. She was actually smiling for what seemed like the first time in weeks. "Now we've got that many less books to find room for somewhere else. You've just got to be careful not to overload. We need to be able to carry them, too, remember."

"Great," I said, looking down at my perfectly packed cardboard box.

"What's wrong?" she said.

"Nothing, nothing's wrong. You were right."

"It's not about anyone being right. I'm just trying to help us, that's all."

"I know," I said, looking up. "I know you are."

"HANK."

"Frank."

Frank's coming out of the Price Chopper near the Gladstone just as I'm going in. We split the difference and stand in the store vestibule beside the bubble gum machine and the miniature hockey helmet machine and the coin-operated rocking horse. Three white plastic grocery bags sag from each of his hands. I'm out of Sudafed and could use a good-quality black magic marker that won't run in the rain. We don't shake hands in deference to the bags of groceries.

"How have you been keeping, Hank?"

"Good, good. You?"

"Excellent. And Mary?"

"She's good too." I don't mention the new house or the move or Mary's upcoming show. I can't even remember if I've told him about my job at the Gladstone. The Duke isn't where you go to tell people things.

"I'm glad to hear that, Hank. I always liked Mary. I knew she was smarter than the rest of us when she quit showing up at the bar."

Frank's grin borders on becoming a laugh as he rocks back and forth slowly, rhythmically, on the balls and toes of his feet. Something's different about him, I know, but I can't place what. He sets down his groceries.

"Hey, this is great, I was really hoping that I'd run into you," he says, reaching between the buttons of his coat and pulling out a pen and a small notepad from inside. "If you don't mind, Hank, I'd like to get your mailing address." He hands me the pen and pad like he's asking for my autograph.

"Sure," I say, not certain if I should write down where we're living now or where we will be. I scribble down our old address since I can't remember the new postal code. Handing it to him, "What's up?"

"Thanks," Frank says, reading over what I'd written. "Thanks a lot." He puts it and the pen both back away. "What I'm hoping, Hank, is that you won't be opposed to the idea of me dropping you a line now and then about some of the things that I'm reading. Nothing major, don't worry, nothing more than the kinds of things we've talked about in the past. Just a way for me to make sure that I'm on the right track with what I'm thinking."

"No problem," I say, "but we can always talk like we always have at the Duke. I've just been kind of busy lately, but I'm still around."

Which is true, but not the reason I say it. I need to read Frank's perky reports on his continuing world tour of history's great thinkers like I need Mary to present me with another snapshot of myself at twenty-five years old and not yet aware that a tapered waist and a determined gaze don't come with lifetime guarantees.

"Well, you see, that's just the thing, Hank. You see, I finally got my place up north. I move up there at the end of the month."

"Really. That's great." I don't know what else to say, so I shake Frank's hand. Then it hits me what's different about him. His grip is tighter, his fingers fleshier, his eyes clear and focused. He's got a steady hand and a lifetime's worth of Penguin classics to puzzle over and a place to make his stand. I'm happy for him. I'm jealous of him. I'm happy for him.

"I'm happy for you, Frank," I say.

"Well, we'll see how it goes. I do like the location, though. And I am looking forward to getting started putting some things in the ground."

"Where is it?"

"Washago."

I shake my head.

"Just a couple hours north of Toronto. The town's nothing special, but I got a good deal on a nice little place that's right on the river, I do like that. You can actually see the river go by right from my kitchen window."

"That's fantastic."

"Knowing my luck, I'll probably get flooded my first spring."

"Yeah, but you probably won't."

"We'll see."

There's nothing left to say, so neither of us does; we shake hands one last time, Frank picks up his grocery bags, and the electric doors usher him out into the night.

Two East Asian kids no more than six or seven, a boy and a girl, probably brother and sister, are messing around with the rocking horse, the girl up in the saddle, the boy down below and running his hand up and down the horse's head like he's trying to pet it to life. The girl says something to the boy that I don't understand, something that sounds like a command, something sharp, anyway, but the boy doesn't answer, doesn't look up from rubbing the horse's hard plastic head.

I drop a loonie into the silver coin slot and the horse immediately starts moving up and down, up and down. The little girl shrieks, wraps all ten fingers around the horse's neck. The little boy turns around and stares up at me. I pick him up and set him down behind his sister.

"Hold on tight," I say.

TONIGHT'S A STAY-AT-HOME night. Winter's gasping its frozen last, a final whack of mid-March sleet and snow howling farewell for now outside, but that's not why Barry and I are in the kitchen and not out prowling the neighbourhood after work tonight. I've got a dry cough and achy limbs, but those are just symptoms, not what's what. You can't feel heroic all the time. Human nature doesn't let anybody be that happy.

By the time I hang up my coat and get the bowl down from the cupboard and the soya milk from the fridge, Barry's joined me downstairs. Once I shut the door behind him I switch on the radio and pour out some Mini-Wheats. I catch "Walk Away Rene" almost right from the first note and hum along while I wait for the milk to do its thing, to make my cereal nice and soggy just the way I like it.

CHUM-AM, All Oldies All the Time, is, for me, a relatively new late-night experience. A couple of weeks back I'd had about all I could take of some basketball general manager explaining on the Fan how he'd had to fire his coach because of "philosophical differences," like the real reason he'd canned the guy was because there was simply no way a Cartesian rationalist and a stone-cold empiricist could work together harmoniously running a successful NBA franchise. I flipped the dial, desperate for some kind of less epistemologically sophisticated sports yak, and stopped at Dionne Warwick doing "Walk On By."

Music makes you more alive, more awake, the opposite of what I need when I get home from work. But Bacharach's clean strings and smoky horns and Dionne's elegant sighs and yearning crooning kept the dial where it was. I stood there beside the fridge through the end of the song and the beginning of the next, "Sixteen Candles" by the Crests, a '50s doo-wop group, before finally sitting back down. Let no man dare judge the aesthetic worth of AM radio until he's sat alone at a kitchen table at 2:43 in the morning listening to thirty-, forty-, fifty-year-old pop songs rise from the dead from a single tiny tinny speaker and bite him square in the soul. The good pain of the dearly departed Top Forty. Sometimes the sublime is as simple as a two-minute tune with a strong melody and a great hook.

"Walk Away Rene" is everything a good song shouldn't be — a 4/4 rock and roll beat syruped over with gobs and gobs of cellos and flutes and surging violins — but somehow it works, and to ask anything more of anything is just plain wrong. I eat my cereal by the faint light of the thin fluorescent bulb hanging from underneath the cupboard over the sink and spot a piece of mail addressed to Mary and me propped up on the table against a cardboard box half-packed with newspaper-swaddled highball glasses we never use and a crock pot. I set my spoon in my bowl and tear open the envelope across its top.

BUSHWHACKED EDITIONS

IS PLEASED TO INVITE YOU TO THE LAUNCH OF

PHILIP SUMNERS' NEW BOOK OF POETRY

FUTURE TENSE

READING MARCH 28 @ 7:30 PM
AS PART OF THE HARBOURFRONT READING SERIES

PRIVATE RECEPTION @ 10:30 PM UNTIL ?
1186 KING STREET WEST

What stings worse: our friends' success, or their being humble about it? Phil and I haven't spoken since the evening I fled the Duke, but this new book of his must have been in the works for months. And the celebratory reception, of course, at Rebecca's tastefully decorated King Street condo, she the hostess with the absolute mostest, wine and cheese and fraudulent smiles all the way around, help yourself, please. At least he's still writing, whatever it is that he is writing. I used to read Phil's poems as soon as they were finished. I guess Rebecca must look over his stuff now.

The Righteous Brothers' "You've Lost that Lovin' Feelin'" was made to be played on a transistor radio with the blankets pulled up over your head and your heart in your throat and the radio tight to your ear and the volume turned low so no one else can hear. Bill Medley moans, white soul brother Bobby Hatfield wails, and Phil Spector keeps the whole thing together with his biggest, thickest Wall of Sound treatment ever, kettle drums and swelling strings and miles of miles of undertow echo. I want to go upstairs and wake up Mary and tell her that we're going to be all right, that we're not like them, that we're not like everybody else, that we're going to be just fine.

I don't, of course. I've got a cold, I'm not crazy. I wait until the song is over and flip off the radio and take my jacket down from its hook. "C'mon, Barry," I say, "let's go for a walk."

I pat myself down to make sure we've got everything we need. I pull out the box of Sudafed. I suppose this stuff works when you're actually sick, too.

THE DAYS ARE GETTING longer, the sky stays lit later, Mary flies west early tomorrow morning. First to Vancouver for one night, for the opening of her show, then to Victoria for five more to visit her parents and her sister. That, and to cart back as much as she can of the stuff that her mother's been keeping around for her for when she got her own house someday.

"We'll probably never use the silver service, but it belonged to my grandmother, and my mum really wants us to have it. I mean, it's nice. Now that we've got an above-ground kitchen I guess we could actually have someone over to our place for dinner for a change."

Mary's talking again. Not a lot, and not without sounding like she's still getting used to the sound of her own voice, but she's talking. And smiling once in a while, too, even if her smiles are more like sighs that say, *Whew, that's over*, rather than a sign that she's actually feeling good right now.

I knew a week ago that the thaw had begun. I was sitting at the kitchen table after work listening to the radio when I smelt it. The paintings for the Vancouver show had been done weeks before, had been hanging in Mary's studio only so that they could completely dry before being shipped west. This was the smell of fresh oils, of turpentine, of paint thinner; the smell of Mary back at her easel, back at work, back at being Mary. I didn't say anything because I didn't want her to think that I was watching her. I didn't say anything because I didn't want her to watch herself.

"Hank, would you bring me the hair dryer when you come up?"

"Yep, be there in a second."

Another reason I knew that Mary was waking up was that she told me she'd bought a plane ticket. Mary's always on her way back when she decides to go away. Where she travels to doesn't matter, only that she leaves town, as soon as she's home again bursting with not so much as what she saw and did as what she'd been thinking about and all of the things she wants to do now that she's back. Travel as purgative, I guess. Getting lost to help you find out where you are.

I grab the hair dryer from the bathroom and carry two cans of Budweiser in my other hand upstairs. When Mary gets back we'll only be here for another few days before we move, so I'm boxing up the last few dozen albums I've waited until now to seal away while she finishes packing for her trip. I'll keep out some essentials so there'll be something to listen to until then — *Exile on Main Street, The Georgia Peach* by Little Richard, *Patsy Cline's Greatest Hits* — but I don't plan on doing much but working and skulking after midnight while Mary's away. We're almost ready to go. The apartment looks like a warehouse full of cardboard boxes with a futon on the floor and some of the night watchman's scattered clothes and dirty dishes.

"Thanks," Mary says, tying the cord around the handle of the hair dryer four tight times, tucking it inside her bag. Odds are good that her parents still have a hair dryer of their own and that she can probably make do for a single night in Vancouver without one, but that's not how Mary operates, even Mary on the mend. She's packed too many pairs of shoes, more books and magazines than she'll ever have a chance to look at, and isn't willing to risk not being able to get the Guatemalan dark roasted coffee she buys at the fair-trade place on Ronscevalles so has stowed away a freshly ground pound which she's double wrapped in two clear plastic bags even though the package itself hasn't been opened yet.

I pop the tabs on our beers. "Keith Richards once showed up at the airport for a Stones world tour with only a bottle of HP Sauce in his coat pocket," I say, handing one to Mary. She takes it, takes a sip, sets it down on the little raft of box-free floor space she's cleared for herself in order to pack.

"He probably has twenty people who get him whatever he wants when he's on the road," she says. She folds a blue cardigan in three neat movements and places it on top of the pile of clothes bulging her bag. One of her bags.

The return of her sense of humour comes last. Until she's entirely Mary again, logic and common sense win out every time over going with the flow simply because it's more interesting that way. It's coming, though, it won't be long now. Like winter inching, inching, inching its way out the door so that it feels like spring is never going to show up and kick its tired ass into last season, your brain knows better, has seen the impossible happen every year that you've been around to doubt that it would. Only a fool or a philosopher would make a practice of it, but sometimes you just have to listen to your head.

Over the music, over Patsy purring from the stereo speakers, "Is this too loud?" I say.

"It's nice," Mary says, looking up, an almost-smile loosening, softening her face. I'd forgotten how beautiful she is when she smiles or has just cum or is laughing at something small and silly. I get down on my knees beside her.

"Is this everything?" I say, hand on the zipper of her bag.

Mary looks around. "I think so."

Before she can change her mind, I pull the zipper which gets about halfway across before it slows to a stop, unable to make it up the mountain of clothes swelling the bag. I unzip it and give it another tug, this time getting maybe half an inch further.

"Don't break it," Mary says.

"I'm not going to break it," I say. I try again, stopping only when I think that if I pull any harder, I'll break it. "Are you sure you need everything that's in here?" I say.

"I wouldn't have packed it if I didn't."

"What about the other one?" We both look at her other, smaller bag. It looks like an overinflated black nylon football that's about to blow its seams.

"Leave it and I'll deal with it in the morning," Mary says.

"It won't be any less stuck then."

"I don't want to deal with it now. It's my last night before I go, just forget it."

"Maybe if ..." I pull out a couple of sweaters and a pair of blue jeans and a clear plastic overnight bag and rearrange them inside, push down and hold everything in place with one hand while working the zipper with the other. I lose about an inch for my effort.

"Just leave it, Hank."

"I want to help you," I say. I stand up and put the sole of my Blundstone on the hump of clothes sticking out of the bag. "Now try it," I say.

"What are you doing?"

"Just try it, I think it'll work this time."

"Hank, stop it, you're getting my clothes all dirty."

"Just the ones on top, and hardly at all. C'mon, try it again."

Mary stands up and goes downstairs.

"Fine, I'll do it myself," I say. "I just thought it might be nice if we spent some time together before you left." Mary doesn't answer. My foot still on the bag, I crouch down and grab the zipper, give it a yank good and hard and quick.

A torn lining isn't the same as a broken zipper, it's not the end of the world.

"Pardon?" Mary yells from the kitchen.

"I didn't say anything," I yell back.

WHEN MARY GOES AWAY I can wear what I want. I can wear what I want anytime, but it's just good relationship etiquette to listen to your partner when they suggest that you might want to save that red check sports jacket, that black leather biker vest, those imitation white rattlesnake cowboy boots for when she's not around. Provided that she returns the favour when it comes to an adored pair of ass-sagging long johns, ideal for sprawling around the house in, or an old boyfriend's cashmere sweater, it's only fair.

When it's just me and the Bubs I can also crank open what few windows we have as wide as I want. Bundled up as usual for Barry's walk this morning, I wasn't halfway out the door when the first sweet body blow of spring knocked me back inside the house, letting me ditch my hat and gloves and scarf on the couch. Mary would have said it's barely sixty degrees out, still way too early to open up all the windows. When Barry and I came back from our walk I got a good cross-current of fresh air going and took off his collar. I let him give it a good sniff before tossing it across the room where it skidded to a stop against a big box full of clothes.

When you live with someone, the first couple of days you're alone at home are nice. Clothes, for example, become optional, underwear being the standard uniform of suddenly single living. You eat what and when you want, sleep in the middle of the bed and stretch out whenever you feel like it, and tend to let personal hygiene drop a notch or two in the pecking order of one's priorities. For my part, I very much welcome the opportunity to screech, grunt, and pound my chest like an agitated ape while chasing Barry around the apartment, an activity Mary tends to frown upon as much as he and I plainly enjoy it. Marriage is about making sacrifices.

I'm not due at the Gladstone for another couple of hours and the Bubs has already been given an extra walk, I've called the mover and confirmed what time he's going to be here next week, and I've washed and dried the only dishes I've dirtied since Mary's been gone, my cereal bowl and spoon. The book of poetry I've been pushing through is boring, reads like somebody trying to write like a poet, and I can't figure out which box something surefire might be packed away in, some Miss Emily, some Uncle Walt, some good old Li Po. I could pop by She Said Boom and roll the dice on something new, but with Mary gone, Barry's stuck inside until I get home late from work tonight and I don't want to leave him alone more than I have to. I could take him verse shopping with me, but he'd pulled his protest act once already today, sat down on the sidewalk only a few minutes after we'd headed out on his bonus walk and refused to go any further. Must be the humidity, winter into spring meaning moist, damp air meaning sore joints and hips.

I leave Barry sleeping upstairs in the reading chair and plug in my laptop in my studio. I haven't checked my e-mail in months, not since around the time I started patrolling the neighbourhood. It's not as strange as it sounds. The only reason I'm on-line at all is because Phil thought it might help fool people into thinking that I'm a responsible freelancer committed to keeping up with the times. The correspondence course aside, though, the need to hang my shingle along the information super highway never really materialized. You can fool some of the people some of the time ...

The usual anonymous cybernetic offers to buy things, go to things, go to things and buy things, and lots and lots of SUBJECT: LENORE SHIPLEY along with just as many SENDER: SCHOOL OF CONTINUING STUDIES. The phone messages were easier to ignore. As soon as I heard the school secretary's voice on the answering machine, a quick stab of my thumb on numeral seven and instant erase: What stern reminder of what a delinquent instructor of course number SCS 6236 I am? Not that I thought I was anyone's instructor anymore. AWOL after your name isn't nearly as impressive as M.A. or Ph.D.

I click 'em and weep, confirm what I already knew. The only one I actually feel bad for in all this is dear old Lenore. I don't need the money anymore, and now that I'm out of the picture maybe the students will actually get someone who knows what they're doing, someone who even cares. But lonely voices everywhere you listen hollering themselves hoarse into the void, and here I am, just one more A-1 a-hole adding to the lonesome echo. What I should do is dig up Lenore's manuscript and read it and mark it up and send it off pro bono.

Yep. That's exactly what I should do.

WHEN I WAS A KID, every March the custodian would go up on the roof and throw down all of the balls that had gone missing over the course of the school year. Maybe according to the calendar it wouldn't be officially spring yet, but us kids knew and so did Mr. Cross, our janitor. The rumour that today was the day that he was going up would usually start spreading right after first class, and by noon it would be official, all of us attacking our brown bag lunches and slurping down our boxes of milk and heading for the blacktop as quick as we could so as to start the Mr. Cross sightings and to stake out a good position for when the sky began to rain weather-bleached grey tennis balls and little white plastic footballs and waterlogged baseballs and more.

Because here was the deal. Whatever you had lost playing foot hockey on the basketball court or twenty-one on the baseball diamond or by way of a badly shagged punt on the playground was gone for good, non-returnable, your's in deed of ownership no more. The moment that your ball landed on the roof it was no one's and everyone's and that was just the way it was. Until March arrived and Mr. Cross went up on the roof. Then, whatever he threw down that you managed to grab you could call your own and take with you home and nobody could say that you couldn't.

Mr. Cross always wore a brown work shirt and green work pants and had a hound-hanging, troubled face, deep black half-moon creases under his eyes. Whenever he wasn't mopping up some grade two's puke or setting up a gymnasium's worth of metal chairs for a school assembly, he was working outside. You couldn't say he looked happy then, but he did seem a little less sad. Maybe it was just because he got to smoke.

But the one day a year when he lobbed down the balls from the roof it felt like maybe it was something else. If you only had your eyes on the balls you'd probably miss it. The sideways smirk when the kids would cheer when he'd first appear. The actual smile when two boys would go for the same ball and collide and knock each other over, another kid swooping in from behind and scooping up the prize. The way he'd soft toss a Frisbee or a tennis ball to the littlest ones among us to make sure that almost everybody went home with at least something.

The roof emptied off, Mr. Cross would wipe his long forehead with the back of his arm and take off his jacket and it swing it over his shoulder and climb on down and stamp out his cigarette on the blacktop. Even for those who didn't get what they wanted, had to settle for a scuffed-up softball instead of a Tony Gabriel-approved football, one thing was for sure. It was spring. And now nobody could say that it wasn't.

"AYE, HAVE YOU EVER been to sea, Billy?"

I look behind me. "I don't get it," I say.

"The Captain Highliner shirt," Bob says. "Your old lady lets you out of the house dressed like that?"

"She's out of town."

"You should have called her," Bob says, adjusting his headphones, cueing up the next song. "You should have called somebody."

As a matter of fact, I did telephone Mary — last night before bed and today, twice, before I left for work — although

not to ask her opinion on the advisability of wearing the ruf-
fled, powder blue puffy shirt I've got on tonight. I've always
maintained that it allows me an elegantly decadent, Keith
Richards circa 1977 look. Mary contends that I'm only an eye
patch and a plastic parrot on my shoulder away from putting
together a prize-winning Halloween costume.

I don't care if she does share Bob's flawed fashion sense, I'm
tired of playing bachelor. Even a less than completely recon-
structed Mary is a better occasional dinner companion than a
cardboard box marked FRAGILE: KITCHEN, as well as a lot more
fun to talk to than a dog who's admittedly a great listener but
who rarely has anything new to say. It's been four nights now,
time and space enough for her to have gotten a good start on
doing whatever it is she's got to do by going on the road solo,
although I know that she'll get there quicker if I don't slow
her down with long distance chit-chat all because I'm sick of
sleeping alone only a couple of days after thinking what a swell
change it was not to have to hear her alarm go off in the morning. I called her parents' place anyway. And got their service.

When no one picks up the phone at my parents' house I
tend to worry, assume that if they're not out grocery shopping
then someone's in the hospital. Mary's parents do things. They
ski in the winter, hike in the summer, enjoy wine tasting,
blueberry picking, antique hunting. I left a short message from
the pay phone near Sid's desk, mindful that Mary might not
be the first one to hear it. Naturally, I was in the shower when
she called back later that night. Her message was shorter than
sweeter, too, although I was the only one on this end in danger

of overhearing anything embarrassingly lovey-dovey. She said that the show had gone fine, one piece had already sold and another two were on hold, and that she hoped I was taking good care of her dog. She finished off by saying not to bother calling back because her parents were both sleeping. This afternoon, when I did call back and waited around so that I could hear her voice again and not her father's on the machine, of course I ended up getting her message only after I'd put off walking Barry for as long as I could.

"I guess we're playing telephone tag," she said, before reminding me to make sure to call the movers and get a firm time and price and to make it clear that we want the two-man crew and not the third guy like they'd pushed on us, all of which I'd already done days ago. "Okay, well, I guess you're it," she said before hanging up. I called right back but the machine flipped immediately over, someone must have been on the phone. I kept trying right up until I had to leave for work but never got through.

"Hey, Big Guy, what do you say about grabbing that brewski at the Greek's we've been talking about after we shut this dump down tonight?" The Greek's is a tiny after-hours grease pit in Kensington Market that I once made the mistake of mentioning to Bob one night still has the same very liberal last-call policy that it did ten years ago when Phil and I would sometimes hit it on the stumble home from the Duke after closing time.

Visions of bellying up to the bar next to the skinheads and junkies and ordinary problem drinkers in a place not much bigger than my parents' kitchen with Bob, a guy, who, at his best, looks like the reason most heterosexual women don't get turned on by porn, "You know," I say, "if I didn't have this thing I've got to go to later —" I pull the invitation to Phil's book launch out of my back pocket and unfold it for him to see "— I'd be up for it."

Bob leans closer to the rail and reads it. "A poetry reading," he sniffs, picking up the APPLAUSE! sign and lifting it high over his head, giving the two giggling university girls on stage the auditory goose they need to continue shrieking their way through "These Boots Are Made for Walking." "I can just imagine what kind of trim goes to one of those things." Bob puts the sign back down and leans back in his chair on two legs, moves the toothpick in his mouth from one side to the other with his tongue while giving the girls' collective rear-end a long, thoughtful once over.

"Yeah, well, I told a friend that I'd drop by, and ..." I shrug, shove the invite back in my pocket, turn around to face the crowd with my hands locked in front of me like a good door-man should.

I didn't tell anyone that I'd drop by anywhere. I'd actually tossed the invitation in the recycling bin the day it arrived, only to be surprised to see it resurrected the next day and stuck up on the door of the refrigerator. In sickness and in health, Mary the great reconciliator. Putting on my coat for work today, hitting the recall button on the phone one last time hoping to get though to Mary, I plucked it off the fridge and stuck it in my back pocket not because I intended to go, but because if I took it with me it meant that I didn't necessarily have to come straight home after work.

The girls finish their song, hug, skip down from the stage. The only good thing about the university kids packing the place every night now is that Miss Pamela and Pistol Pete and Michael can't hog the microphone anymore. Good for the ears, but not so good for the eyes. All three of them, and a handful of the regular boozers, too — neighbourhood drunks and welfare cases getting by upstairs who've hung around in spite of Sid jacking up the alcohol prices just because he can — swallowed up by long, beer-pitcher-cluttered tables of loud, laughing twenty-year olds. Miss Pamela is the hardest to watch. Sitting by herself in her gold lamé dress and ice-pick high heels and elbow-length, white silk gloves a little dirty at the finger-tips, she looks like a lost little girl gone missing from her own birthday party, like she's been waiting around for sixty years for her parents to realize that she's disappeared and to come back and get her.

"It's showtime, Big Guy," Bob says.

"Touch Me" by the Doors, the official house band of Hank the Doorman, and I shut my eyes and squeeze the mic tight and belt out Jim just as Jim as I can. I try not to hear myself sing.

I CAN'T REMEMBER THE last time I ran anywhere, and now I know why. Sprinting to catch the Queen streetcar in order to make last call at the Duke, thankfully I had the cars not trying very hard not to run me over to help keep my mind off my gut jiggling around underneath my shirt like an untouched Jell-O mold. Now how the hell did *that* get there?

I could have hopped a cab to make sure that I made it on time, but with the move only a few days away, money is tight. I shouldn't even be doing what I'm doing, but it's either the Duke, home, or Phil's party. Ten dollars in my pocket, two quick pints, and three old Stones tunes on the jukebox, music so good that even Mick Jagger couldn't ruin it. And who knows? When I do get home, maybe Mary will have called.

I pull on the door of the Duke and nearly dislocate my shoulder. I pound twice and wait for Lenny or Sam or Julio to unlock it and let me in. It can't be after last call already. The tattered red curtains covering the bar's few dirty windows are all pulled shut, but even if it was past closing time Lenny at least would still be at it, putting up chairs and putting down a few last glasses of draft beer before climbing the stairs in the back to his tiny room over the bar.

I wait, pound twice more, and jump up to see if I can see anything over top of the curtain on the door. It looks completely dark inside, not even the light behind the bar that Len puts on when he's closing down is lit. Maybe it's later than I thought.

"Everybody's gone."

I turn around. Julio, swaying in place in front of me, takes a drink from a small bottle inside a brown paper bag.

"Everybody's gone where?" I say. When Julio's doing his drinking in the street I know to keep things simple.

"Ah, those ..." he says, dismissing the Duke with a wave and a sharp frown. He lifts his bottle again, winces this time when he swallows.

"Everybody's gone where, Julio? Sam and Lenny went where?"

Julio's body suddenly stops moving; he stares at me like he's trying to recall who I am or is contemplating slugging me.

"Hank," he says. He Frankensteins toward me until he's about a foot away, lifts a shaky hand and squeezes my forearm. "Go home, Hank, go home to Mary, you don't have to be here." The smell of alcohol and wet cigarettes and rotten cheese; I try to breathe through my mouth.

"I am," I say, putting my hand on his, which is still on my arm. "I'm going home to Mary right now. But where is everybody, Julio, where are Sam and Lenny?"

Julio lets go of my arm, staggers carefully backward four heavy steps and stops in the middle of the sidewalk, points. I walk around to the front of the bar.

FOR SALE

CONTACT BOWMAN REALTY

(416) 251-5729

We both look at the sign leaning up against the dust-caked curtain inside the front window. "They're gone, everybody's gone," Julio says. He forces down what's left in his bottle and lets it drop to the ground. I wait for a crash that doesn't come. The top of an empty plastic container of Listerine pokes out of the bag. I look back up at the sign.

"Why didn't anyone tell me?" I say.

Julio wraps his hand around my arm again. "I did, I did tell you, Hank."

"HENRY. YOU MADE IT."

"Yeah, I ... Is Phil here?"

"Of course," Rebecca says, "come in, come in. Philip will be so glad to know that you stopped by, just let me hunt him down."

People, food, drinks; lots and lots of each. The people, all except for Rebecca and Phil, talking to some guy I don't recognize on the other side of the crowded living room, I don't know. The food and drink, long silver trays loaded down with rows and rows of sushi and plenty of pretty little fishy things bundled up in seaweed dinner jackets, a glass of red wine or white wine or a bottle of Heineken in everyone's hand, are abundant and everywhere although it's after two in the morning and the party's presumably been going on for hours. There's jazz on the stereo, but not loud enough to listen to, only to barely register underneath the buzz of conversation floating above the guests.

"Oh, he's still talking to Nathan," Rebecca says. Turning to me, "Have you met Nathan yet?"

"Uh, no, I don't think so."

"But you know his book." It's not clear whether she's asking a question or issuing a threat.

"No, I don't —"

"*Nuon.*"

"No, I don't think I've —"

"Oh, you must have. It's the biggest-selling book in the history of Canadian poetry."

Just then, Phil and the biggest-selling poet in the history of Canadian poetry both burst out laughing, the latter putting his hand on Phil's shoulder to help steady himself. I can't actually hear them laugh above the chattering going on around me or tell what it is they're breaking up about, but every time one of them puts his wine glass to his mouth he ends up bringing it back down for fear of not being able to take a sip without having to spit it right back out.

"It's a book made up entirely of nouns," Rebecca says, watching her boyfriend and the best-selling poet finally get a drink in, each calm enough now to wipe his eyes with his fist. "It's quite ingenious, obviously, but I ask myself, why hadn't anyone else thought of doing it before? I mean, it's really such an elemental idea. But I guess that's what genius is, isn't it? Noticing what was there in front of everyone's nose all along."

I'm not sure if this is a question or not either, so I say the only sensible thing I can think of. "Is it okay if I grab a beer?"

"Oh, I'm sorry, of course, you know where the refrigerator is, help yourself, Henry. I'm afraid that with all the excitement this evening I haven't been the world's most attentive hostess." A man and a woman who wouldn't look out of place in a Gap ad except for the NO JUSTICE/NO PEACE buttons pinned to their sweaters dip their sushi into a bowl in the middle of one of the trays. Rebecca smiles at them. "Don't forget the pickled ginger," she says, pointing.

"It looks like you're doing just fine," I say, and head for the kitchen.

I get my beer, but only barely. The kitchen is just as congested as everywhere else, plus twice as loud and overheated, and I've got to say *Excuse me* four times just to make it to the refrigerator. I find a couple of empty feet of counter space near the sink and back myself in, take a long drink from my Heineken. On either side of me, two guys talking across me.

"You've got to apply."

"It sounds great."

"It *is* great. The foundation pays your airfare there and back, supplies the cabin and covers all of your utilities, and every day they drop off a little picnic basket with your lunch in it."

"Nice."

"Every day, there it is, waiting for you outside your door."

"Very nice."

Wine-sip pause.

"What were you working on when you were down there?"

"My novel."

"Right. The one about the Holocaust. What's it called again?"

"*Testament of Ash.*"

"Right. How's that going, anyway?"

"Amazing. You wouldn't believe how much writing you can get done when you don't have to worry about life's BS."

I spot Phil trying to push himself toward me through a bump of bodies, a roomful of floating, jabbering faces, but every other person stops him, wants to hug him or shake his hand or has something that he or she needs to pull him close to tell him. I meet him in the middle of the kitchen. No one tries to stop me on my way there.

"The Duke's closed," I say.

Phil's eyes cut from the crowd, connect with mine, but it takes him a moment to recognize who it is he's looking at, to shout, "Hey!" He puts his hand on my shoulder the same way the best-selling poet did on his. "When did you get here?"

"Just a few minutes ago. Didn't Rebecca tell you I was in here?"

"No, I just came in for a refill." He holds up his empty wine glass.

"The Duke's closed," I say again.

"What?"

A man with perfect hair and wearing too much cologne steps in front of me before I can answer, grabs Phil's hand. "Fantastic reading, Philip, and the book looks absolutely incredible," he says, tapping one of his jacket pockets.

"You're not going, are you?" Phil says. "Stay for one more drink."

"You know I'd love to, but I've got a shoot tomorrow morning at eight."

"Ouch."

"Yeah, but seriously, great book, and get your publicist to call me about what we were talking about."

"That would be great, Aaron, I'd really appreciate that."

Phil and Aaron shake hands one more time.

"Do you know Aaron?" Phil says.

I shake my head, run my arm across my forehead to mop up a line of sweat.

"Damn, I should have introduced you. He's a good guy to get to know. He's got his own book discussion show on A&E."

"We don't have cable."

"Right. Well, you don't have to subscribe to a channel to be on it. He could be useful when you publish your book. I'll make sure to bring up your name when I see him again."

"Great," I say, taking a drink. "What about the Duke."

"Right, right, you were saying. It's closed. Geez. That's too bad, I guess."

"It's too bad. You guess."

"Well, it's not exactly shocking news. That place is like a cemetery now. I bet you Sam got an offer he couldn't afford to turn down. Everywhere along Queen Street down that way is hot property these days. Who bought it?"

"I don't know."

"Did he say if it's going to be a restaurant or a clothing store or what?"

"I said I don't know."

I take another drink. Phil looks into his empty wine glass.

"Hey, where's Mary?" he says, looking up.

"Her parents'."

"Just visiting?"

"And bringing a bunch of stuff back for the house."

"Oh, yeah, how was the move? What's it like being king of your own castle?"

"We haven't moved yet."

"Why did I think you had?"

I wipe some more sweat from my face. "I don't know."

A trick of the hostess too quick for the human eye: Rebecca with her arm entangled with Phil's, there she wasn't and here she is. "Philip, Judith's leaving, I want you to come and say goodbye."

Talking to her but looking at me, "I want to give Henry a copy of the new book. Is the box of extra copies still in the bedroom?"

Rebecca tugs at his arm. "She's my editor, Philip, it's important, give it to him after you say goodbye, it'll only take a minute."

"So will this."

Tugging harder, "Philip ..."

"It's okay, go, go," I say, waving them away with my beer bottle. "Besides, aren't I supposed to buy a copy, isn't that the way this whole poetry business works?"

"See?" Rebecca says, smiling, looking at me for the first time.

"Henry doesn't have to pay for my books," Phil says.

Towing him away, "Henry's a big boy," Rebecca says. "Henry can do whatever Henry wants to do."

MARY SAID SHE WANTED me to get rid of the half-empty liquor bottles left in the kitchen cupboard anyway. Not much sense in taking them with us since I don't do high-octane anymore and Mary never really did, but it seemed like such a waste to just empty them down the drain. In a way, then, I'm not sucking on a pint of sour mash while Barry and I prowl the neighbourhood, I'm just putting the finishing touches on the packing, I'm just reducing, reusing, and recycling.

"Stay, Barry," I say, leaving him sitting behind on the sidewalk, looking both ways before I start my stalk of the water sprinkler doing its thing in the middle of the dark lawn. April showers bringing May flowers aren't enough for this guy, he just can't take the risk that the grass isn't going to be greener at 243 Geoffrey Avenue than anywhere else on the block this summer. Most nights, only old men conscientiously watering their driveways and sidewalks after dinner because a tidy home is a happy home make me want to pull out my blade and exact some slash and dash justice in the name of freshwater conservation. But tonight isn't most nights.

I wait for the sprinkler to fall the other way; crouch down, get on my mark, get out my knife. The sky dry for approximately the next fifteen seconds, I make my move, manage to saw through the hose — harder than you'd expect, like it's been double-dosed coated with green shellac — before getting too, too wet on the return shower. I pick up Barry's leash from the sidewalk and we're gone. Gone, but taking our time doing it. I tug the pint from my back pocket and have a nip. Always walk away like there's no reason to run, especially if there is.

The more Jack Daniels I drink, the more things I see that make me mad. A black Beemer with a licence plate that reads MY BMW. A mother skunk with two baby skunks trailing behind her across somebody's front yard looking to outwit starvation for one more night. Satellite dishes like cancer cells crawling up the sides of vine-covered, century-old homes. A squashed squirrel in the middle of the road whose insides have poured out of its mouth like paint squeezed out of one of the silver tubes in Mary's studio. The stubborn red light on the phone cradle staring me down when I'd come through the door, letting me know that Mary hadn't called.

Barry's barely keeping up, keeps pulling toward home, but this is my walk. As long as there's bourbon left in the bottle, nobody's safe tonight. I drag my house key along the side of a SUV without bothering to admire what kind of damage I've done, don't even remove the bottle from my lips. I put the key back in my pocket and lick a dribble of Jack off my chin with the tip of my tongue. Whoever invented whiskey wasn't fucking around. Probably the same guy who came up with God.

"Asshole, come back here!"

I don't need to turn around to know that whoever's yelling from the other end of the street is yelling at me. I pretend that I don't hear him, keep looking straight ahead, keep walking.

"Asshole with the dog, you're going to pay for what you just did to my car!"

I also don't need to turn around to hear the sound of the soles of his shoes slapping against the empty sidewalk. I stop and turn around anyway, see a guy in tiny wire-framed round glasses and wearing a red and black checkered housecoat charging my way, one hand holding onto the housecoat where it ties together to keep it from falling open, most of the rest of it flying behind him at his knees like a tartan cape. Suddenly he blows a shoe, stops, looks at the stranded sandal in the middle of the road, looks back at me. He pushes his glasses up his nose and then points at me with the same finger. "I saw what you did through my kitchen window."

I don't say anything, just look at the blown black plastic flip-flop like it's a loaded gun lying between us. The man is still pointing. "You're going to have to pay for what you did."

I yank Barry's leash and now we start running, run long enough that we hit an unlit back alley and make a sharp left. I lean up against somebody's garage door and listen to hear if the man retrieved his shoe and went home. Ten seconds later, the advance guard echo of both sandals pounding the pavement, and Barry and I are back on the move. We're close enough to home now to cut up the alley to Roncesvalles and then down to Parkway, but unless I'm lucky enough that this guy drops dead from a heart attack, I can't run the risk of having him find out where I live. Before I can figure out what to do, we're across the street from Sorauren Park.

The park is dark, only a couple of dim streetlights spreading a thin, yellow fog, the moon hiding behind a heavy sky full of mashed potato clouds. We walk toward the rear of the park, where it's even darker.

I hear the dog speeding toward us before I see him, which is more warning than Barry gets who growls and snorts and growls again only once the small dog has slammed to a stop less than a foot from his face. The other dog's little white tail is whipping back and forth like an out of control metronome, though, so Barry does the same, only slower. He lowers his head so that the two of them can touch noses.

"Omar! Come!"

And then the dog is gone again, shoots off back into the darkness. I hear twigs snapping underfoot, a "Heel, Omar," and then there she is, her dog walking right beside her.

"Beverly," I say.

She doesn't answer until Barry and her dog are sniffing each other hello again. "I'm impressed," she says. "You actually remembered my name."

I don't realize that I've taken the pint of Jack out of my back pocket until I'm unscrewing the cap. "Sorry," I say, shaking my head, putting the cap back on.

"Don't be sorry," she says, "just don't hold out on me. May I?"

"Sure," I say. I hand her the bottle.

She takes a drink, passes it back. "Omar and I don't usually have any company this late. Certainly not the sort furnishing their own refreshments."

"You come here a lot?"

"My God," she says, "that sounds like the world's absolute worst pick-up line."

"No, no, I just meant —"

"I know," she says, squeezing my hand, "I'm only having a bit of fun with you." She takes back the bottle. "I'm afraid that

I haven't been sleeping particularly well recently. And Omar is always game for a bit of a stroll, so ..." She shrugs. Hearing his name, Omar looks up at her for a moment before going back to sniffing the damp night grass. Barry is lying down with his head between his paws.

"You should be careful," I say. "It's kind of late to be walking around in a park by yourself."

"Yes, look at who you might run into, strange men brandishing bottles of spirits." My eyes are getting adjusted to the lack of light. I can see her brush some hair off her face.

"I'm strange, not dangerous, there's a difference. You should be careful."

"All right," she says, smiling. "Distinction made and point taken."

Barry yawns, sounds like he's swallowed a doggie dose of helium. We both laugh.

"Well, it looks like somebody's ready for bed, doesn't it?" she says. Beverly bends down and rubs Barry between the ears. Barry immediately flips over and offers up his belly. She rubs him up and down his stomach and chest until she hits his canine G-spot and his back right leg starts to twitch uncontrollably. "I'm sorry, sweetheart," she says, "but I'm afraid that that's all for now. I think that your father will have to finish the job at home."

Beverly stands up and pulls Omar's leash out of the back pocket of her jeans. She's wearing a clear plastic rain poncho over top of a white turtleneck sweater. "And where exactly is home," she says, clipping on the leash. "Perhaps we'll walk you if it's on our way."

Looking at the entrance to the park, scanning the street for any sign of an enraged man in his housecoat still on the prowl, "I think we're actually going to hang around for a bit," I say.

"In the rain?"

"It's not raining, is it?" I put out my hand like I'm asking her for some spare change. "I can't feel anything."

"I wouldn't be surprised, in your condition," she says, nodding toward the pint of Jack still in my hand.

"I —"

"I'm only joking again," she says, squeezing my hand again.

"I wasn't going to deny it. I was just going to say that it's been a long night."

"Is that why you don't want to go home?"

"Something like that."

Barry and Omar are both sitting up now, leashes on and ready for whatever's next.

A fat raindrop hits me square in the eye. I rub it. "It is raining," I say.

"Yes, and you're going to catch your death if you stay much longer in this park."

"I guess." I scan Sorauren Avenue again.

"Here's an idea. Why don't you and Barry walk Omar and me home, and then you and I can have a proper drink with a roof over our heads."

"Thanks, but ..."

"Oh, right, your wife. She'll probably be worrying where you are."

"No, she's, she's away. I just don't want to ... I don't want to put you out."

"Nonsense," she says. "Have a drink, and maybe by then you'll feel like going home. Besides, you were the one saying how dangerous it was for me to be out walking this late."

"That's true, but ..."

"I only live on the other side of the park. If you feel like passing on the drink once we get there, you can turn right around and come back here and commune with nature and your bottle all night if you like."

"You live over there?" I say.

"On Sterling, yes, why?"

"That's good, that actually works," I say. "Sure, we'll walk you home. I think we might take a rain check on the drink, though. C'mon, Bubs, let's go." As if on cue, Barry yawns again.

We both laugh. "Well, you might not be in need of a bit of a sit-down," she says, "but I'm fairly certain that I know someone who is."

III

WHEN I WOKE UP, her dog was sleeping between us and there was a red plastic bucket on the floor on my side of the bed. On the chance that I was only dreaming I closed my eyes then slowly reopened them, but all I got for my effort was a spark of throbbing pain that quickly ignited into an inferno of suffering inside my brain. I shut them again without much hope of things being any different next time.

I lie there beside a sleeping woman in her four-poster bed with her thin, naked back facing me, butterscotch shoulder blades like broken wings, just as naked myself underneath the blue silk sheets, and contemplated the delicate logic of destroying one's life. If the Duke had been open I wouldn't have ended up at Rebecca's condo trying to tell Phil about it being closed, wouldn't have ended up tromping up and down

Roncesvalles an hour and a half later looking for trouble. If the guy whose SUV I'd scraped had been in bed where he should have been instead of gawking out of his kitchen window I wouldn't have ended up as a fugitive in the park at four o'clock in the morning. If I'd gotten rid of the bottle of bourbon weeks ago like I'd intended to I wouldn't have ended up in the park at four o'clock in the morning drunk.

Oh, Mary, I thought, she means nothing to me.

When the deepest truth sounds the same as the cheapest cliché, you know you're in trouble.

But, really, it's not what it looks like, I can explain ...

Oh, Mary, I thought.

We finished my pint of Jack Daniels with her glasses and ice, switched to gin and tonics when the bottle was finally empty, and the rain outside came down and down. We could see it, thick liquid curtains of it hanging across the sky, from the living room where we drank and listened to her stereo, her dog and Barry both busy on the kitchen floor with fresh rawhide chew bones. Barry appreciated the bone but couldn't understand why he wasn't allowed to bring it into the living room where we were. "No, Barry," Beverly would say from the couch every time he'd try to sneak it past her, snapping her fingers and directing him back into the kitchen. Somebody else ordering your dog around is like somebody poking fun at your parents: it's all right when you do it, but ... But it was her house and her floors and her gin and tonics, and the rain outside kept coming down.

Me in an antique rocking chair not rocking by the stereo, she on the couch with her bare feet tucked underneath her, the tips of her exposed toes wiggling hello whenever she'd set down her drink on the glass coffee table or reach over to pick it up, we talked about what strangers talk about: how she was here in Canada as part of the first wave of British barristers setting up a Toronto office specializing in insurance defence litigation; what she thought of Canada so far; how she was having a hard time making it to the gym as much as she wanted to, what with the crazy hours she was keeping and her still trying to get used to being here. I told her the same things about me, the same things that don't matter to anyone but who they happen to happen to, and tried not to look at her toes.

"Do you like Miles Davis?" she said. She'd asked me if I'd heard the remastered version of *Kind of Blue* with two previously unreleased bonus tracks, and I'd said that I hadn't, which was true.

"Sure," I said, which was and wasn't. Miles Davis was jazz, and jazz to me had always been another language, something I could hear but could never really understand; at best, background noise, at worst, just noise.

Holding her drink to her lips with both hands, "Well, would you like to hear it?" she said.

"Sure," I said.

"You're a pretty easy fellow to please, aren't you?"

I looked at her toes and lifted my glass too fast; ice cubes collided with upper front teeth, gin and tonic splashed down the front of my shirt.

"Oh, dear," she said, setting her own drink down with a clink on the coffee table. "Let me rinse that out for you. You'll stain your — it's some sort of pirate shirt, isn't it?"

"Forget it," I said, taking another sip, this time hitting the target. "Let's hear some Miles."

It started with a kiss in the kitchen, more ice cubes needed and none frozen-through ready yet, and somehow this all very, very funny. Her perfume wasn't Mary's, and her bra fastened in the front, not in the back. There was a plush stuffed monkey lying on her bed, on his back, his head resting on the pillow, and I backhanded him to the floor as I fell to the bed on top of her.

She slid her fingers underneath my underwear and clawed at my ass with both hands, chewed at my neck. "Don't you like Mr. Geebers?" she said, lifting her mouth, trailing her tongue across my throat before taking another bite from the other side.

"Fuck Mr. Geebers," I said.

I grabbed both ends of the waist of her peach thong panties between pinched fingers and she lifted her legs high in the air, allowing me to more easily slide them off. The last thing I remember thinking before crawling between her thighs was, What kind of woman without a boyfriend wears peach thong panties to the park to walk her dog?

She had a pretty cunt. It was small and neatly trimmed and reddish brown, sort of the colour of Mr. Geebers. I felt a rumble in my gut but didn't stop what I was doing. I managed to get puke on only one of her kneecaps before I swung my head over the side of the bed.

"My God," I heard her say.

When I was finished, I rested my head on the bed and wiped my mouth on the blue duvet. The duvet matched the freshly painted blue walls. For the first time all night I felt happy. I didn't fuck her, I thought. Mary, listen, this is important, I didn't fuck her.

I started to laugh. I closed my eyes. I started to laugh harder.

"What are you laughing at," she said.

"I hate jazz," I said.

Grabbing a hold of the sheets and pulling them up to her armpits, "What?"

I started laughing again, but this time I made it to the bathroom.

MOVING SOUTH ON THE midnight Greyhound to Chatham — the 12:17, actually, with stops in Oakville, Brantford, and London along the way — my mind is back in Toronto, further proof that no matter where you end up, you're rarely ever there. The university kid next to me on the bus is slumped up against the window and snoring loudly with his mouth wide open, a balled-up jean-jacket a makeshift pillow cushioning his head, a copy of *Maxim* magazine resting on his chest, but I don't bother nudging him awake. Even if he's suffering a silent nightmare, there are far worse things than waking up and realizing that none of it was real.

Barry and I walked home from Beverly's through an obscenely beautiful early April morning — the ground under my feet in the park alive to my nose as only the still-damp earth after an all-night spring shower can be; a warm breeze blowing in from the direction of the empty baseball diamond an unwanted caress across my face. When I unlocked our door, the first thing I saw was the blinking red light at the base of the phone stand winking at me hello. Of course it was Mary. Who else could it have been?

Until I heard her voice, I wasn't too bad. If my body hadn't smelled like a counterfeit of some other woman's, my brain might have even believed it was only suffering the sort of cerebellum-corroding effect that comes from forgetting that 40% spirits rapidly consumed in extra-large quantities is a bet that no one can win. I punched in our phone code, pushed eleven to hear the one new message, and sat down on the arm of the chair that Barry was already curled up in. He looked happy to be home.

"Hi. It's me. Sorry I didn't call back before, but we left really, really early this morning and — oh, Hank, the snow was so beautiful today, I really wish you could have seen it. I know you don't like skiing, but I want you to come with me next time, just once, there was hardly anybody out there and it was just like miles and miles of pure white, it was so bright you had to wear sunglasses, you couldn't take them off. And then we drove into Blackcomb for dinner and — anyway, it's about — hold on, let me check, I'm leaning over the side of the couch to look — I'm watching TV downstairs but there's absolutely nothing on — oh, my God, that hurts so much, my God, I am so out of shape, the backs of my calves and my hamstrings are already killing me from today — it's about two-thirty our time, so I guess that means you're still at work, I guess I'm just talking to myself. It doesn't matter, I'll talk to you when I see you tomorrow. I just wanted to tell you that I'm looking forward to coming home and getting settled into our sweet little house and spending more time with you and the Bubs. And making our schedules work better together, even if they're not perfect. I love you, Hank. I love you a lot. I want you boys to take good care of each other until I get back tomorrow, okay? I love you both very much. I love you."

Some things you don't talk about, even with yourself. Especially with yourself. I don't remember the next five, ten, fifteen minutes very well except that I ended up on my knees with a handful of peanut butter dog biscuits from downstairs that I proceeded to feed to Barry, still sitting in the chair, one after the other. He seemed surprised every time I'd give him another treat, but by the time my hand was empty he didn't seem to believe it, kept sniffing my fingers and licking my palm.

"That's all there is," I said, pressing my forehead to his.

The kid on the bus sitting beside me has woken up. "Do you mind if I put on the light?" he says.

"Go ahead," I say.

He reaches up and clicks on the overhead light that shines a thin beam onto his magazine. I don't know what the article he's reading is about, the type is too small for me to read, but underneath a picture of some blonde model in a bathing suit and heels there's a block of larger letters that say "Show me a beautiful woman and I'll show you someone that somebody else is tired of fucking."

"You were snoring," I say.

"Pardon?" the kid says, looking up from his magazine.

"If you fall asleep and start snoring again, I'm going to wake you up."

THE BUS BRAKES TO a slow, sighing stop outside of the station, a one-room glass office sandwiched between a Zellers and a Payless shoe store, with barely enough room inside for a pop machine, a pay phone, and a single ticket booth. It's close enough to my parents' place that I could walk home in fifteen minutes, could use the spare house key I've got in my pocket to disappear for a few sweet amnesiac hours underneath the piled-high heavy blankets on the king-size bed downstairs without anyone even noticing that I'm there, but I head across the empty parking lot in the pre-dawn dark in the opposite direction. I'm going to have to be utterly exhausted to finally get some sleep, and right now I'm only unbearably weary. Besides, I haven't spoken to anyone since I talked to Mary after she got home from the airport, and I don't want the first person I do speak to to be my mum or my dad. The first thing they'll ask me after what I'm doing here is where is Mary.

By the time I get to Brad's parents' house half an hour later the sky is beginning to hatch; soft blues and pinks and yellows, birth colours of a brand new day. I kneel beside the basement window and knock twice, once, twice more, but the curtain stays shut. If he's in bed he likely hasn't been there for very long. I rap-rap, rap, rap-rap again, and this time the curtain pulls to the side. "Come round back," he says.

Brad meets me at the screen door with red eyes and dressed in the same terrycloth maroon bathrobe he's had since high school. Two decades of wash, rinse, and dry have softened it, permanently wrinkled it, made it, if anything, only more thickly thirsty looking.

"Hey," I say.

"Hey," Brad says. He rubs his hand across both eyes like he's trying to massage them awake. He drops his hand to his side, looks at me, yawns.

"Can I come in?" I say. "Or is there a cover charge now?"

"When did you get in?"

"I don't know, a half hour ago." I'm holding the screen door open with my shoulder, my hands in my pockets.

Brad nods, yawns again. He scratches his head. Thin patches of blond hair stick straight up all over the place. "When are you going back?"

"For Christ's sake, I don't know, a couple days, maybe less, maybe more." I'd arranged it with Sid a month ago to get a full week off work for the move. "Can I come in or not?"

"Come by Friday night. What a minute, that's tonight. Come by tonight. I'm not used to going to bed so early yet, I need some more Z's."

"You're working?"

Brad shrugs and almost smiles like I'd just asked him how far he'd gotten with Margaret Wilson at the post-football game bash at Jamie Dalzall's house. "I got my lift-truck license a couple months ago. I'm at Siemens in Tilbury four days a week right now."

"Shit, sorry." I shake my head, look at my shoes, look at Brad's bare feet.

"Don't sweat it," he says. "Can't you go to your parents' place?"

"Yeah."

"You've got a key, right? Cause if you don't, you can crash here until they're up if you're worried about waking them."

"No, I've got a key." Now I rub my eyes.

"So go home and sack out and come by tonight around nine. I got some killer weed from this guy at work, and you won't believe the bootlegs I've picked up since the last time you were here. Unbefuckinglievable."

"Great," I say, but I don't move.

"What's wrong? How come you don't want to go home?"

"Nothing's wrong," I say. "I'm going home right now."

I WAS WAITING FOR her by the front door like a cop for a thief. Her plane was due in Toronto at 8:22 a.m. our time, so I'd set my alarm for seven. I shouldn't have bothered. The last time I remember looking at the clock was at around four, and I woke up just after dawn. I'd walked Barry and showered and shaved and was sitting in front of the upstairs window by half-past six.

I heard Mary's taxi arrive, stop, and drive away down the alley before I saw the backyard gate open and her come through it. When she saw me see her, she smiled a shy lover's next-morning smile and I thought I was going to vomit. Her hands were full, a piece of luggage in each plus a cream-coloured paper shopping bag, so I got up and let her in.

"Hi," she said.

"Hi."

By the time she set down her bags and gave late-waking Barry the rubs and hugs he demanded and deserved, the only thing left to do was for her to ask me what was wrong and me to tell her. The autopsy of our love in one hundred words or less. She sat down. I stayed standing.

"You betrayed me?" she said.

She could have been asking me if she'd really heard me right, if I'd really just said that I'd traded the down-payment on our new home for a copy of last Thursday's newspaper and a tennis racket without any strings in it. Barry had fallen asleep with his chin resting on one of her shoes.

"I betrayed both of us," I said.

She took a moment before she answered.

"No, Hank, you betrayed me. You, you just made a fool of."

IT'S NOT QUITE SEVEN o'clock in the morning and my mother is scrubbing the kitchen sink. On the radio, Anne Murray wants to know if she can have this dance for the rest of her life.

I take my key out of the door.

"What's this?" my mother says.

"Nothing. I just thought I'd come home for awhile. Is that all right?"

"Of course it's all right." The SOS pad in her hand is cobalt blue, looks like a fat, foamy diamond. "Where's Mary?"

I put the key back in my pocket. "Mary stayed home."

"Well, I can see that, Henry. Why didn't she and Barry come with you?"

"She's at home taking care of some things."

"What kinds of things? Things for the move, you mean?"

"Yeah, things for the move."

"Why aren't you helping her?"

"It's not worth going into, believe me. Don't worry, everything's under control." I kiss her on the cheek, inhale her perfume of always, Bounty clothes softener and Nabob coffee. "I'm going downstairs," I say.

"Not to bed?"

"I need to get some sleep. Is the bed still made up from the last time we were here?"

"Of course not, I remade it with fresh sheets right after you left. What time do you want me to get you up?"

"Just let me sleep," I say.

"If you sleep all day, you know you'll never get to sleep tonight."

"Just let me sleep," I say. "I'll wake up whenever I wake up."

HAPPY DAYS: SOMETHING'S BROKEN so my father has something
to fix. Evenings are okay, there's usually a hockey game or a
baseball game or a football game on TV, but unless the washing machine is making a funny noise or the eavestroughs need
cleaning out or the toilet in the downstairs bathroom won't
stop running, chances are he'll eventually start poking around
in the old lady's business, which will only result in her ending
up being just as bored and restless as him. Thankfully, Mum
doesn't have to worry about sharing the excitement of cleaning out the refrigerator of any past-due-date food stuffs with
anyone else today, the general consensus being that the vacuum
cleaner just doesn't have quite the sucking power it used to.

"Do you know what needle-nose pliers look like?" my dad
says.

"Yeah." The vacuum cleaner is on its back on the workbench downstairs, its grey plastic casement popped up like the
hood of a car.

"Well, give them to me then. This son of a bitch of a wire
doesn't want to come through, and if I'm going to thread this
other bastard back in there then it's going to have to go."

I hand him the pliers.

I'm pretty sure that I never intended to end up as hopeless
around the house as I am, but either way, it worked. I was
seventeen when the old man finally gave up on trying to
teach me how to mow the lawn properly. First the vertical cut,
then the horizontal, and every ten minutes or so be sure to
remember to empty the side pouch of grass clippings into an
extra-strength black garbage bag. But less than razor-straight

lines; occasional embarrassing tufts of uncut grass; forgetting to empty out the pouch and clogging up the side blower: somehow I always ended up not quite making the mulching grade. I guess I was supposed to feel embarrassed or maybe even angry at being denied the opportunity to illustrate what a crackerjack gardener I could be if only I set my mind to it and applied myself, but relief was about as close to feeling anything as I got. Likewise when, not long after, I lost my job as my dad's car-repair assistant and number-one house painting helper.

"C'mon, you son of a bitch, get out of there." He's got both hands inside the vacuum cleaner, looks as if he's trying to coax an obstinate baby out of an artificial birth canal. "Bring that light down a little closer to the right. Not that far. About an inch to the left. There, keep it there." There are certain tasks for which even the admittedly useless are qualified to perform. Holding the flashlight for the person who knows what he's doing is one of them.

His nose no more than six inches from the vacuum cleaner, "You want to tell me what's going on at home?" he says.

"What do you mean, in Toronto?"

"That's the only home you've got, isn't it?"

"Nothing's going on. Like I told Mum, we've just been stressed out with getting everything ready for the move and we both just thought it'd be a good idea to give each other some space before moving day. Things'll probably get pretty crazy after that."

"Bastard, get back here." His face even closer to the machine now, his busy hands buried still deeper inside, this time he looks like he's tying to remove somebody's bum liver that doesn't want to let go. "Except your moving day is today."

"No, it's next week," I say.

"That's not what you told me two weeks ago."

"No, it's next week."

Not moving his head or his hands, only his eyes, "Listen, pal, I *know*. You told me it was today."

"Well, if I did, I gave you the wrong date then."

"Uh huh." He finally gets the pliers around the wire he wants and slowly brings it to the surface. "Keep that light where you had it, you're all over the place now."

"I moved it half an inch."

"Well don't move it at all, I've almost got this bastard." He tugs and snips and sets down the pliers on the bench and quickly splices. "All right, let's see what she can do." He snaps shut the cover and flips the machine over and plugs it in and clicks on the power switch. He holds the nozzle to his palm. The vacuum cleaner keeps attempting to suck up his hand and he keeps pulling it away then letting it get sucked back.

Over the roar, "It's none of my business," he says, "but if you've got things to take care of, you should be there doing them, not here."

"If I knew coming home was going to be such a problem, I wouldn't have bothered."

"Don't be stupid. I'm just thinking of Mary."

"What about Mary?" I shout, just as he flicks off the switch. The basement is quiet again. I can hear the ticking second hand of the SIEMENS clock hanging over the workbench.

"You'd know better than me. I'm just saying don't leave things until they're too late." He unplugs the vacuum cleaner from the wall and lifts it to the floor. The mini-gym he'd bought himself for Christmas three years ago is covered in jackets and hats and baseball caps. He plucks a blue toque from one of the arms of the bench press.

"Do you need a hat?" he says.

"Not really, no."

"Here, take this one."

It's the cloth watch cap he used to wear when I was a kid, when he'd keep the sidewalks clean or shovel out the end of the driveway when the snowplow would block it off with a barricade of slush and dirty snow. I try it on. It feels as if I'm wearing a warm shield. It feels good.

"Don't you need it anymore?" I say.

"We don't get snow around here like we used to. The winters aren't the same anymore."

"Yeah, but you might need it."

"Take it," he says.

"Maybe I'll take it in the fall."

"Take it now."

My dad pulls the vacuum cleaner into its spot in the corner. I rub my head through my new hat.

"You know," I say, "you really don't know what you're talking about. About Mary and me, I mean."

"Whatever you say," my dad says. "And like I said before, it's not any of my business."

IT WASN'T MY FAULT; I wanted to be there, I wanted to help. All right, it was my fault. But I still wanted to be there. Insisted on it, actually.

"What do you want me to do, just go away?" I said.

"I really don't care what you do," Mary said. "Just don't get in the way tomorrow when the movers get here."

"How is me helping us move getting in the way? Look, I know things are ... but be reasonable about this."

"I'm serious, Hank, stay out of our way." Her unpacked bags were still where she'd set them down on the floor to greet Barry hours before, but we weren't talking about me or her or us or the other her anymore. It didn't seem like it, anyway.

"C'mon, you need my help, you can't do this alone."

"Yes, I can," Mary said, looking up from the cardboard box she was retaping, one of several I'd been responsible for packing while she was away. "And do you know what else? You don't deserve to be here tomorrow, Hank. You don't deserve to get to help."

I said something else — I said a lot else — but I can't remember what.

"WELL, WHAT DO YOU think?"

"Sounds good," I say.

"I checked it all out on-line. I can catch the afternoon train out of Chatham after work on Friday and come back home on the evening one out of Toronto on Sunday. Plus, if I buy my ticket two weeks in advance I get can get forty percent off."

"Sounds great."

Brad's lying lengthwise on his bed with all of his pillows piled up and jammed behind his back and his head. There's a bottle of Blue between his legs and an ashtray balanced on one of his thick thighs. The curly tips of his hair are still wet, he must have got out of the shower just before I showed up.

"So what do you say?" he says. "I can check out your new digs and hit some of the record stores downtown and you can finally take me to the Duke. I can't wait to see that place. And it'll be cool to hang out with Mary on her own turf for a change."

The handful of times Brad's visited me in Toronto were all pre-Mary. Now that he's forklift flush, though, a big screen TV and a vibrating recliner — the kind you see advertised on television at four in the morning for people with chronic back problems and creaky retirees ready to get a piece of the good life — aren't the only signs that things are looking up. Brad's been talking about coming and seeing me for years. Apparently, plenty of disposable income is only one of the benefits of not sitting around all day in your parents' basement telling yourself that you're really going to get your shit together one of these days.

"It sounds great," I say. "Really. I'm just, I'm just bagged, that's all."

"Didn't you crash this morning?"

"Yeah."

"Not like sleeping in your own bed, though, is it?"

I drink from my beer, tilt it back until it's empty. "More than you know," I say. Brad takes my cue and guzzles from his bottle too. I lean back in the recliner and shut my eyes. He's got the Yardbirds in the CD player, Jimmy Page's first band.

"Hey," I say, opening my eyes. "Remember trying to dance to 'Stairway to Heaven'?"

"The last song of the night."

"It was okay for the first three or four minutes, until it started to pick up."

"Until the drums kicked in." Brad goes to the bar fridge to get us two more Blue. He turns up the stereo, but not too loud. We're only on our third beer.

"But even that was okay, even then it was still ..."

Squatting at the fridge, "You could still slow dance to it," he says.

"Right, you could still dance to it. But it was awkward. Here you were trying to get as close as possible to the girl you're dancing with, and John Bonham's laying down this big fat Bonzo drum beat. You couldn't help moving faster than you wanted to. Neither of you could."

Brad hands me my beer. Tonight's the first alcohol I've had since the gin and tonics at Beverly's house. The first sip tasted like treason. After that, it was just Labbat Blue. I twist off the cap.

"And then —" I pause, take a drink.

"The guitar solo," Brad says.

Struggling to swallow, "The fucking guitar solo!" I say. "Here's Jimmy Page, just wailing, just blasting away on his double-neck Fender, and then Bonham kicks in with all these huge rolls and fills and monster cymbal smashes, and then there you are, your damp hand still on the small of her back, the two of you rocking back and forth by now like a buoy in a fucking hurricane, and even though the song is unbelievably lame, all you want to do is push her away and drop your hands and —"

Brad's face lights up; ten wiggling fingers mime a blistering guitar solo.

"Exactly," I say, shaking my finger at him, "exactly. You just, you just want to ... go."

And we do, to "Stroll On," the Yardbirds' absolutely smoking rip-off rewrite of the Johnny Burnett Trio's "Train Kept A-Rollin'," each of us picking and plucking and fretboard slithering until both the song and the CD arrive at their impossible end. We pick up our beers in silence, drink from them standing up.

"But nobody did, though," Brad says.

"No."

"Everybody wanted to, but nobody ever did."

MY PARENTS' TELEPHONE IS driving me crazy, won't leave me alone, hasn't rung the entire time I've been here. No, wait a minute, it did ring once, somebody calling during dinner last night wanting to know if my mother would consider changing long distance companies. Anyway, it wasn't Mary.

"Let's get going here," my dad says, several Pro-Line betting tickets lined up side-by-side in a neat row across the breakfast nook counter. "I want to get these in to the store before suppertime. Colorado, they've got to beat Pittsburgh tonight, don't they? They're only paying one and a half to win, but that could be our lock pick."

He's sitting at the counter on a wooden stool perched over his tickets, my mother at the kitchen table thumbing through today's *Chatham Daily News*. She skims the headlines but reads most of the ads. The paper's on the front doorstep by four-fifteen and in a cardboard box on the garage floor for recycling by quarter-to-five, when she starts to make dinner. CFCO, dim but deliberate in the background — in this case, "The Wreck of the Edmund Fitzgerald" — doesn't disturb her concentration.

"I guess," I say. I'm sitting a few feet away in the living room, in my mother's easy chair, facing the TV. The television isn't on.

"Don't guess," my dad says, "you're not helping me by guessing. What about a tie? That pays three. Do you think they can get a tie?"

He's trying his best to distract me, even if he doesn't know from what, which means that I should probably meet him halfway and at least try to try to be interested. Except that the last thing you feel like doing when you're low is try. When you're low, except for thinking about the thing you're low about, what energy you've got left over goes into thinking about things like all of the thousands of times you've got left in your life to brush your teeth, to even out your sideburns when you're shaving, to be put on hold by the bank only to get cut off before you're told what you don't really want to hear to begin with.

"They could," I say. "Or the Penguins could upset them. What does that pay?"

"Pittsburgh's not going to beat Colorado. Christ, they're second from the bottom overall and the Avalanche is first in the west."

"Even the worst teams have to win once in awhile."

"Yeah, well, it isn't going to happen tonight."

"Your batteries are on sale," my mother says from the table. My father looks up. "What kind?"

"Nine volt, double A, triple A."

In the event of a natural disaster or a nuclear attack, the Roberts residence will not lack for fresh batteries. Nor for cases of Diet Pepsi, three-packs of grey work socks, or individual cans of WD-40. My mother does her part, lets the old man know whenever somebody's running a special on one of life's essentials. Mary's parents go skiing and play doubles tennis, but my mum and dad know when it's time to move on a limited time pop sale at Zellers.

"Where at," he says. "BiWay?"

"Wal-Mart."

"Until when?"

"Monday."

"That only gives me two days, I better get over there today."
To me, "Let's get one more here, I can drop this thing off on

the way over. How about Detroit and St. Louis?" It's a trick question. No matter what the odds, you never bet against the Red Wings.

"What are they paying?"

"Only 175."

"But they're at home, though."

"Yep."

"I'd take Detroit."

He puts pencil to paper, shades in the box. "That's what I'd do, too."

The phone shrieks. Although it's only a few feet down the counter from the old man, my mum pushes herself up from the table and limps over and picks it up on the third ring.

"Hello." My mother always answers the phone like she's expecting a call from a kidnapper with his ransom demand. Her voice lightens, lifts, when she hears who's on the other end.

"Well, hello, stranger, we were wondering how you were. Mr. Secret here just grunts when I ask him how things are with you ... Oh, I'm fine ... No, no more than usual, a little sore, I'll live. We missed you this time ... Oh, I know, you're busy. All ready for your move, are you?"

My heart changes gears, downshifts to third, picks up the pace. I can feel my palms go sweaty, the blood drain from my head. I don't know whether I'm excited or scared. It's probably fifty-fifty.

"Okay, little girl," my mum says, "I'll put him on, you take care." I'm standing right beside her now, but she mouths the words *It's Mary* to me as she hands over the receiver. I press the plastic to my face. It's warm from being next to my mother's.

"Hello," I say.

"Hank, something's wrong with Barry."

I turn my back to my parents. "What do you mean?"

"He doesn't want to go for his walk, he's hardly eating, and his nose is as dry as a bone."

"He's probably just freaking out because of the move. Dogs hate to have their routines upset." I put the phone to my other ear. "How did it go?" I whisper.

"Fine. We're here, it went fine. But I'm worried."

"He's most likely just upset because of all the excitement. And me not being around right now probably doesn't help, either."

"I've seen him upset, Hank, he's not upset, there's something wrong."

"Okay, okay. Look, I'm sure everything's fine, but just to be on the safe side and to make you feel better, make an appointment at the vet. Their number is on their magnet on the fridge. I guess we packed that up, though, didn't we?"

"I already called them. They got us in today at five-thirty, the earliest they could."

"Good. You'll see. He's fine, don't worry. Remember when he ate that plate of chocolate-chip cookies you brought home from work last Christmas? He's got a stomach of steel, he's Super Barry, he's indestructible." I don't hear anything on the other end. "Are you okay?" I whisper.

"I want you to come home," she says. "I want you to come home tonight."

If only the liquor store sold something that could make you feel as good as I feel right now. "Do I still have a family to come home to?" I say.

"Don't push it," Mary says. "Just get here as soon as you can."

I'M NOT SO BAD.

I did bad, but I'm not so bad.

I don't pretend to like rap. I've never been able to finish a Margaret Atwood novel. Every Christmas, in lieu of gifts, I cut cheques in our names for the Ontario S.P.C.A. and the Toronto Humane Society. I can take a joke. I knew the Ramones were the real deal the first time I heard them. Ditto for Howlin' Wolf, Gene Clark, and Gram Parsons. I own a 1932 Oxford University edition of Bertrand Russell and A.N. Whitehead's *Principia Mathematica* that I'll never read and couldn't if I wanted to, but let's just see someone try to take it from me. I'll eat pickled eggs directly out of the jar if that's what the situation calls for. I understand the idea behind Kant's categorical imperative and see his point. I've never owned an album by Journey, Styx, or REO Speedwagon. I know the location of every above-average jukebox in the greater metropolitan Toronto area. I don't believe that Jesus died for my sins, that the mountain came to Muhammad, or that the Buddha was anywhere near as cool a customer as he led people to believe. I do believe in the existence of the perfect pop song. I've been a vegetarian for nearly a decade but fully realize the appeal of Sloppy Joe's. I'm glad I can't even begin to comprehend how Carson McCullers managed to write *The Heart is a Lonely Hunter* at the age of twenty-two. I've never been able to tell north from south or east from west but it's never stopped me from getting where I've needed to go. I've read the classics and don't go around talking about it. I've never watched Janis Joplin's performance of "Ball and Chain" at the Monterey Pop Festival and not gotten goosebumps up and down both forearms. I hold the following truths to be self-evident: that marijuana should be legalized; that homosexuals have the right to marry; that four-on-four hockey is the only sensible way of unclogging the neutral zone. I stop to pet strange dogs. I don't know why rainbows happen, how the Internet works, or what keeps jet planes in the sky, and have absolutely no interest in having any of them explained to me. I'm not opposed to knowing who wrote the book of love. No one can convince me that one-hundred-dollar haircuts aren't immoral. I own the first five Elton John albums and, for what they are, I stand behind them all. I don't need subtitles to enjoy softcore porn. I don't get opera, and feel no compulsion to try. Mary loves me.

Fuck if I know why, but Mary loves me.

"Brantford is next," the bus driver announces over the intercom. "Brantford in five minutes."

Only one more hour. I'm almost there.

I DON'T HAVE A key to my own house so I ring the bell. Somewhere inside, Barry barks, and I know that he's all right. I can see the skyscraper silhouettes of boxes stacked upon boxes through the closed blind hanging in the front window. I'm standing on my own front porch looking into my own living room and I can hear my wife and my dog coming down the stairs to let me in. No one deserves to be this happy — I don't deserve to be this happy — but thankfully deserving something doesn't always have a lot to do with getting it.

"Hi, guys," I say. I squat down and let Barry kiss me; it seems like the safer bet. Mary stands there with her arms crossed but can't help smiling. I know it's because Barry's licking my face and wagging his tail and going around and around in circles and looking like anything but a dog on his last four legs, but adulterers can't be choosers. I stand up, take a look around.

"Wow," I say. Mary leans back, an elbow on the end of the banister, and joins me, surveys her hard work. She's wearing her oldest, most faded jeans, and a grey sweatshirt, no shoes or socks. Her hair is tied up in a single fat bob.

"There's still some stuff left in the backyard," she says. "The lawn chairs and the Hibachi and our rake and some other stuff."

"I'll go get them tomorrow," I say, too quickly, too confidently, I know, for someone who feels lucky just to be standing inside the front door. But before I can backpedal:

"Go before noon," Mary says. "The new people aren't supposed to be there until two or three."

I nod, look down at Barry lying with his head resting between his paws, search for something to say before Mary can change her mind and decide that I'm not worthy of hauling home our torn lawn chairs and rusty tools after all. "How did it go at the vet?" I say. "Everything check out okay?"

"Let's sit down in the kitchen," she says. I push my bag into the living room with my foot and follow her down the hallway. Barry, his nails clicking on the hardwood floor, follows me.

The kitchen is in the same state as the living room, boxes and more boxes, most of them still unpacked. But Mary's made sure that everything that's supposed to be here is here, the kitchen table and chairs and the microwave oven already staking out their rightful places. We manoeuver our way to the table through the cardboard labyrinth and sit down.

"You did great," I say.

Mary works a fingernail underneath a strip of tape holding shut a small box marked FRAGILE in her own handwriting. "I know it doesn't look like I've done much, but ..."

"It does, it looks like you've done a lot. I can tell. I appreciate it. Thanks."

She slides her fingernail along the length of the box top; when she gets to the end, tears the tape free. "The movers you got were good," she says, rolling it into a sticky plastic ball. "You did a good job picking them out."

"It wasn't that hard. I just called the cheapest one with the biggest ad in the Yellow Pages."

We both smile, at each other. Both of us look down.

Mary arcs her hand a couple of times like she's going to attempt a basketball shot with the tape, but there's nowhere to toss it, so she sets it down on the table instead.

"They think Barry might have cancer," she says.

A beat of silence, two, before I speak. "Not those lumps," I say. "Those aren't cancerous. I told you, the vet told me, they're —"

"Liponas. No, not those. Those are still just fatty deposits." Mary pulls her chair closer to the table, rests both hands face down on top. "There's another lump now, a different one, a hard one, one that doesn't move around. That's the one they think might be cancerous."

I take another moment. "Where?" I say. "Where is this hard one?" Standing up, "Barry, come here. Show it to me," I say to Mary. "I want to see it for myself. Barry, come here *now*."

Mary stands up. "Don't yell, Hank, he's coming. He's lying right in the doorway, he's just a little slow."

"He wasn't slow when I came home," I say. "He looked all right then."

Barry finds us through the maze of cardboard, sits down in front of me, wags his tail likes he's doing double-duty sweeping the floor.

"That's because he was so excited to see his dad," Mary says, more to him than to me, laying down long, smooth strokes from his almost invisible eyelashes to the crown of his head. "Weren't you, sweetest Barry Boy?" Barry closes his eyes and lifts his nose; Mary gently scrubs him underneath his chin. I stand there, watch her rub him. His eyes stay shut.

"Come here," Mary says without stopping, without looking at me. I bend over like she is. "Put your hand where mine is." Still massaging Barry's chin, she places her other hand halfway down the right side of his ribs, closer to the bottom than the middle of his torso. I do like she says, and she slowly withdraws her hand. She lightly presses my fingers to Barry's flesh. "Feel it?" she says.

It isn't like his other lumps; this one is tiny and hard, like an acorn, like it's a part of the bone that it's attached to. "I feel it," I say.

"Okay, let it be now," Mary says. I keep my hand where it is. "Hank."

I straighten up. Mary pulls a dog biscuit out of her jeans pocket and offers it to Barry. He sniffs it, then slides to the linoleum floor, lazily licks his coat. Mary puts the treat back in her pocket. We sit back down at the kitchen table. I don't say anything, so Mary does.

"Because of the way he's been acting lately and the way the lump feels, they used a needle to take out a few cells so that they could test them. If they're abnormal, then they do a biopsy. We should know by Thursday at the latest."

"If it's cancer and they cut it out, though, then it's gone, right? He'll be all right then."

"If that's the only tumour," Mary says. "There could be ones that we can't see yet."

"How do we know if they're there if we can't see them?"

"If it's what they call a high-grade or aggressive tumour, the tests should show it."

We both look at Barry. Finished cleaning himself, he's already asleep, or at least his eyes are closed.

"Why didn't I notice anything," I say.

"I didn't notice anything either until yesterday."

"But I was here, you were gone. I should have noticed."

"The vet said it might have been there for a month or even two."

"He told us to keep an eye out, he told us to watch out for lumps that —"

"— I know," she says. "I know. We should have caught it. But I've already beat myself up about it, so don't bother, I've done enough for both of us."

"And the other things, not acting normal, not eating as much, not wanting to walk as far ..."

Neither of us speaks. Eventually, "Maybe it's no wonder we didn't notice," Mary says. "Things haven't been exactly normal for anyone around here recently."

"They should have been, though," I say. "They shouldn't have been like they were."

Mary picks up the ball of tape from the table and squeezes it a couple of times, puts it back down.

"Look," she says, "let's just be glad we noticed what we did when we did and hope that the biopsy comes back negative. And if it doesn't, let's hope that they get all there is."

"And what if they don't?"

"Well, then we'll deal with that too."

Barry snores. I smile. Mary smiles.

"Since when did you get so brave?" I say.

"I don't have any choice," she says. "And neither do you."

HOME HARDWARE SMELLS LIKE everything's going to be all right. Yards and yards of waxy yellow rope ready to be cut to any length you want; clear plastic drawers overloaded with shiny screws and nails of every imaginable size and shape; cans of paint, bags of lawn seed, boxes of light bulbs big and small. I came in for a bottle of Murphy's Soap and a twelve-foot extension cord and leave with four full plastic bags and a VISA receipt for $107.56. I've got two arms, though, so I'll drop by the old place on the way home and grab at least the shovel and the rake. It's been less than seventy-two hours and we're already calling 81 Parkway the old place.

Old doesn't always equal *over*, though. *Over* takes time and talking. And how do you talk about something when there's really nothing to say but you can't not talk about it; that needs to be talked about if there's ever going to come a time when there's no reason left to talk? You talk about it by talking about something else until you end up talking about it.

"Have you seen my Red Wings hat?" I'll say. "We packed it, right?"

"Maybe you left it at your friend's house," Mary will say.

"Who?"

A look — a long look — and I'll know who my friend is. Isn't.

"She wasn't a friend," I'll say.

"Oh, yeah? What was she then?"

"A mistake."

"You obviously didn't think that the night you went home with her."

"I told you, I wasn't thinking anything, that was the problem."

"The problem will be that if you screw around on me again you'll be looking for a new place to live."

"I wouldn't. I won't."

Without looking at me, "Your hat's in one of the boxes in the upstairs hallway."

"Oh. Great. Thanks"

"Bring the whole box with you when you come down. I want to get that hallway emptied out so I can get to my studio without worrying about breaking my neck."

"Sure."

I turn left at our old street, all four yellow Home Hardware bags swinging in rhythm at my sides.

The downside of the warmer weather — more people clogging the sidewalks, bad music blaring from the open windows of the cars on the road, longer lines at the cash registers — hasn't outweighed the upside of spring's soft surprise yet. Opening up the front door in the morning and bracing yourself for what isn't there anymore is still worth the price of too many people too much everywhere. A program I saw on TVO the other night said that the population of planet earth is increasing by approximately 13 million human beings per year and that we're quickly running out of food, water, clean air, and places for them to live.

But Mary and I are talking — we're not telling each other anything that the other one doesn't already know, but we're talking — and the box of steel wool I bought came with a peel-off coupon for seventy-five cents and the sun on my face as I walk down Parkway Avenue is like easing into a hot bath on a howling cold day.

Come on, apocalypse, bring it on, let's see what you've got.

"OKAY, THEN," I SAY.

"Okay," Mary says. "Bye."

I stay standing where I am, one foot on the bottom step, the other on the sidewalk. Mary's on the porch cutting up empty cardboard boxes with a yellow X-ACTO knife; every time she's done slicing one open she crushes it flat with her foot and adds it to the growing pile. Barry is stretched out beside her. It's early evening, around six-thirty, daylight's last orange decaying, and whenever the sun slides a few inches to the right across the wooden slats of the porch Barry moves with it. When he's sleeping, it's easy to believe that it's all been one great big mistake, that the vet's going to call tomorrow and tell us that Barry caught some sort of stupid virus and that there's a pill he can take in order to get better and that before we know it he'll be banging his food dish around when it's five minutes past his supper time and bugging us to take him for his walk when neither of us feels like it.

"I'll see you when I get home," I say. My time off is over, tonight's my first night back on the door. Mary's still got another week's holiday left.

Stamping around the perimeter of a partially collapsed box, "Okay," she says.

"I'm coming home right after work."

"Okay."

"Okay, see you then."

"Bye."

"Bye."

I suppose I could leap up the steps and take her by surprise, make happen the kiss that hasn't happened since she's been back, but it's not my kiss to steal, only hers to give. What needs to happen will happen when it happens. When she says so. Or does so. Or ... God, I want to kiss Mary. No. I want Mary to kiss me.

I step up, reach up and pet Barry goodbye. "Take it easy, old boy." His fur that's in the direct sunlight is warm, almost hot. His eyes stay shut.

"Okay, bye," I say.

"Bye."

When I get to the Gladstone there are two guys camped out front on the sidewalk sharing a litre bottle of Maximum Bull malt liquor. They're both white and stringy and dirty. One of them is wearing a red bandana, the other a filthy Blue Jays World Series Champion 1992 baseball cap and a matching blue fanny pack sagging around his waist. The one in the hat springs to his feet when he sees me coming.

"Hey, bro, want to buy a stereo?" I stop walking; he's standing directly in front of me.

"I'm okay," I say.

"No, really, check it out, I've got what it's all about right here." He unzips the fanny pack and produces what looks to be a paper wad of instructions and a warranty still tucked away in an unopened clear plastic pouch. "It's a good one, bro, check it out, two hundred bucks, can't beat it."

"No, I'm okay," I say, stepping around him. I open the door of the Gladstone. *Asshole*, I hear, as it shuts behind me.

Not much has changed in the week that I've been gone.

"You missed it, Big Guy," Bob says. "Saturday night, some art college threw some kind of graduation party, took over half the room, I swear. And guess what? They were *all* girls, all except some limp-wristed Nancy boys, maybe five of them, ten at the most. Christ, you wouldn't believe it. You've never seen so many sweet young things in your entire life."

"Really," I say.

"Oh, yeah, you really missed it, you really should have been here."

Later, while I'm helping Bob put out the songbooks and little yellow pencils and slips of blank paper, I see Sid through the doorway at his desk motion me over with a single, gnarled finger. He's wearing the same brown carpet slippers and white knit cardigan he had on the day he hired me. His feet are up on the desk, the racing form on his lap.

"We're going to stay open until two from now on," he says. "That okay with you?"

"Every night?" I say. One more hour of Bob, of blaring bad singing, of getting home even later than I already do.

"No, no. Just the karaoke nights, the nights you work. Is that a problem?"

"No," I say. "It's not a problem."

By the end of the night, by the time Bob announces the return of Hank the Doorman, I haven't had my usual cold medicine and black coffee pick-me-up, hadn't even realized until then that my box of Sudafed was in my army jacket at home. I tell myself on the jog up the stairs to the stage that I don't need it, that it's always just been about the music.

I keep my eyes closed while I sing. At some point, a loud cheer, and I open them, see the backs of a roomful of heads; that, and three girls standing on top of one of the tables at the rear of the room with their shirts pulled up to their armpits. The audience roars.

I lean into the chorus, but no one's listening, everyone's looking the other way.

IT'S A NICE NIGHT, I thought I'd walk.

At the corner of Queen and Roncesvalles where there used to be a youth hostel there's now a McDonald's. I honestly don't remember seeing it before, but now that it's there, I can't imagine anything else in its place. I'm lacking ammunition and my four-legged running partner is out of action on the sidelines, but spray paint wouldn't do the job I've got in mind anyway. Everything's closed, the McWorld is deep asleep, all the Happy Meals have been served and swallowed, so I get a four-step start at the curb and deliver my best kung-fu kick to the glass door.

I mean: to what looked like a glass door. Picking myself up off the sidewalk, ten fingers massaging my tender tailbone, it's better to have fought the power and lost then never to have ...

Jesus Christ, my ass hurts.

Ten minutes later, on the front lawn of a house a few doors
down from where Roncesvalles meets Fern Avenue, street-
light-lit like two actors alone on a grassy stage, there's a woman
and a Dalmatian that's missing its back right leg. I feel like
someone or something has knocked the air out of me, like
what it felt like when you were a kid playing road hockey
and you'd get hit square in the stomach with an errant elbow
during a goal-mouth scramble and you'd drop your stick and
couldn't move or breathe or even tell anyone you couldn't
breathe. I don't want to look at the dog, but I can't stop myself.

The woman smiles at me, says hello — it's two o'clock in
the morning, we're the only ones around — and rolls a small
red rubber ball underhand halfway across the lawn. The
Dalmatian takes off after it just like a dog taking off after a ball.
He gets to it before it stops rolling, snaps it up with his mouth,
and trots back to where the woman is standing, drops it at her
feet. He crouches low, waits for her to toss it a second time,
eyes never leaving the ball.

I can feel myself breathe again, I can feel my mouth smile.
Hope is a three-legged dog chasing a small red rubber ball. I
can't wait to tell Mary. I can't wait to get home.

THE VET IS SUPPOSED to call today with Barry's test results so
the ringer is on, we're picking up. So far we've only had to

field one false call, someone from Mary's work hating to bother her at home but wondering if she knew where some PDF files were and, by the way, how was B.C., how were her parents, did she go skiing like she'd said she wanted to, what was the snow like? Mary was Mary, knew exactly where the file was and filled the woman in just enough about her trip before telling her that she should probably get off the phone because Hank was expecting an important call.

Mary thumbs the TALK button off. "Sometimes I forget why we never answer the phone."

"Now do you remember?"

"Yep."

She sets the receiver down on top of a chest-high stack of boxes and takes the X-ACTO knife back with her into the kitchen; the kitchen is connected to the living room by a door-less doorway, and as we unpack, we can see each other work. All either of us is really doing is waiting for the telephone to ring, but we're both doing a pretty good job of pretending like we're not. It's okay, though. It's good, in fact. Two liars are better than one. Delusion by consensus.

The reading chair is pushed into the corner by the front window, on an angle so that Barry can see outside. That was one of the things we were most looking forward to, making a place for him to sit and scratch and watch the world slide by in his old age. He's up in the chair, but sleeping. It seems as if all he ever does now is sleep.

I look out the window instead. There's a big maple tree in the middle of our little patch of a lawn with a bird perched on one of its just-budding branches and a squirrel stopped half way up its trunk. Neither of them is moving, not even the squirrel hanging upside down six feet off the ground. Finally the squirrel shakes its tail, like it's sassing somebody or is particularly proud of just how bushy and black it is. That it's probably just shaking off some lice doesn't make it look any less sassy. I'm tempted to wake up Barry — he despises squirrels, and what could be more infuriating than one of them showing you up in your very own yard? — but I don't. There'll be plenty of time for barking at snotty squirrels later, when he's better.

From the other room, "What's with this?" Mary's opened up the winter clothes box, is holding up my can of red spray paint. It must have fallen out of my army parka.

"I was going to use it for something at the old place."

"For what?"

"You know, I don't know. I forget now."

"Well, what do you want me to do with it?"

"Just throw it out."

"You can't just throw it out, this stuff is incredibly toxic. Let's keep it downstairs until there's one of those Earth Day things and we can drop it off."

"Sounds like a plan," I say.

The phone rings, and Mary and I look at each other. I wait for it to ring once more and pick it up in the second of silence before it can go off again. I clear my throat before I answer.

"Hello?"

"Henry? This is Rebecca James calling."

It takes me a moment to place the full name. When I do, because it's anyone but the vet, I'm almost glad it's her. "Hey, Rebecca. How's it going?" I shake my head and wave a hand in front of my face. Mary looks as relieved as I feel and pulls some dishes out of a box on the kitchen table. I turn around and face the window.

"I'm afraid not very well," she says. "I'm afraid Philip's mother has passed away."

"Jesus. I didn't even know she was sick." Wait a minute, yes I did. I think. Maybe. "How did she ... I mean —"

"She'd had a mastectomy several months ago which the doctors thought was entirely successful, but the cancer came back. The only saving grace was that it hit her so hard she didn't have long to suffer."

Breast cancer. Now I remember. Phil had told me. I did know.

"I'm sorry," I say. Both the bird and the squirrel are gone from the tree.

"I'm calling because the funeral is this Saturday, after which there'll be a small reception for family and close friends at Philip's parents' house in Etobicoke."

"Right?"

"I'm calling to invite you and Mary, Henry."

"Right, of course. We'd love to come." Christ, man, get off the fucking phone.

"Henry, I know that you and Philip have had your differences of late, but I think it's extremely important that you be there on Saturday. He needs you there."

I change hands, press the phone to my other ear. "I'll be there," I say. "We'll both be there."

"Good. I'll call within the next couple of days with the details. Goodbye."

"Goodbye."

As soon as I hang up, "Was that Rebecca?" Mary says.

Before I can say anything: the small red flashing light on the phone stand meaning that there's a message waiting. Someone called when I was on the line. Less than a minute later I click the telephone back off.

"Well?" Mary says.

"The doctor wants us to come in."

"When?"

"Today."

"When today?"

"As soon as we can."

"HOW MUCH IS A pound of ground beef?" I say.

"It goes by the kilogram. It's $6.78 a kilogram."

"Okay, how much is —" I hold my hands apart like I'm describing a small fish that I'd caught.

The kid behind the counter — and he is a kid; in spite of the white deli apron and the black Loblaws visor there's no way he can be much more than eighteen — scoops a clump of raw hamburger onto a red sheet of butcher's paper he holds in the palm of his other hand. It looks like a decomposing human brain or an enormous worm orgy.

"Just a little more," I say.

Another quarter clump, and he sets the entire thing down on the electronic scale. The computerized numbers start flipping forward. "$5.23 okay?" he says.

"Yeah, that's great."

While I wait for him to package up my hamburger and slap on a price sticker I wonder how old he must have been the last time I ordered anything over a deli counter. Eight, nine, ten at the oldest. Around Barry's age.

I pay for the meat and the other things that were on my list — garbage bags, a box of baking soda, dish rags — and cut across the grocery store parking lot in the direction of the old place. There's another potter left and one or two gardening tools and then that's it, we're ghosts, we never lived there. It's not hot out, not even T-shirt weather yet, but every day feels a little bit warmer than the one before, so I can't dawdle, I've got to get Barry's meat home and in the refrigerator before it starts to go bad.

The raw ground beef was the vet's idea.

"What's basically happening is, Barry doesn't feel like eating because he's associating food with feeling bad." The doctor stroked Barry head to back while he spoke. Barry, lying flat on the metal examination table with his head between his paws, ignored our conversation. "So don't push him, but try to give him small amounts of really tasty stuff, stuff you might not have thought of giving him before, and try to serve it to him in places where he doesn't usually eat. Make it seem more like a really nice treat than a meal."

Barry felt bad when he ate, the vet had explained, because he had cancer. Not just in the tumour they'd tested, but in his liver, his kidneys, and most of his internal organs. Surgery was out, but there was chemotherapy. It was expensive, but it could prolong his life and make the time that he had left closer to normal than otherwise.

"Let's do it," Mary said.

"Do you have pet insurance?" the doctor said.

"Pet insurance?" I said.

"No," Mary said, "we don't. It doesn't matter. When can we get started?"

Technically, your mother was wrong: dogs can't smell fear. They don't have to. If you're blubbering away and moaning their name and covering their confused face with eye salt, of course they'll know things aren't right, that something's wrong. Then and there in the examination room, without a spoken word passing between us, Mary and I decided that Barry had enough to deal with, that he didn't need us making him feel worse than he already did and would. We walked home from the vet — we'd taken a taxi there, but the doctor said that a little exercise every day was still okay, just make sure to let Barry set the pace — and stopped to let Barry sniff whenever and wherever and for however long he liked. None of us was in a hurry.

When I get to our old place I peek over the fence on tiptoes before I open the gate. The landlady told the new people that we'd be dropping by to pick up some of our stuff, but I still can't help feeling like a thief somehow. The blinds in the front window are shut tight, though, so I let myself into the back-yard. By the time I gather up the clay potter and the hand weeder along with my bag of groceries and turn to leave, George is watching me.

"Christ, George. You scared me."

George doesn't say anything. Somebody's dressed him for summer, bypassed spring altogether. He's got on a loud Hawaiian shirt that hangs over his baggy bright blue shorts, and cheap white running shoes and black socks that ride up over his white calves, the long veins in his skinny legs the same colour as his shorts. He looks like a bewildered tourist who got off in the wrong country.

"You'd make a good spy, you know that, George?"

"I will not see you again," he says.

"Sure you will. I'll run into you around the neighbourhood all the time." Not that I've ever seen him anywhere but here before.

"The cavalry has called me. It is not my decision."

"You mean the army? You mean the Polish army's called you?" What am I supposed to say, tell him that he's an old man and mentally ill and that the only thing anyone's likely to call him for anymore is dinner?

"It is not my decision," he says. "I must go."

We both stand there, me with my garden supplies and bag of groceries, George staring at the ground with a furrowed brow like he's trying to figure out a secret message encoded in the dirt. He thrusts out his hand.

"Goodbye," he says.

I set down my stuff. "Good luck, George."

He drops my hand and then grabs me by the shoulders, kisses me once on each cheek. "Take care of yourself," he says.

"You, too," I say.

"It is not our decision."

ETOBICOKE IN THE SPRINGTIME almost makes sense. Birds busy in the trees, children on bicycles in the streets, lumpy old men and women stooped over in silent tandem working side-by-side to resurrect their mushy lawns from the short death of another long Ontario winter. At its best, like Chatham at its best, a good place to grow up or die, ideal for anyone who doesn't know any better yet or is old enough not to care anymore. To every city there is a season.

"Turn here," I say.

"Are you sure?" Mary says.

"I've been here before."

"These streets all look the same. Read me Rebecca's directions again."

I lean over and flip on the turn signal. "Just turn here, we're almost there."

"Hank ..."

Mary does turn, though, and we are almost there, on Edgecroft, Phil's parents' street, their house the second red brick rancher from the end.

In all of the years I've known Phil I've been to his parents' place maybe four or five times, met his mum and dad exactly twice, once when their son was down with the flu and still living at home and I hand delivered a list of essay topics from our History of Aesthetics class, the last when I helped him finally move out with the aid of their Oldsmobile. I remember being doubly surprised: that they were both at least a decade older than my parents and that they were Polish, Sumner, apparently, one of those Immigration Centre name changes for the New World better. His father had laid line at Toronto Hydro for twenty years, wore a Maple Leafs toque when he worked around the yard, and had as thick an accent as his wife's. When we'd finished dropping the last load of Phil's stuff off at his new apartment downtown and returned to Etobicoke with the car, she'd made us sit down to an early-afternoon supper of cheese and potato pergogies from the freezer served up with fresh cucumber and tomato slices and plenty of bread and butter. There was a framed picture of the Pope on the wall of the kitchen and photographs of Phil's older brother and sister and their spouses and children on the refrigerator door. On the street, when I asked Phil why he'd never said anything before about his parents being Polish, "Why would I?" he said. "It doesn't matter."

"Look at all the cars," Mary says. "I'm going to go around the block and see if I can find somewhere else to park."

"Must be all the people for the wake," I say.

"They're Polish, right?"

"Yeah."

"It's not a wake, then."

"Okay, then, what is it?"

"I don't know. A reception?"

"Too bureaucratic."

"A get-together?"

I shake my head. "Too cheery."

"Oh, look, a spot," Mary says. Mary parallel parking is like watching an expert golfer line up a pivotal tee shot. I know better than to bother her while the wheels of geometrical conjecturing are turning the steering wheel.

She'd picked up the car from Hertz this morning before I was awake. The plan was to get to Etobicoke and be back home as quickly as possible so that Barry wouldn't have to be alone for any longer than he had to be. Chances are we'll find him just where we left him, in the chair in the sun by the half-opened front window, but the price of a day's car rental is worth knowing that we'll probably be home before he even wakes up. Besides, riding around suburbia feels right. When in Etobicoke ...

Bumper to bumper snug, as parallel as anyone's ever going to be, Mary cuts the engine. "I'll lock the doors," she says. "You grab the wine and the book, I want to put them in the trunk." Mary being Mary, after she'd picked up the car, she'd used the opportunity to go to the liquor store at Queen's Quay to buy some new vintages that were released just this morning and, passing by a Book City on the way home, popped in and bought us a copy of Phil's new book. "It seemed right," she'd said.

I unbuckle my seat belt. "It's Etobicoke, not Jane and Finch, nobody's going to break into our car," I say.

Doing up the windows from the driver's seat, "It'll make me feel better, okay?"

I grab the bags from the backseat. "Pop the trunk," I say.

I lay the bottles of wine in their LCBO paper bags down carefully on the carpeted lining of the trunk, hesitate for a moment, then drop the book into my suit jacket pocket. Locking away poetry in a darkened place — even if it's by someone you know — seems wrong. I slam the trunk shut and we head back the way we came, toward 17 Edgecroft.

The front door is wide open so we go right in, careful to wipe our feet first on the black rubber WELCOME mat.

"Shouldn't we ring the bell or something?" Mary says.

"Everybody's probably downstairs," I say.

A round man in an old brown suit around Phil's father's age, a long strand of black hair combed up and over his otherwise bald head, is doing up his zipper as he comes out of the bathroom off the hallway. "Hello, hello," he says, finishing zipping up. "Leave shoes on, leave shoes on, everybody downstairs."

We follow him through the kitchen to the top of the stairs, where he turns around. We can hear the heavy murmur of voices down below. "I am Nicholas," he says, pointing to himself. "You are friends of Phil's, yes?"

We say that we are; introduce ourselves.

"It's good you here," he says. "Everybody today is old, old friends of Teodor and Eva, good to have young people here today."

We both smile; Mary webs her fingers through mine.

"You two married, yes?" Nicholas says.

"Yes," I say.

"How long?" He says it like a challenge.

"Ten years this August," Mary says.

"Ah, babies," he says, waving away the decade, and we all go downstairs.

Where everyone *is* old, the basement full of retirement-age and older men and women standing mingling in small groups or sitting and talking with their neighbours in grey metal folding chairs pushed up against the walls. There's a white paper plate of food in most people's hands, or at least a cigarette or a drink, Styrofoam cups of something steaming, coffee probably, in the women's, brown quart bottles of beer in the men's. A mix of almost-English and pure Polish floats to the low basement ceiling, just below the accumulated cigarette smoke. Phil and Rebecca in the middle of the room tower above everyone else. Mary and I make our way over. We're still holding hands. It's the most physical contact we've had since ... since since. Mary and I are still holding hands.

"Hi," I say.

Phil turns around and his eyes are red, puffy, it's obvious he's been crying. The funeral was this morning, for immediate family only. While he accepts a long hug from Mary, Rebecca says, "Did you guys get something to eat?"

"We had lunch just before we came," I say.

"How about a drink, then? There's coffee and tea and pop and some Polish beer that Philip's dad and all his friend are drinking. What's it called, Hon, I keep forgetting." She slides her hand around Phil's waist.

"Zywiec," he says.

"Right. How about a couple of Zywiecs?" She looks from me to Mary.

Mary seems as caught off guard by Rebecca's hyper-hospitality as I am. "Uhm, I'm driving," she says.

"Okay, how about something else?" She leans closer. "I'd seriously take a pass on the coffee if I were you, but there's hot water and some tea bags. How about a nice hot cup of tea, Mary?"

"Okay," Mary says.

"And a Zywiec for you, Henry?"

"Sure."

Rebecca wraps her other arm around Phil's waist, turns him to face her. "Why don't you have a beer with Henry, baby?"

Phil shakes his head. "I don't think I should."

"Sure you should, if you feel like it you should. And if you don't want to finish it, you don't have to, okay?"

Phil nods, lowers his head.

"Okay."

She gives him a short, hard hug and heads for the couple of card tables set up on the other side of the basement covered with kelbosa slices and pieces of bright orange cheese speared with toothpicks and dill pickles and sweet pickles and deviled eggs and tidy rows of unopened bottles of beer and cans of No Name cola and a black-spouted, chocolate brown coffee maker like the kind I remember my parents putting out for Christmas gatherings in our basement when I was a kid.

"How's your dad doing?" Mary says.

"He's okay," Phil says, nodding, as if in agreement with himself.

"You know, I've never met your dad. How long were he and your mother together?"

Phil lifts his head, considers. "I think it'll be their fifty-fifth anniversary this July."

"Wow," Mary and I both say.

Phil smiles. "It's a total cliché. They met on the boat over as teenagers, got married after they docked in Montreal, and had my sister practically nine months to the day later. It turned out that they knew each other when they were like four or five, their parents knew each other in this same little town in Poland, and they used to play together until one of them moved away."

"Are your sister and brother here?" I say. Phil never talked about them and I'd never met them, but I knew that they were both much older than him and that one of them lived in Oakville and the other somewhere on the east coast.

"Yeah, they're around here somewhere." We all scan the room for anyone under the age of sixty. "Both sets of kids are at my sister-in-law's place in Oakville. A Catholic funeral is a long day for children, I guess."

"For anybody," I say.

Phil shrugs, puts his hands in his pockets.

"Is that your sister?" Mary says, pointing a half-concealed finger at the profile of a short woman talking to someone I think I remember as Phil's dad. Phil definitely got the tall genes in the family.

"Yeah, that's Alexandra," he says.

"She looks like you," Mary says.

"Oh, God, don't tell her that. She's convinced that she's the one who got mum's looks."

"Well, you both must have. And your mother must have been a very attractive woman."

Rebecca arrives with Mary's tea and our beer. "Are you talking about Philip's mother?" she says.

Mary nods; Rebecca patiently waits for all of us to take our drinks.

"You met her, right, Henry?" she says.

"Just a couple times, years ago."

"She really was beautiful, and not just when she was young, either, although if you look at the pictures she's drop-dead gorgeous. She had the most incredible long, grey hair, even for a long time after she got sick. I used to comb it for her sometimes at the hospital." She puts her hand back around Phil's waist, smiles up at him. "She was incredibly vain about her hair."

Phil takes a first, tentative sip of his beer. "Yeah, she was." He smiles too.

"I want to meet your dad," Mary says.

"Okay," Phil says. He looks at his father still talking to Phil's sister and an older woman, even older than his dad. "Why don't I ..."

Rebecca takes Mary by the hand. "C'mon," she says. "I'll introduce you. You'll see where Philip gets all his charm."

Mary waves at me as Rebecca drags her off. Phil and I drink from our beers.

"I've got to admit," I say. "Given all that stuff you told me about Rebecca having a death phobia, I thought you'd be the one having to take care of her today."

"She's terrified," Phil says. "Has been all week."

"She sure doesn't seem like it."

"Believe me, she is."

We both take another drink. I read the label on my bottle.

"6.2%? This is high octane," I say. "How come you never turned me onto this stuff before?"

Phil looks at his own bottle. "It's what my dad always drank."

"So?"

"I don't know." He lifts his Zywiec to his lips. I do the same.

"Where'd you get those shoes?" he says. We both look down at my feet. "I didn't think you owned anything that required the tying up of laces."

"When the appropriate situation demands it, I can be per-suaded to sacrifice my couture integrity." I lift a Doc Martin Oxford like a horse ready to be shod. "Value Village, ten bucks, no tax, just a little black shoe polish and almost as good as new."

Phil's grinning with me, not at me. We both drink.

"Remember what a big deal it was in public school what kind of running shoes you wore?" I say.

"I went to Catholic school, but, yeah."

"Best of all was high-top Nikes."

"*Leather* high-top Nikes."

"Right. Leather high-top Nikes and leather high-top Converse were 1 and 1-A."

"Then high-top canvas Nikes and Converse."

"Then low-top Nikes and low-top Converse."

"Then North Stars."

"North Stars!" I say. "I haven't heard that name in years."

"I wore North Stars," Phil says.

"Me too."

"I wanted leather Nikes so bad, but my mother said there was no way she was going to spend fifty bucks on a pair of running shoes."

"Same here."

"At least we didn't have to wear Sparks."

"Oh, God, Sparks. From the BiWay. You might as well have had a face full of zits or a sign on your back saying I JERK OFF TEN TIMES A DAY. Praise be our parents for sparing us the social horror of having to grow up wearing Sparks."

"Here, here," Phil says, and we clink bottles. A couple of old ladies look our way and we lower our eyes. I remember the book in my suit jacket pocket.

"Have you got a pen?" I say.

"Maybe." Phil puts his hand inside his jacket and pulls out a ballpoint. I pull out his book.

"Sign this for me," I say.

He takes the book from me and stares at its cover for a moment. "You shouldn't have had to buy this," he says.

"Well, unfortunately the Canada Council for the Arts hasn't deemed it required reading for all Canadian citizens yet, so Mary had to actually pay for it. You can compensate me in pints next time we're at the Duke."

"You said it was closed, didn't you?"

"Right. Well, that doesn't mean you can't still buy me a beer."

"That's true," he says. He opens up the book and slashes something down on an inside page, hands it right back.

"You want me to read it now?" I say.

"It's your book, you paid for it."

I open it up to where it's signed and can't help being disappointed when I see that *Best, Phil* is all that he's written. Then, above it, I read the typeset dedication.

> For Hank Roberts
> *If you would not be martyred slaves of Time; be*
> *drunken continually!*
> *With wine, with poetry, or with virtue, as you will.*
> Brother Drunk

"You're not forcing poor Henry to read your book now, are you?" Rebecca says, locking her arm around Phil's. I feel Mary at my side. I forget that I'm not supposed to and I kiss her on the cheek. I slip the book back in my pocket.

"Of his own free will entirely," Phil says. "Apparently he finds my conversation a trifle on the dull side."

"What was that, old boy?" I say. "I'm afraid I wasn't listening."

"Okay, I think one Zywiec each is enough for you two," Mary says.

"Yes, but you can make sure that this one —" Rebecca slips her hand around the bicep of Phil's already entwined arm "— gets out of the apartment this week anytime you want.

I don't need him moping around while I'm trying to work. Don't you two have some sort of pool game that's been going on forever?"

"They lost their pool table," Mary says.

"I don't need the Duke's pool table to kick his ass," I say, looking at Phil.

"No doubt," Phil says. "For that, you'd only need to learn how to play pool better."

"Okay, boys, save it for when you're alone," Mary says.

"Right now, Philip, I think it's time you talked to some of your parents' friends," Rebecca says. "Some of them have come a long way and are getting ready to leave."

"We should get going, too," Mary says. She doesn't need to say anything else. I take her hand.

To Phil and Rebecca, "Barry's sick," I say.

I WAKE UP ALONE, Mary's back at work. Today's not a chemo day so Barry and I are still in bed at just after eleven. My ears are ringing from the music of the night before and I've got to be back at the Gladstone in less than eight hours. When I told Mary the other night that I'm getting too old for this shit, she said, "Why don't you do something else then?" It sounds so easy when she says it.

We let Barry snuggle as high on the bed as he wants to now, put up with any snout-twitching or limb-shaking or even the occasional outright sound-asleep mule-kick that we wouldn't have tolerated before. It's a chore to get him to eat and he's not interested in much anymore except sleeping, so him being a pain in the ass throughout the night somehow feels comforting, helps us — helps me, anyway — sleep better.

It's almost May, so we make sure that our bedroom window is open a crack before we go to bed. But evening's chill, no matter how warm the night when we fall asleep, always manages to find us. When I wake up to take a leak at four in the morning all three of us are packed tight together, each of us keeping the others warm by trying to keep warm ourselves.

The front door bell rings and I brace myself for Barry's bark and his lunge off the bed. Except that the bed isn't located fifteen feet from the door anymore — we're on the second floor now, right beside the bathroom, just down the hall from Mary's studio — and he doesn't hear it. I toss off the blankets and pull on Mary's baby blue housecoat and close the bedroom door behind me. I don't want Barry waking up to strange voices down below and come tripping down the stairs trying to protect me.

Whoever it is only has time for one more ring before I open the door. It's a nice clean, clear ring, too; lately I've been spraying things around the house with WD-40. A toolbox in a can, my father called it over the phone.

"Sears Delivery," the man at the door says. He's wearing a dark blue polyester Sears jacket and holding a clipboard. There's another man standing behind him on the porch in an identical blue jacket leaning with both forearms on a red metal dolly that supports a cardboard box taller than it is wide.

"I think you've got the wrong house," I say.

The man looks down at his clipboard. "Is this 11 1/2 Wright?" he says.

"Yeah."

"Then this is the right house. Just sign here and we'll put this inside where you want it."

"But I didn't order anything from Sears," I say.

The man looks down at his clipboard again. "Do you know a Mary Calder?" he says.

"She's my wife."

"Well, I've got an invoice here and a delivery request form with her name on it for one Schwinn stationary bike, $549.00, and one bathroom scale, white, $24.99. Paid for in full. Paid for with VISA." He turns the clipboard around so that I can see Mary's signature, places a finger underneath her name.

"Oh," I say. "Okay."

The one with the clipboard steps into the hallway and holds the door open wide so that the other one can wheel the dolly inside. I take a step back, get out of their way. I can just imagine what they're thinking: What kind of man is still in bed at 11:30 on a Wednesday morning and doesn't have a clue what his old lady's been up to with their credit card? It might help if I was wearing something other than my wife's bathrobe. I pull the tie tighter around my waist.

"So where do you want this?" the man says, offering me the pen from his workshirt pocket. I scrawl my name on the bottom of the invoice and look around the small living room filled with all of our books and some of Mary's paintings and a bunch of others that she's collected over the years. I know it's the last thing any mover wants to hear, but I say it anyway. "Can you put it downstairs?"

The man with the clipboard looks at the man with the dolly. Their eyes meet. To me, but still looking at him, "Where are the stairs?"

I lead them to the kitchen and open the basement door. I turn on the basement light and let them go first. I'm on the fourth step down by the time they're already coming back up. I turn around.

"Okay, you're all set," the man with the clipboard says, not even slowing down as he hands me my yellow copy of the invoice. The man with the empty dolly nods as he passes by me through the kitchen.

"Okay," I say, and watch them leave. They shut the door behind them, hard, the bell issuing a faint after-effect ringing. There's a plain white envelope on the kitchen table with *Hank* written on it. Inside:

AN EARLY BIRTHDAY PRESENT

XXOO

Mary

Another man might be upset. Another man might be insulted. From where I'm standing, though, all I'm seeing are two kisses and two hugs. And that's a whole two more of each than what I had yesterday.

"HOW MUCH DID IT cost to get the phone hooked up?" my mother says.

"Sixty," I say.

"That's not too bad. What about the gas?"

"One twenty-five, I think."

I'm sitting in the kitchen with the phone tucked between my shoulder and my ear, carrying on a conversation with my mother while unpacking a few final boxes. The last ones are always the most difficult to get rid of. The clothes and the dishes and the bath towels were on hangers and in drawers and helping us get dry before we'd memorized our new postal code. The ones containing fat manila envelopes stuffed full of old income tax returns and even older frayed files labelled *Bifurcation (Whitehead, Alfred North)* remain uncuriously untouched. You are what you unpack.

"One twenty-five," she says. "Just to turn on the gas." I can hear her tsking. "How about hydro?"

"Two hundred, but you get it all back with interest in three years if you pay all of your bills on time."

"Two hundred dollars just to get the hydro turned on." She tsks again. "Well, what are you going to do." It's not all bad. Being shafted by the utility companies is at least one more thing the two of us have in common now. "How's Barry?" she says.

"He's okay," I say.

Aside from getting thinner and always sleeping, he is, he does seem okay. Animals don't know they're going to die and wouldn't complain about it even if they did. Forget about Socrates drinking his hemlock while squeezing out a final speech or two, you want dignity, take care of a dying dog.

"That's good," she says. "Just make him feel as comfortable as you can, that's all you can do."

"We are."

We are. I've folded four blankets in half and laid them down on top of each other on the kitchen floor so that he can stretch out beside me while I unpack. Just before that, I hand fed him a few small pieces of Salisbury steak I cooked up in a gravy mix out of a pouch. Sometimes I feel like telling the guy behind the deli counter at Loblaws that the meat's not for me, that I'm a vegetarian, that it's for my dog, but it doesn't make any difference. It is for me. It's for my dog.

"Did dad tell you Mr. Hanna died?" Mum says.

I lift a stack of files out of a box, set them down on the kitchen table. "No, he didn't."

Mr. Hanna is — *was*, now, I guess — Jamie Hanna's dad, a guy I used to play pee-wee hockey with. He taught me high-school math, grades nine, ten, and eleven. He played hockey with my dad when they were both kids. "Cancer?" I say.

"Stroke. He was golfing in Florida. You know he'd retired from teaching."

"No, I didn't know that," I say, and let my mother tell me all about Mr. Hanna's final holiday in the sun while I go through the stacks of files. I need some fresh folders to keep track of all of the bills that we have to pay now that we're homeowners. Before, as renters, all we'd had to worry about was making sure that the telephone didn't get cut off.

Most of the files are from my two-drawer filing cabinet sitting empty in the basement. The plan is to clean up and winterize the small mud room off of the kitchen once things settle down so that I can have a room of my own again, but although Mary keeps saying how guilty she feels that she already has her studio — big and bright and with windows that actually open up all the way — the truth is, I don't miss being behind four walls. Actually, now that I don't have them, it's hard to see why I ever needed them. What I am looking forward to is setting up some shelves and putting my records, currently exiled to the basement, in order. Mary says that as far as she's concerned I can do whatever I want down there. It's too cold for her, she says; too damp, too dark.

"So they took him back to the hotel," Mum says, "and that's when they found out it was a stroke."

"Right."

I flip through the folders — extracurricular undergraduate keener stuff mostly, yellow highlighted and heavily annotated photocopies and class notes — like we used to do with our O-Pee-Chee hockey cards as kids at recess. *Got him, got him, got him, need him, got him.* I figure I have to come up with at least eight new files for the house, so the contents of *Rorty, Richard*; *Free Will*; and *Heidegger (Naziism)* get dumped into a recycling pile right off the top. I decide to spare *James, William.* Although I couldn't tell you what *The Varieties of Religious Experience* is about other than I'm pretty sure it has something to do with a variety of religious experiences, I can remember finishing reading it: a Thursday evening in late March just before the end of term, a rusty can sun setting through the grimy, bird-shit-splattered windows of the thirteenth-floor view from Robarts Library, and hours until I was supposed to meet Phil at the Duke for a late beer, all of my work done for the day and all of the rest of the night all mine.

"It turns out he had high blood pressure and he wasn't taking his medicine like he should have been."

"Oh?"

"If he had been, he might have made it, they say."

"Really."

I dig back in, pick up a bright blue folder stamped with the U of T logo. Across the front, *INDEPENDENT WRITER'S CLASSROOM*; inside, Lenore Shipley's carefully typed, double-spaced, never-read manuscript, *The Wounded Mirror*, along with a neatly labelled self-addressed stamped envelope. Trouble never really goes away, it just ends up at the bottom of the last box you look in.

"So Ellen, she had to get the body flown back down here, but because of SARS, they had to do all sorts of tests and it took them nearly a week to get it back."

"That's terrible," I say.

Correction: second from the bottom of the last box you look in. In a crisp, unthumbed file folder that would be just perfect for our property tax statements, *WORK IN PROGRESS*.

"Her husband for thirty-nine years, and she can't get him back down here to get him ready for his own funeral."

"Up here, Mum," I hear myself say.

"You know what I mean. Anyway, they got him back eventually. Hinnegan's did a good job on him, your dad said."

I look at the folder in my hands. It's hard to look a lie straight in the eye.

"Do you want him to call you when he gets back from Canadian Tire?"

"What's that?"

"Do you want your father to call when he gets back in?"

"Sure, that'd be good, get him to call me."

"All right, take care. And say hello to Mary for me."

"I will."

"I love you, son."

"I love you, too, Mum."

I set down the phone.

An old bandage. A piece of string tied to a loose tooth. Something that should have been done a long, long time ago. Rip it off, tear it away, yank it out by its rotten, rotten roots. I open up the *WORK IN PROGRESS* file.

A thirty-eight page, fifteen-year old A-honours thesis essay, the undergraduate acorn that never became the book-length mighty oak. Three chalk-blue note cards, two of which have actual notes written on them. An unopened package of five-hundred sheets of cellophane-wrapped white printer paper.

I hear Mary's steps on the front porch.

I go to the junk drawer and pull out a pen and a yellow Post-it note. A house becomes a home when it sprouts its very own junk drawer.

> *Lenore:*
> *Sorry for abandoning you.*
> *Good luck with your novel.*
> *Sincerely,*
> *Hank Roberts*
> P.S. *Maybe you can use the enclosed more than I could.*

I stick the Post-it to the package of blank paper and stuff it inside the envelope with Lenore's name and address written on it. Burying the dead isn't nearly as bad as watching them die.

"Hi, guys," Mary says.

"Hi," I say, taking her bicycle helmet from her, giving her a hug.

Thump thump thump.

We turn around.

A month ago Barry would have charged to the door to greet her. Two weeks ago he would have gotten up and gone to her as soon as she was inside. His head is resting on its side on the blanket like he's sleeping on a pillow, but his eyes are open and his tail is banging hello against the floor.

Thump thump thump.

Mary looks at me. For the first time since he's been sick, I think she's going to cry.

"Group hug," I say, and we both squat down.

Barry moves to lift himself to meet us, but I put a hand underneath his neck and ease him back down. "Lay down, Bubs, it's okay," I say, and he does. We bring our faces to his. We let him lick our noses, first Mary's, then mine.

WE LET BARRY'S BODY tell us when it was time to say goodbye. Bad days began to outnumber good days until every day wasn't very good. He stopped cleaning himself, would give his coat a few desultory licks before giving up and staring ahead at nothing, slightly panting, as if the effort had exhausted him. The bite-size slices of raw sirloin I held in the palm of my hand in front of his nose were sniffed at and then ignored. Sometimes he'd attempt to lift himself up from the floor only to have his back legs betray him. We had to move our futon down to the living room and sleep on the main floor because he couldn't climb the stairs anymore. The first week of June, the weather warm enough at last to retire our duvet to the closet, his tail gave out and when he'd defecate, bits of faeces would cling to its underside undetected.

We called the vet and made the appointment. For an extra forty dollars they'd administer the needle in your own home if you lived within the 416 area code. We did. I gave the receptionist our credit card number and our new address.

MARY WORKED IN HER flower bed while I dug the hole. It couldn't have been a nicer day: bright, warm but not hot, dry. The vet informed us that disposal of the body was included in the agreed-upon price, but we told him we wanted to keep it with us. He asked us if we knew that privately burying a body was against city by-laws. We told him we were keeping Barry with us.

There wasn't any favourite spot to favour, spring hadn't

come early enough for him to lie out in the yard in the sun and find one, so I chose a shaded area in the rear left-hand corner of the backyard underneath the overhanging branches of a small birch tree. A couple of weeks before, Mary had come home with a large black plastic compost, our first, which we installed in the same general part of the lawn. The irony of the location of the hole I was digging wasn't lost on me. I didn't bother to share it with Mary.

When I was finished I stuck the shovel upright in the muddy lawn and went over to the flower bed and watched Mary plant Cala lillies, her favourite. Flowers are like food to me: I can enjoy them, I just can't understand the appeal of the work that goes into them. Mary scooped out a handful of dirt with her trowel and stuck a bulb into the ground, pushed the disturbed earth back where it came from with her bare hand.

"What are those?" I said.

"Lilies."

"I know, I mean what colour."

"I don't remember," she said, patting the dirt flat. "It doesn't matter, does it?'

"No."

We waited until all of the bulbs were gone. When they were, Mary stood up, wiped her dirty hands on the thighs of her jeans, and we went inside. Barry was on the floor of the mud room in the dark blue plastic bag that the vet had brought with him the day before. Mary held the door open for me and I picked him up. I told myself not to be surprised if he felt stiff, but couldn't help it when he was.

I set him down on the lawn in the sunshine. I got down on both knees and unzipped the bag. His eyes were closed so I was okay. I heard Mary start to cry, so I got to work, peeled back the plastic from the body. Tiny black bugs jumped off his coat and out of the bag and onto the lawn, already on the lookout for a new warm home. I picked him up again, this time without the bag, his fur on my bare arms, and I got down on my knees beside the hole. He was in a sort of fetal position, and thankfully the hole I'd dug was wide enough.

I lowered him as far I could, until I felt the cool of the damp earth on my knuckles and then on my face, and let him drop. It wasn't far, only another four or five inches. I don't think Mary heard the soft thud of his body hitting the bottom.

I didn't look inside the hole again until I'd filled it more than halfway up. When I did: dirt, just dirt. I shovelled in the rest and patted it down with the back of the shovel. Mary got on her knees beside me and helped flatten it down with her hands. By the time we were done, it looked like the rest of the grassless yard, only a little smoother.

Standing up now, "What do you think about a rose bush?" Mary said.

"I like roses."

"A nice big red rose bush."

I nodded, looked at the ground.

"Let's go to Home Hardware and get one," she said.

"What, you mean right now?"

"Yeah."

"Okay. Just let me get washed up and grab some money."

"Bring your wallet," Mary said. "I might want to get some more lilies, too."

I LIKE IT HERE underground.

The sun and sky we've bought are part of it, sure — surfeit morning sunlight tap-dancing across the kitchen floor, second-storey windows breathing early-evening breezes — but I also like my musty green couch with the broken springs that I found in front of somebody's house down the street, I like getting horizontal on it and watching Blue Jays games on our old TV, especially late games from the west coast when Mary's asleep upstairs and I'm downstairs alone with a cold can of Diet Canada Dry in one hand and the remote control to mute the commercials with in the other. Sometimes I'll call up my old man during a Toronto rally or when the Blue Jays are holding on to a late inning lead with men on second and third and there's only one out and he'll be watching the same game as me downstairs in his basement. That's usually when I'll ask him about the best way to fix a toilet with low water pressure or when he'll remind me that I've got to remember to clean my furnace before I turn it on in the fall because just one quick cleaning job will end up paying for itself in no time.

I like my walls of records. The octopus-arm heat vents of the oil furnace have taken some getting used to, have dinged me more than once, but I'm learning when I have to duck and when I can stand up. Best of all, any wall space I can get to is mine, no more books or artwork to compete with anymore, meaning that if I manage to find a battered but still quite playable copy of Tim Hardin's *Suite for Susan Moore and Damion* — a mediocre and overproduced album, no argument, but Hardin's last decent LP of completely original material before the heroin finished off his body after already doing in his brain — I don't have to worry about subtracting one of my other records in order to make space. I figure that at my present pace I've got about fifteen years before I'll start to run out of room. Fifteen years is a long time.

I even like my stationary bike. The scale, I'm not so crazy about. The first time I stepped on it I couldn't believe that it was right, kept pushing it around the basement floor thinking that it had to be sitting on an incline, in a gully, on a ridge. Everywhere I went, though, 198 pounds followed me. Eventually I got tired of running and let the little red needle go where it wanted to go. I weigh myself every Sunday afternoon now, and today was a good day, I came in at 192, down one more pound from last week.

But my bike, my bike is a guaranteed good time. At first, okay, not so good; Sisyphus on a hamster wheel with sweat burning his eyes and an embarrassed ex-athlete's sharp pain in his side. Soon enough, though — not soon, but soon enough — a torn white T-shirt with stains underneath both arms that Mary'd been bugging me to get rid of for ages scissored up and tied into a headband and what do you know, remembrance of muscles past every Monday, Wednesday, Friday, and Sunday.

First I close the basement door at the top of the stairs. Then I climb aboard my bike, then I tie on my sweatband, then I set the needle down on the record, then I slip on my headphones, and then I start pedaling. I never ride for less than one entire album side, and lately I've been making it up to two if the records are short. I stack the turntable three LPs thick so that when one is over, the next one falls into place. I've never made it to album number three, but that doesn't mean it couldn't happen someday. Will be disappointed if it doesn't, actually.

In the beginning, I always made sure that the basement door was shut because I worried that Mary might hear me wheezing or gasping or maybe even worse, but now I don't want her to hear me humming or singing along with the music or shouting out loud or yelping or whooping when my legs catch the rhythm of this or that song and I pick up the pace and the sweat rivers down my scalp and I close my eyes, and even though I know I'm not going anywhere, I'm going, I'm going. When I'm all done, I towel off — me first, then my bike — and shut off the stereo, hang my headband on one of the bike's handlebars to dry, and head upstairs to take a shower.

I can hear the water running in the bathroom when I stop in the kitchen to get a drink of water. Mary's put today's mail on the kitchen table. For me, a hydro bill. I'll pay it by phone and file it away later.

Upstairs: me, staring at Mary, Mary, naked, staring into the bathroom mirror, her face less than a foot from her own reflection, her hand slow but steady as she traces a tube of red lipstick over her puckered lips. The bathroom is still filled with the steam from her shower. Freshness, warmness, squirts and sprays from little green and blue bottles of womanly redolence

— girls smell better than boys. What they want with fuggy us, I have no idea, only hope that they keep getting fooled just a little while longer.

"Quit your staring," Mary says, returning the lipstick case to the clear plastic bag on the toilet tank and pulling out her eye works. I don't quit, of course, only pan my eyes lower.

Ten years on seeing the same person's every same body part in action and at rest 3,661 times over, you take whatever illusions of fresh lust you can get: a red wig she wore at a Halloween party that started out as a joke but ended up in the host's bedroom; a Fu Manchu moustache she bugged you to grow because, just like that cute guy on the New Jersey Devils, you know, what's his name, it'd look great on you, too; spying a beautiful naked woman in the bathroom, her face less than a foot from her own reflection, her hand slow but steady as she traces the tube of red lipstick over her puckered lips.

I get down on my knees behind her and do what I don't need to tell myself to do; gently at first, soft kisses to the softer still insides of her soap-scented inner thighs, gradually moving upward, then in.

"Stop it," she says. "We're going to be late for the movie."

Longer kisses, now; lingering to suck, bite, lick.

"Stop it," she breathes, moving her feet apart, helping me help myself. "You're making me wet."

Oceanic face wash.

I don't hear the swipe of her brush applying her blush anymore, only the loud tide in my ears of two thighs now two seashells such a nice vice clamped tight around my head. I ride out the stirring and shaking and final shudder of her orgasm. Take back my tongue and drop my sweaty workout shorts and put myself inside.

I may not know much about art, I may not know much at all, but I know that I know this: you can keep your Lichtenstein and your Diebenkorn and your Agnes Martin. The woman you love best bent over the bathroom sink with her ass in the air getting fucked — long tangled wet hair falling over her face, clenched knuckles as white as the porcelain sink she holds on to for support — put that in your National Gallery, pal. No art appreciation class necessary.

I'VE BEEN STAYING CLEAR of the park for the same reason that we stowed away Barry's water dish and his food bowl and his tennis balls. Absence makes absence more bearable. A rubber ball covered in green fuzz on the living room floor can be hazardous to your mental health.

If I'm going to walk to work today and not be late, though, a short cut through Sorauren Park is probably in order. Anyway, it's July, it's been over a month since Mary and I planted the red rose bush in the backyard. As long as there aren't any aging Black Labrador Retrievers with greying muzzles answering to two-syllable names beginning with the letter *B*, I think I'll be all right.

I hear the park before I see it. The ting of an aluminum baseball bat meeting a softball. An excited chorus of high-pitched children's cheers. A bicycle bell. A soccer ball being thumped. A dog barking.

Cutting across the middle of the park, I can't avoid the dog people. Fraser and his policeman dad, Casey and her family and Hunter and his, Lucille and her mum: they're all here, all except for Barry and Rover and Beverly and Omar. But there are new people and new dogs that I've never seen before, too, including a Chocolate Lab puppy jumping up on Casey's back and nipping at his neck and whose Labrador lineage is just a little too strong for my emotional well-being at the moment. I make a sharp turn at the irrigation grate, walk with my head down behind a lonely trio of ten-year-old outfielders.

Posted to the side of the padlocked grey metal equipment shed, there's a computer-generated sign.

INTERESTED IN BEING A DOG WALKER?
BETTY K.'S DOGGIE DAY CARE IS LOOKING FOR RESPONSIBLE,
PHYSICALLY ACTIVE ADULTS TO JOIN OUR GROWING BUSINESS
GOOD HOURLY RATES AND VERY FLEXIBLE HOURS
CALL: 416-583-3766

A woman standing by herself beside the shed is watching the softball game. There's an unopened juice box in one hand and a hand-held computer game in the other.

"Excuse me," I say. "You don't happen to have a pen do you?"

The woman looks away from the game. "I might, in my bag. Can you hold on just a minute? My son's at bat and he'll be furious if I miss him getting a hit."

"No problem," I say.

We both turn to watch the pitcher — an unshaven guy in a Maple Leafs baseball cap, the team's coach, no doubt — bring back his arm with an exaggerated slowness and let go of the softball. He's pitching to one of his own players, so the ball couldn't float across the middle of the plate any slower unless they were playing on the moon. Except for his too-big batting helmet that tilts down almost over his eyes, the woman's son looks the same as all the other kids sitting on the bench, short and scrawny with skinny arms poking out of baggy red jersey tops with *Film Buff Video Rental* written across the back. The boy swings, misses the pitch by at least a foot.

"Almost, Todd, almost," the woman shouts. She sticks the computer game underneath her armpit and opens up her beige canvas bag, briefly rummages around inside before producing a pen. "Is red okay?" she says.

"Sure," I say, taking it from her. "Thanks."

I copy down the phone number on the inside cover of the book in my back pocket, Edgar Lee Masters's *Spoon River Anthology*. I go to give her the pen back, but the woman's watching the game again. She cups her hands over her mouth. "C'mon, Todd, you can do it."

The boy's coach lobs the softball again and this time the kid makes contact, if only barely. The bench explodes, his teammates go bananas, scream and jump up and down and windmill their arms around and around like Todd was on his way home on an inside-the-parker instead of just trying to beat out a weak grounder to the shortstop. "Go, Todd, go," the woman yells.

The kid loses his helmet halfway down the baseline, it bounces off one of his pumping arms and disappears in the trail of dust he's kicking up behind him. He'd still be out by a good three feet if the throw to the first baseman didn't soar over his head. Todd hits first base surprised, relieved, proud, starts to walk back towards home plate to pick up his helmet.

"Keep going!" the coach, his teammates, his mother scream. "Keep going!"

Todd gets the message, turns around and takes off for second. The other team's first baseman finally retrieves the ball, runs down the line a few steps, then hurls the ball to the second baseman. "Slide," Todd's coach yells, and he does, does surprisingly well, head first into the bag. There's dust everywhere, but it's not even close. Todd stands up and waves to his mum.

"ARE YOU HUNGRY?" MARY says.

"I don't know, I could eat," I say. "Are you?"

"I don't know."

"What have we got in the fridge?"

"Not much. We need to go shopping."

"Well I guess that settles that."

"Not necessarily." Mary gets up from the kitchen table and goes to the refrigerator and peeks inside, starts pulling things out. She was in her studio working when I got home from the Gladstone and came downstairs when she heard me come in. It's Thursday night, she doesn't have to get up early tomorrow.

"How was work?" she says, unloading what she'd come up with on the countertop.

"All right."

"Just all right?" She opens up the silverware drawer and pulls out a knife, starts chopping an onion on the cutting board.

"Just all right."

Actually, better than just all right if you count the job interview I've got for tomorrow afternoon, but I don't want to count my dogs until they've been walked. Betty, she of Betty K.'s Doggie Daycare, lives only a few streets over it turns out, and is going to be out walking with her usual Friday lunchtime canine charges in Sorauren Park at around 12:30. When I asked her on the phone if I should bring along a résumé or references or anything, she said no, just make sure to wear some comfortable clothing that I don't mind getting dirty. What matters most, she said, is if the dogs like you.

"Do you want to take a shower while I get this together?" Mary says. She's got her back to me, is whipping eggs in a metal bowl.

"You know, I know I should, I know I probably smell like an ashtray, but all I really feel like doing is just sitting here."

"So just sit there then."

"Do you want me to do anything?"

"Nope. Unless you want to pour what's left of that bottle of Vielle Ferme. If we don't drink it tonight or tomorrow, it's going to go bad."

I get two glasses down from the cupboard and grab the bottle off the counter. Mary's melting butter in the frying pan on the stove. I pull the plastic wine pump cork out of the bottle and fill each glass a little less than half way.

I hand her her glass; we clink, drink.

"What do you think," Mary says. "Does it taste vinegary to you?"

"It tastes fine."

She takes another sip, looks at me while she considers. "It's still good," she says, and sets her glass down on the counter and goes back to her pan.

While I'm up, I click on the radio on top of the refrigerator. Different fridge, same radio. It's set to the Fan, two guys yelling at each other about how the New York Yankees' two-hundred million dollar payroll is or is not ruining professional baseball. I flip the dial until I hit 1050, CHUM 1050.

We get lucky. An oldie but truly a goody, Doug Sahm's first band's only real hit, "She's About a Mover" from '65, just a tiny taste of the Tex-Mex soul stew he'd eventually cook up, but a sweet tease of country-fried raunch and roll to hear on your AM radio at 2:27 in the morning nonetheless. Mary sings along with the chorus as she takes two plates from the cupboard.

"How do you know this?" I say.

She ladles out the eggs. "You think you're the only one around here who knows good music?"

"No, but —"

"It's Mister Something-or-Other, right?" She carries the plates over to the table waitress-style, two in one hand, her glass of wine in the other. She sits down across from me.

"Sir Douglas Quintet, but close enough," I say. "I'm impressed."

"Toast me then," she says, and I do. We drink, set down our glasses, pick up our forks.

The omelette is delicious. How six free-range eggs, a mushy but not-yet mouldy Shitake mushroom, a pad of butter, and some onions and garlic and basil and salt and pepper can come together to taste this good just doesn't make sense. Eggs perfecto *ex nihilo*.

"This is delicious," I say.

"It's just an omelette."

"I don't care, it's great." I didn't know how hungry I was until I started eating. I'm already halfway done.

Mary holds her glass of wine in front of her while she finishes chewing. When she does, and before she drinks, "It is good, isn't it?"

"It's fantastic."

We finish our omelettes and drink our wine and listen to the radio. Doug is gone, has become the Everly Brothers' "All I Have to Do is Dream."

"Do you know who this is?" I say.

Mary frowns. "Please. Everybody knows who this is."

"Okay, who is it then?"

"The Everly Brothers."

"All right," I say, raising my glass.

Mary drinks without clinking. "That's too easy, that doesn't even deserve a toast."

I smile, drink from my glass, too.

"Are they still around?" Mary says.

"Who, the Everly Brothers?"

She nods.

"You mean still recording, or still alive?"

"Alive."

"Oh, yeah, they're still around. They broke up for awhile in the seventies, but they're both still kicking."

"What about Sir What's-His-Name?"

"Doug Sahm. He's the one who wrote all of their stuff and sang lead."

"Okay. Is he still alive?"

"No. He died just a few years ago, actually."

"How?"

"They say heart failure. He was alone in a motel room in New Mexico when they found him. He was only fifty-eight."

Mary lifts her glass, finishes what's left of her wine. I'm already there.

"But both Everly Brothers are still alive," she says.

"Oh, yeah. They even tour once in a while."

"Really. How old are they?"

"God, I don't know. In their mid-sixties, anyway."

"And they still tour."

"Sometimes, yeah."

We listen to the song fade out and end, to the D.J. start talking.

"So what do you want to do?" Mary says.

"What do you mean?"

"I mean, do you feel like opening a new bottle and having

another glass, or do you want to just go to bed?"

"Can't we do both?"

Mary smiles. "Yeah, I suppose we can."

"Then I guess I don't understand the question."

RAY ROBERTSON graduated from the University of Toronto with High Distinction with a B.A. in philosophy and later gained an M.F.A. in creative writing from Southwest Texas State University.

He is the author of the novels *Home Movies* (Cormorant, 1997), *Heroes* (Dundurn, 2000), *Moody Food* (Doubleday, 2002), and a collection of non-fiction, *Mental Hygiene: Essays on Writers and Writing* (Insomniac, 2003).

He is a contributing book reviewer to *The Globe and Mail*, appears regularly on TVO's *Imprint* and CBC's *Talking Books*, and teaches creative writing and literature at the University of Toronto's School of Continuing Studies.